WELCOME TO
HOMETOWN REUNION

Twelve unique stories set in Tyler.

*Where you can find romance and adventure,
bachelors and babies, feuding families, a case
of mistaken identity, and a mum on the run!*

*Join us in America's favourite town and
experience the love and the laughter, the trials
and the triumphs of those who call it home.*

*First published in Great Britain 2000
by Harlequin Mills & Boon Limited,
Eton House, 18-24 Paradise Road,
Richmond, Surrey TW9 1SR*

UNEXPECTED SON © Harlequin Books S.A. 1996

Marisa Carroll is acknowledged as the author of this work.

ISBN 0 373 82549 8

110-0700

*Printed and bound in Spain
by Litografia Rosés S.A., Barcelona*

MARISA CARROLL

Unexpected Son

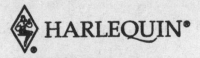

HARLEQUIN®

TORONTO • NEW YORK • LONDON
AMSTERDAM • PARIS • SYDNEY • HAMBURG
STOCKHOLM • ATHENS • TOKYO • MILAN • MADRID
PRAGUE • WARSAW • BUDAPEST • AUCKLAND

WELCOME TO A
HOMETOWN REUNION

Twelve books set in Tyler.
Twelve unique stories.

Marisa Carroll is the pen name of sisters Carol Wagner and Marian Scharf. The sisters live in a small Northwest Ohio town, where they are surrounded by five generations of family and friends. They are contributing two books to Hometown Reunion: *Unexpected Son* and *Mission: Children*, the finale of the series.

CHAPTER ONE

THE LITTLE TOWN was spread out below him, church steeples glinting in the autumn sun, the lake beyond its outskirts the same crisp blue as the October sky. The village and the lake were ringed as far as the eye could see with fields of corn and soybeans, heavy and golden with grain waiting to be harvested. Horses, sleek and shining, ran in pastures on the gentle hillsides, and cows fed in haylots beneath giant silos that rivaled the church steeples in height and grandeur.

In the center of the business district the grass in a parklike square was still green. The trees that graced it—tall, stately oaks and maples—were clothed in autumn colors, a subtle reminder that although the afternoon was reasonably warm, winter was coming to south-central Wisconsin. But he doubted that even wily Old Man Winter whistling down from Canada would catch the little town unawares. The two- and three-story brick buildings that framed the park, and the stately Victorians that lined the wide, straight streets behind them, were as solid and foursquare as the Swedish and German immigrants who had founded the place a hundred years before.

"Welcome to Tyler," he said aloud, reading the greeting painted in elaborate Gothic script on the sign by the side of the road. His words echoed in his ears— gruff, a little rough around the edges, as though it had been a long time since he'd spoken his thoughts aloud. "Yeah, right."

It was a nice sentiment, but in reality, how would the good citizens of Tyler react to a stranger in their midst?

He wasn't certain exactly what it was he was looking for here. A house or building that seemed familiar? A man or woman walking down the wide, tree-lined streets who would wave him over to explain what in hell a Miami street kid was doing here in this small, Mom-and-flag-and-apple-pie kind of town? Usually when the shipping season ended on the Great Lakes, he headed home to Florida. But this year there was no one to go home to, and maybe, when all was said and done, that was why he was here.

Michael Kenton put the truck in gear. The transmission of the aging pickup groaned in protest. And the brakes were touchy, too. He was going to have to take a look under the hood when he got the chance. It wasn't that he couldn't afford something more impressive to drive; he could. But the old blue Ford didn't look too beat up, and he sort of liked the idea of being able to stretch out under the tarp in the back alongside everything he owned if he had to. He didn't mind sleeping under the stars. As a matter of fact, he preferred it. He'd done it often enough on the decks of the lake freighters he'd served on during the past three years.

He turned the corner onto a narrow side street lined with small, twenties-era bungalows, and, oddly enough, a woman did walk out onto the pavement and wave him over to the curb—a young woman with red hair and freckles and a shy, sweet smile. A superstitious chill waltzed up and down his spine. But she didn't offer him a magic talisman, or pose him a riddle he must solve to be allowed to remain in her small, enchanted town.

"I'm sorry," she said, smiling some more. "If you could wait a moment, please, they're trying to get that tree off the roof."

"I can see that." Michael was impatient to get where he was going, although he still had no idea where that was. He rested his forearm out the window and watched as two burly individuals in canvas coveralls wrestled a chain around the thick branch of a maple that had fallen onto the roof of a brick building directly in front of him.

The woman didn't notice his impatience. "We had a terrible thunderstorm day before yesterday." He'd figured something like that had happened. There were a lot of fallen branches piled by the curb in town, and here and there he'd seen a boarded-up window or section of roof with the shingles torn off.

She wasn't looking at him as she talked. Instead, she shaded her eyes with one hand as the older of the two men got in a truck that had definitely seen better days and began to back slowly away, trying to pull the severed branch of the tree off the roof of the church. Michael knew it was a church because even though there was no steeple, there was a sign in front of the remarkably ugly brick building that proclaimed it to be the Tyler Fellowship Sanctuary:

Sunday School 9 a.m.
Worship Service 10 a.m.
Prayer Hour: Wednesday. 7 p.m.
Pastor S.C. Fleming

Nearby stood a second sign shaped and painted to resemble a happy clown. It seemed that the Tyler Fellowship Sanctuary was also home to TylerTots Community Day Care. An arrow pointed around the corner to a side entrance into what was probably the basement of the building. Michael realized he couldn't remember the last time he'd set foot inside a church.

The tree continued to resist the men's efforts to dislodge it, the shattered branch swinging dangerously, dragging down a rain of shingles and eaves trough.

"Oh dear," the woman said, biting her lower lip. "Thank heaven we covered the window." He wondered if it had been the two men or the woman at his elbow who'd had the foresight to nail a sheet of plywood over the stained-glass window directly under the damaged roof.

"They should have taken off the smaller branches before they tried to pull it off."

She turned to look at him, frowning at his tone. "Randy is afraid of heights and Jonas had a pacemaker installed just last winter," she said, as if that explained everything. Her eyes, now that they were no longer shadowed by her hand, turned out to be hazel—an intriguing combination of green and gold that looked just right with her red hair, her pale ivory skin and the smattering of freckles across her nose. "I couldn't ask either of them to climb up on the roof."

"Then what the hell are they doing taking down trees for a living?"

"They don't take down trees for a living. Jonas Phillips is a butcher by trade. And Randy is his son. He drives a delivery truck for Yes! Yogurt."

So Jonas was the old guy's name. He seemed to be the one in charge of the uncoordinated operation. "If neither one of them knows what he's doing, they sure as hell shouldn't be pulling that tree down off the roof.''

"They're only trying to help. With all the damage from the storm the other day, I couldn't get any professional tree cutters to come until Saturday. And it's supposed to rain again tonight. Something has to be done about the hole in the roof before then.''

"You're the preacher's wife?'' She wasn't wearing a wedding ring, but that didn't mean anything these days.

"No. I'm the pastor,'' she said, a tiny frown drawing her nicely arched eyebrows together over her nose. She smoothed her hands down the front of her sweater and stood a little straighter, which would bring the top of her head just about level with his chin, he figured. She offered her hand. She had small hands with long graceful fingers and delicate wrists. A flare went off inside him, exploding at some deep, instinctive level that warned him not to touch her, not to become involved.

She might look shy and sweet and virginal but she was still a woman and there had been no women in his life for a very long time. "I'm Sarah Fleming. This is my church. Randy and Jonas are two of my parishioners.''

Just then the heavy chain the two men had wrapped around the branch slipped and the old pickup Jonas was driving lurched forward. The tree rolled drunkenly and lodged itself more firmly in the hole in the church roof.

"Oh dear,'' Sarah Fleming said again.

"One of those two is going to get himself seriously hurt or killed.''

"I agree with you.'' She moved away from the truck, not seeming to notice that he had not shaken her hand. "I'll tell them to stop at once.''

"Don't bother." He got out of the truck. Sure enough, the top of her head barely reached his chin. She was small all over. Her breasts beneath a prim cotton blouse and shapeless brown cardigan were sufficiently rounded to warrant a second glance, and her hips flared below her waist, nicely filling out the pair of faded jeans she wore.

She was looking at him again and caught him giving her the once-over. A delicate tint of pink spread up her throat and highlighted her cheekbones. He'd embarrassed her, staring like that, and surprisingly, he wished he hadn't. It was obvious the Reverend Sarah Fleming wasn't used to being checked out by strange men in front of her own church. "I can't ask you to help Mr...." She paused, waiting expectantly for him to supply her with his name.

"The name's Kenton," he said. "Michael Kenton." He grabbed a pair of work gloves and a crowbar from the toolbox and headed over to where Jonas and Randy were investigating the damage to the truck's bumper. "Do you have a ladder and a chain saw?" he called over his shoulder.

"I...yes. There's a big ladder in the garage behind the parsonage. And I think Jonas brought his chain saw."

"I did that." The older man straightened, eyeing Michael suspiciously from beneath dark, bushy eyebrows. With ingrained, small-town courtesy he stuck out his hand. "I'm Jonas Phillips."

"Michael Kenton," he said, returning the greeting. "Need a hand?"

"We could use some help. But we don't want any if you're one of them fly-by-night fix-it guys who shows up after there's been a storm like this one and then charges an arm and a leg for shoddy work."

"I'm not a fly-by-night fix-it guy," Michael said, angry with himself for volunteering. He hadn't been in Tyler five minutes and already he was letting himself get caught up in one of its small dramas. It wasn't what he'd planned. But it was too late to back out now. He'd only draw attention to himself, make it impossible to stick around for any length of time if he turned on his heel and walked away, leaving them to get themselves out of the mess they'd made. No, the best thing to do was help the two men pull the big branch off the roof, cover the hole and be on his way. He still had to find a place to stay for the night.

Jonas took a moment to consider the offer. "Pastor Sarah, there, is mighty anxious to get that tree off the roof."

"Then let's quit wasting time. I can climb a ladder and I can use a chain saw. Do you want some help or don't you?"

Both men were silent for a moment, still not quite sure what to make of him. "We need the help," Randy said.

"Okay. What do you have to cover that hole in the roof?"

Randy pulled a heavy-duty plastic tarp from the bed of the pickup. "I brought cement blocks to hold it down."

The tarp would do. But not for long. The lady preacher would have to get someone up there on the roof to fix that hole before the next rainstorm. Michael nodded. "That ought to work for now."

Randy nodded, too, then stuck out his hand in greeting. "We appreciate the help. I'll get the ladder."

SARAH WATCHED the three men work on the tree. The stranger, Michael Kenton, hadn't been there half an hour yet and already he'd dealt with the severed branch that had punched a hole in the roof and had hooked the big log chain around the trunk in preparation for lowering it to the ground. If work continued at this pace, they would have the makeshift repairs finished before sundown.

She couldn't keep her eyes off the stranger, although it made her nervous to see him moving around on the steep pitch of the roof. He was a good-looking man, surefooted and smooth moving. Quite a contrast to Randy and Jonas's stolid presence. He certainly looked as if he knew what he was doing up there. But what if he fell? What if he hurt himself and sued the church? Or her? She made herself stop thinking such thoughts. Eric would never have had such doubts. Her husband had believed in the innate goodness of his fellow man. She should just be thankful for this Michael Kenton's help and stop worrying about whether he was the kind of person who dropped a hammer on his toe and then filed suit over it.

He certainly didn't look like the kind of man who tripped and fell over his own two feet. He was about thirty, she guessed, strong and assured. He was tall, an inch or two over six feet. His shoulders were broad and his waist narrow. He wore a dark T-shirt that strained across his chest as he worked and his soft, faded jeans couldn't hide the well-muscled contours of his hips and thighs. His hair was a little short for her taste, almost a military cut, dark as a raven's wing, with a hint of auburn in the shining depths. And his eyes. She'd noticed his eyes right away—blue or black, or some combination of both, bright and hard, reflecting everything he saw and giving nothing of himself away in return.

What was a man like him doing in Tyler? Was he here to visit friends or relatives? Or to look for a job? Neither option seemed likely. If he had relatives in Tyler he would have mentioned them when he introduced himself to Jonas and Randy. She'd lived in the Midwest only a little more than four years herself, but that was long enough to learn how things worked. If you had blood ties to a place, you made them known right up front.

And Tyler wasn't exactly the center of the universe. People didn't flock here looking for jobs even when Ingalls Farm and Machinery, the town's main employer, was running at peak capacity. There just wasn't much of a turnover at the F and M. Most of the people who worked there measured their employment in decades or years, not months or weeks.

Sarah narrowed her eyes against the coppery glare of the setting sun and continued her study of Michael Kenton. She wondered what he did for a living. If he didn't look like a factory worker seeking employment, he certainly didn't look like a waiter or bartender on his way to a job interview at Timberlake Lodge, Tyler's other main employer.

Maybe he was just passing through, as unlikely as that might seem. Tyler didn't have the kind of reputation that attracted drifters. Most of the people who came here had a reason for doing so. But when all was said and done, this man's reason was none of her business. He was a Good Samaritan, stopping to offer his help in her time of need. What he did for a living or where he was going was his business, not hers.

While she watched, the stranger finished anchoring

the chain with sure and practiced gestures, and two minutes later, with Jonas carefully maneuvering his battered pickup, the trunk came free and dropped to the ground with a thud. Ten minutes after that the hole in the roof was covered, the heavy plastic tarp was anchored down with cement blocks and Michael Kenton was back on the ground.

Randy and Jonas were surveying the litter of broken, twisted branches around them as he descended. Randy looked at his watch, shrugged and prepared to yank the starter cord on the chain saw. The gesture wasn't lost on Sarah.

"Wait," she called. She walked toward the three men, her feet strangely reluctant to move from the spot where she was standing. "Don't worry about clearing away those branches this afternoon. It's only an hour until the game starts. You'll miss kickoff if you don't leave now."

"I don't like to leave a job half-finished," Jonas said stubbornly.

"It can wait. You can't be late for Brian's homecoming game." She looked at Michael Kenton and smiled automatically, her Sunday-morning-greeting-on-the-church-steps smile. She would treat him just like all the other men in her congregation, keep a friendly distance. That way he wouldn't seem quite so dangerously male, so compelling. "Jonas's youngest boy, Brian, is Tyler High's star quarterback this season. Tonight's the homecoming game against Sugar Creek. I don't want Jonas and Randy to miss it."

Michael Kenton looked directly at her with those dark, unreadable eyes, and Sarah fought against an unexplainable urge to look away or be in danger of being lost in their depths. Her practiced smile faded away, leaving her breathless and a little unsteady.

"No problem," he said after a few moments. "There's a good hour of daylight left. If Jonas will leave the chain saw, I'll finish up."

"We can come back tomorrow," Jonas said.

"That's not necessary unless you don't trust me with your property."

"Didn't say I didn't trust you." Jonas motioned for Randy to hand over the saw. "Said you didn't have to stay and finish my work. But if you're of a mind to do it, I'll say thank-you and be on my way." He held out his hand.

Michael Kenton returned the handshake. "Like I said, no problem."

After making arrangements to come back the next afternoon and haul the cut wood away, Randy and Jonas climbed into the truck and drove off, leaving Sarah alone with the stranger. She wrapped her arms around her waist and turned back to face him.

"You really don't have to do this. I...it's getting late. You'll probably be wanting to find a place to stay. There's a very nice bed-and-breakfast a couple of streets over. It's called Granny Rose's." He didn't seem like the bed-and-breakfast type. "Unless you were planning to spend the night at Timberlake Lodge?"

"Is that the big place out by the lake I passed coming into town? Lots of gables and chimneys and a fancy gate out by the road?"

Sarah nodded, having trouble meeting his dark gaze. She recrossed her arms under her breasts, noticing the late-October chill for the first time. She felt awkward and tongue-tied in Michael Kenton's presence, as though she'd never been left alone with a man before. She'd never felt that way around men when Eric was alive. And since he'd died three years ago she hadn't felt much of anything at all. That made this stranger's effect on her even more disturbing.

"I think Timberlake's out of my price range."

"Mine, too," she said, forcing a smile. "Especially now that I have to find the money in the budget to fix the church roof."

"It should be a simple-enough job. There was no serious structural damage that I could see."

"Thank heaven for that," Sarah said.

"Aren't you going to ask the Almighty to help you out on this one?" Michael Kenton asked, the beginning of a smile touching his mouth.

"The Lord helps those who help themselves," Sarah reminded him. "One of our local contractors, Joe Santori, promised to send someone over to give me an estimate as soon as he could spare the time. But he's putting up some new condominiums on Lake Shore Road, and what with everyone else who has wind damage to deal with..." She fell silent a moment, then spoke quickly before her brain could censor her words. "Mr. Kenton, would you like the job of repairing the church roof? I can't pay you much, but I can offer you a place to stay. And your meals. I'm a pretty good cook."

Why had she said that? Why had she told this man she would fix his meals? It would have been enough to offer him the use of the efficiency apartment above the parsonage garage. That was what the room was meant for, after all—sheltering travelers and townspeople in need of a place to stay. But there had been no need to offer to share her food and her kitchen. She wished she could take the words back, but it was too late. She was torn between hoping he would accept her offer so that she could quit worrying about the hole in the roof, and wishing just as hard that he would say no, get in his pickup and drive out of town and out of her staid, quiet life before he disturbed it any more than he already had.

Michael Kenton didn't answer right away. His blue-black eyes grew even darker, more unreadable. Or perhaps that darkening, that feeling that he was considering accepting her offer for reasons of his own that had nothing to do with a place to stay and food for his stomach was only a trick of light and shadow as the sun slipped closer to the horizon and the smell of burning leaves came to her nostrils on the evening breeze.

"It would take only two or three days to fix the roof," she said, trying to keep her voice light and untroubled. "If you turn me down I'm going to have to cancel day care until I can get someone who will. Surely you can find enough charity in you to spare me the wrath of the parents of thirty-five displaced preschoolers, can't you, Mr. Kenton?"

He held her gaze for a few seconds more. Then the darkness retreated from his eyes and a smile curved his mouth, a genuine smile this time, one that nearly took her breath away. "Thirty-five preschoolers?"

"Thirty-five," Sarah confirmed.

"TylerTots," he said, still smiling. "Who came up with that name?"

Sarah raised her chin. "I did. I think it's cute."

The smile disappeared. "What will your husband say about me staying here?"

"My husband is dead, Mr. Kenton. He died three years ago in a snowmobile accident. This was his church, his parish. Now it's mine. I have the authority to allow the use of the garage apartment and to offer you the job of repairing the church roof. I don't have to ask anyone's permission.''

''I'll remember that,'' he said.

''Is it a deal, Mr. Kenton?'' she asked, holding out her hand. He had refused to shake hands with her before. She wondered if he would do so again. He hesitated barely a heartbeat, then enfolded her hand in his. Sarah's breath caught in her throat. His hand was hard and strong, his skin warm and rough, and she felt the shock of his touch all the way to her toes.

''It's a deal, Reverend Fleming.''

''Good.'' The one-word reply was all she could manage. He released her hand, and Sarah resisted the urge to rub away the tingling sensation in her palm. ''I'll show you the apartment. You can buy all the supplies you need from Murphy's Hardware and charge it to the church's account. They open at seven, so there's no reason you can't get started first thing in the morning.''

CHAPTER TWO

"THIS IS THE FIRST YEAR since Kellie Jo was born that I haven't had to rack my brains for Halloween costumes," Moira Schweinhagen said as she ran her fingers through Alyssa Wocheck's hair, watching in the mirror to see that every shining strand fell into place. "I mean, fifteen years of ballerinas and pirate hats and wooden swords and the walking dead. Enough is enough."

"It's hard to believe all three of your children are in high school," Alyssa commented with sympathy. The rise and fall of voices from the other occupied chairs at the Hair Affair salon underscored their words. Myra Allen was having her roots touched up in the seat next to Alyssa and, being incurably nosy, was probably eavesdropping on their conversation. Sheila Lawson, the manager at Timberlake Lodge and a high-school classmate of Alyssa's daughter, Liza Forrester, was getting a manicure, while Martha Bauer, the mother of Alyssa's best friend, Anna Kelsey, still spry and active at eighty-four, was evaluating her new perm with a critical eye.

Moira laughed, her blue eyes nearly disappearing into her plump, good-natured face. "It is a pretty high price to pay for not having to be sewing on costumes every spare minute of the month of October," she agreed. "Especially since I'm working so many more hours now that I'm managing this place. But I don't miss all that candy lying around the house. I used to gain at least a pound every Halloween. By the way, how many trick-or-treaters did you have last night?''

''Hundreds,'' Alyssa replied with a smile of her own. She was used to Moira's rapid-fire changes of subject. ''I passed out all the candy I had in the house, and I even raided the cookie jar before I could satisfy all the little ghouls and goblins that came to the door.''

''Well,'' Moira said, brandishing a can of hair spray as she smoothed a final strand into place, ''it's only once a year, after all.''

''Cece brought the twins by,'' Alyssa continued, waving off the hair spray. ''Jeff had an emergency at the hospital so she had her hands full. They were dressed up as little cows, with ears and tails and everything. They were 'udderly' adorable.'' Annie and Belle Baron were Alyssa's grandchildren, the daughters of her son, Jeff, and his wife, Cece. Along with their cousin, four-year-old Margaret Alyssa Forrester, they were her pride and joy.

''Liza and Cliff brought Margaret Alyssa by our place,'' Moira said. She made a clicking sound against her teeth. ''Imagine a four-year-old wanting to be a vampire.''

Alyssa laughed aloud. ''Complete with fangs and fake bloodstains on her lips.''

''That child is just as much of a free spirit as her mother.''

''Liza always did march to a different drummer,'' Alyssa agreed. Five years ago that statement would have caused her heart to ache. But five years was a long time, and her relationship with her rebellious youngest child was now on firm ground.

"They're cute as bugs' ears, all three of those kids."
Moira removed Alyssa's cape. "Did you take pictures
of them in their costumes so we can all see them?"

"Of course." Alyssa brushed off her skirt as she
rose. "Lots. Edward's in London and missed seeing
them in costume. And Dad and Tisha would never forgive me if I didn't send them at least half a dozen
poses."

"I thought that husband of yours was going to be
spending more time here at Timberlake and less time
jetting around Europe."

"He's helping Devon interview candidates for a new
vice president of operations for Addison Hotels International, so that both he and Devon can spend more
time here," Alyssa explained. Devon Addison, heir to
the vast Addison Hotels chain, was Edward Wocheck's
stepson. And since her marriage to Edward he had become very dear to Alyssa, as well.

"That's great. You'd never know that boy is worth
big bucks when you see him on the street. Acts just
like everyone else." It was a high compliment coming
from Moira, and Alyssa took it as such. "Speaking of
my absent boss," Moira said, changing the subject in
midsentence as she led the way to the cash register.
"She called yesterday to check up on us. She says she's
been down to the pool every day. And it sounds like
their condo is really gorgeous."

"Yes, it is very nice. Small and comfy and convenient to shopping and their favorite restaurants." Pri-
vately Alyssa was a little shocked that her eighty-two-
year-old father had decided to move into his fiancée's
Tucson condo. Tisha Olsen, a flamboyant and outspo-
ken redhead was almost thirty years Judson Ingalls's
junior. And although Tisha routinely postponed setting

a wedding date, their engagement was of long standing and their attachment to each other genuine. In Tyler, however, they'd always kept separate residences. Evidently in Arizona they felt more free to be themselves.

"Tisha says Judson has taken up golf," Moira disclosed.

"That's what he told me when we last spoke on the telephone. I can't believe it," Alyssa said with a laugh. "As long as I can remember Dad's said that game was a waste of time. Now he's golfing three times a week."

"It's good for him," Moira pronounced, taking the check Alyssa handed her and slipping it into the cash register. "He's worked hard all his life."

"Yes, he has. And I'm glad that he has a chance to enjoy himself with a woman he loves." Alyssa and Tisha Olsen, although contemporaries in age, were not close friends and never had been. But Tisha had been Judson's staunchest defender when he'd been accused of the death of Alyssa's mother, a murder that had taken place forty-five-years before, and her belief in his innocence had never wavered. Alyssa admired her for that steadfastness. And all other considerations aside, Tisha adored Judson and so did Alyssa. That was their common ground, and they had built a workable relationship on that basis over the past four years.

Alyssa turned to take her coat from the hook alongside the counter. It was a beautiful sunny day, but the sunlight was deceiving. The temperature was only in the mid-fifties, with a bite to the air that seemed to have arrived with the new month.

"I'll bet that's the man that Pastor Sarah hired to fix the church roof," Moira remarked, wiggling her finger in the direction of Murphy's Hardware on the other side of Main Street. "Over there, loading stuff into that blue pickup. That's who it has to be. Pete saw him up on the roof. Told me he looked like he's doing a real good job. One or two other people have hired him to do storm repairs, since Joe Santori and his crew are so tied up out at those new condos on Lake Shore Road.''

Alyssa frowned at the mention of the contractor's name. ''I know Joe's busy. He was supposed to replace the front porch railing for me before winter.'' She glanced in the direction of Moira's pointing finger. She had never seen the man Moira was referring to before, but she had heard about the stranger in town. He was dressed in faded jeans and an equally faded gray sweatshirt. He had short dark hair, mostly hidden beneath a red baseball cap, a strong profile and beard-shadowed chin. It was hard to make out any more details from inside the Hair Affair, but Alyssa caught herself staring at the young man nonetheless.

''Maybe this guy could do it for you,'' Moira said, staring as hard as Alyssa. ''His name's Keating or Carson or something like that.''

His name wasn't Carson. It was Kenton. Michael Kenton. Cece had told her about him, and she'd gotten the information straight from her friend, Sarah Fleming. ''Joe always does our repair work....'' Alyssa adjusted the strap of her purse on her shoulder. The broken porch railing, the result not of the recent storm but of a runaway piano that Liza had moved out to the boathouse, had been worrying Alyssa. The damage was very close to the front steps of the house, and with the twins and Margaret Alyssa always running in and out, she didn't want to leave it unrepaired any longer than necessary.

''Why don't you see if this guy'd be willing to do

the job for you? Joe won't mind, I bet, especially not on a little project like that.''

''Maybe I will,'' Alyssa said, making up her mind. ''It can't hurt to ask.''

Moira nodded, then added a cautious rejoinder. ''The worst he can do is say no.''

''EXCUSE ME—Mr. Kenton, is it?''

Michael straightened to face the woman standing half in shadow, half in sunlight beneath the old-fashioned canvas awning outside Murphy's Hardware.

''Yes, ma'am. Michael Kenton. What can I do for you?'' His grandma had taught him manners once upon a time. He slid the last of the two-by-fours he'd been loading into the bed of the pickup and rested his arms on the side walls.

''I wonder if I might speak to you for a moment.'' She was in her late forties or early fifties, with sleek blond hair lightly threaded with silver, high cheekbones and a long slender neck without a sag or wrinkle in sight. She was one very classy-looking lady. Michael had spent some time around the upper crust in his younger days, and he knew what to look for. Her shoes and purse were real Italian leather and her coat hadn't come off the rack at K-Mart. Her earrings and the watch that peeked out from below her cuff were real gold, heavy and substantial, but elegant and understated, like everything else about her.

''Fire away.''

''I need some work done on my house. Nothing too complicated, but I'd like to have it finished before winter comes. Would you be interested in the job?'' She shifted the strap of her purse a little higher on her shoulder. Her eyes were somewhere between blue and gray, with little lines fanning out from the corners. They were narrowed now, watching him closely, gauging his words and more, he suspected, as she waited for his answer.

He'd been here only three days and already he'd been approached by half a dozen people with offers of odd jobs. Most of them were parishioners of Sarah Fleming or relatives of her parishioners. None of them had the presence and air of gentility this woman possessed. "I'm just passing through, ma'am," he said, not really certain why he did. He hadn't made up his mind to leave town—not right away, anyway. Not till he found out what he'd come to learn about Tyler.

"Oh." She sounded disappointed. "I see."

"Who recommended you see me about the work?"

"Moira Schweinhagen suggested it. She manages the Hair Affair."

"Never heard of her."

She narrowed her eyes. "I don't imagine you have. But Tyler's a small town and you're a stranger here. That gets you talked about."

"I imagine it does. Is that who told you my name? This Moira person?"

"Actually, no. That was my daughter-in-law. She heard about you from her friend Sarah Fleming."

So he'd been wrong about her being so different from the others who had approached him. She did belong here, odd as that might seem.

"Do you want the work or not?" She wasn't about to be cowed by his curt replies.

"What work do you want done?"

"It's my porch. The railing needs mending. There are a few other odd jobs I'd like done, as well. It's an old house. And like people, once you get to a certain age it's patch, patch, patch.'' She smiled, and he was hard put not to return it.

"A broken porch railing doesn't sound too taxing."

"No, I imagine it wouldn't be. But if you're not going to be staying around town…''

"I might be here long enough to fix your porch," he conceded. "Where do you live?"

"One fifty-three Elm Street. It's a big white Victorian. The Ingalls house."

"And that's your name? Ingalls?" So he'd just met one of the members of the most important family in town. The Ingalls name was everywhere, on the factory outside of town, the park down by the school and the street that ran behind it.

She laughed, a pleasant, chiming sound every bit as classy as the rest of her. "I used to be. Years ago. My name is Wocheck now. Alyssa Wocheck."

"I'll be by to take a look at your porch, Mrs. Wocheck. After that I'll let you know if I'll take the job."

"That's fair, Mr. Kenton. I'll be expecting you." She turned and walked away. He watched her go, then looked back to see Murphy standing in the doorway of his store.

"You do good work for Alyssa and she'll treat you right. Good people, the Ingallses and the Barons."

"Barons?" Michael tensed, then went on arranging the lumber he'd just bought from the man. "I thought she said her name was Wocheck."

"It is now. Married Eddie Wocheck four years back. But before that she was Alyssa Baron. Mrs. Ronald Baron. 'Course, she was a widow long before Eddie Wocheck came back to town."

"Ronald Baron's widow?" Michael had trouble getting the words out.

"Yeah. Old Ronald up and blew his brains out one day twelve—" Murphy narrowed his eyes and scratched the top of his nearly bald head "—no, damn it, time sure has a way of getting away from you. It was closer to fifteen years ago that the elevator went bust and old Ronald put that gun to his head."

SARAH LOOKED out her kitchen window at the small square of light spilling onto the landing at the top of the stairway. Michael Kenton was home. She'd heard his truck pull into the driveway more than an hour ago, but he hadn't come down for his meal. She glanced over at the tray on the table, then at the pot of vegetable soup simmering on the stove. He'd only eaten in her kitchen, at her table, that first evening he'd been in town. From then on he'd taken his meals alone.

She wondered if something was wrong. He was usually very punctual coming to her back door to fetch the tray each evening and returning it to her, with clean dishes, every morning. Perhaps something had happened. Maybe he had hurt himself at work, or maybe he was ill.

Sarah's heart sped up, responding to the faint anxiety she was feeling. She'd felt just this way when Eric hadn't come home on time the day he was killed. She hated waiting. Spinning away from the window, she grabbed the soup ladle and filled a bowl with soup, covered it, added three blueberry muffins she'd bought that morning at Marge's Diner to the tray and reached into the refrigerator for a second, smaller covered bowl filled with fruit salad. Balancing the tray carefully on one hand, she let herself out the back door and started across the yard to the garage.

It was already fully dark and there was the promise

of frost in the air, although it was only a little past seven in the evening. The moon was a faint silver arc, low in the sky, and the starlight was no more than a faint dusting of glitter on black velvet. The mournful honking of a flock of Canada geese could be heard in the distance as they settled for the night onto the placid waters of the lake. A car drove by and a dog barked at its passing, and overhead she could hear the rustling of startled sparrows as she walked beneath the branches where they slept.

At the top of the apartment stairs she shifted the tray to her left hand and prepared to knock. The door opened before she could accomplish the tricky task, and Michael Kenton stood in the doorway, tall and silent, blocking the light and making her feel small and awkward standing there with the heavy tray in her hands.

"Hi," she said, slipping into her Reverend Sarah persona, trying to recreate, as always, what she remembered of Eric's easy, friendly way with people. "I brought your supper."

"You didn't have to do that." His tone was as stony as the expression on his face.

Sarah felt the smile falter and fade away. "I…it was part of our agreement that I give you your meals. I'll take it back with me if you're not hungry."

He remained silent. She made a move to turn and leave. "No. Wait," he said. "I am hungry. Come on inside."

Sarah hadn't been inside the garage apartment for months before Michael Kenton arrived. It consisted of one big room with cracked and peeling linoleum on the floor, an old iron bedstead and a warped chest of drawers at one end, a couch and chair and coffee table, castoffs from parishioners, grouped in the center op-

posite the door, and a bare-bones kitchen with a
wooden table and chairs along the back wall. In the far
corner, a partitioned-off rectangle held an even-more-
utilitarian bathroom.

There were overhead light fixtures above the kitchen
table and the bed, and one floor lamp positioned between the couch and chair. At the moment that lamp
was the only source of light in the long, shadowy room.
Sarah couldn't see the chest of drawers and the bed
where Michael Kenton slept, and for some reason she
preferred not to confront, she was glad.

He took the tray from her hands. Sarah followed his
movement with her eyes and saw a half-empty bottle
of whiskey and a glass sitting on the table. He looked
up and saw her frowning at the liquor. "I suppose you
don't believe in a man having a drink, do you?"

"The denomination that my church is affiliated with
does frown on the use of alcohol," Sarah said carefully.
She didn't drink herself, but she personally didn't feel
that it was a sin to have a glass of wine or a bottle of
beer now and then.

"Then I won't ask you to share one with me."

Sarah looked up quickly, but the light was too faint
to allow her to tell for certain if he was serious or not.
It wasn't a joking matter, as far as many of her parishioners were concerned. She didn't want to ruffle any
feathers. "I'd appreciate it if you would limit your con-
sumption while you're staying here."

He screwed the lid onto the bottle and put it inside
one of the dingy, pale green cupboards. "I think I can
manage that."

"Thank you." He was wearing a flannel shirt, unbuttoned over a surprisingly white cotton T-shirt, and
he wasn't wearing shoes, only heavy socks, also white

enough to have been in a detergent commercial. He might have been a homeless drifter, but he thought enough of himself to take care of his clothes.

"You'd better eat your soup. It will get cold." Sarah wrapped her arms around herself. The whole room was cold. Michael Kenton hadn't bothered to light the fuel-oil stove next to the bathroom wall. Perhaps he thought he was responsible for the cost of the heating oil if he used the stove. He saw her looking in that direction and read her mind.

"I didn't light the stove. I planned on turning in early tonight. I've got to get an early start tomorrow."

"Oh." Sarah felt herself flushing. "I—I just didn't want you to think you might be responsible for the cost of the heating oil. The church council okayed your staying here as long as you were doing work for us. That means the utilities are included."

"I agreed to make whatever repairs they wanted done," he said. "If they ever make up their minds as to what they are."

Sarah smiled without thinking—a real smile, her own, not Reverend Sarah's. "Spending money doesn't come easily to the church council. Usually because we have very little extra to spend. The thought of getting so much done for only the cost of materials and your room and board has gone to their heads."

"I imagine the whole batch of them were up all night praying about it."

Sarah's smile faded away. "They're good people," she said. "They have faith in God and themselves."

"Yeah," he said, not meeting her eye. "Early to bed, early to rise. A fair day's pay for a hard day's work."

"Yes," Sarah said, smiling again. "Exactly what you said *you* meant to do tomorrow."

He had the grace to look sheepish. "I guess I did."
He smiled, too—a fleeting, reluctant grin that caused
an unexpected and unwelcome flutter in her pulse.

"I'd better be going." She turned back to the door,
which she'd purposefully left open. Her parishioners
were not mean or vindictive people, but their values
were rooted in time and tradition, and one of the things
that an unmarried female minister did not do was visit
a strange man in his room at night.

"Wait." He didn't move a muscle, but Sarah felt as
if he'd reached out and taken her by the hand. Her skin
actually tingled and she had to stop herself from rub-
bing the feeling away. "Can't you stay for a minute?"

"I shouldn't. I have my sermon for Sunday worship
to work on." He hadn't been at the service Sunday
morning. She hadn't expected him to be.

"It's only Tuesday. It can wait another day. I—I
wanted to ask you something."

"Of course." Sarah wondered what on earth this
hard-edged, self-contained man could need her advice
about.

"Do you know Alyssa Wocheck?"

"Everyone knows Alyssa," Sarah replied, surprised
by his question. It wasn't what she had expected. "Her
family helped build the town. She was Alyssa Ingalls.
Her father is Judson Ingalls, founder of the F and M."

"Ingalls Farm and Machinery. Ingalls Park. Ingalls
Avenue."

"Yes."

"Is Alyssa all that's left of the family?"

"No. Although Alyssa was an only child. Her
mother was killed many years ago." Sarah felt uncomfortable gossiping about Jeff and Cece's family. Cece
was her friend. Cece's first husband had been one of

Eric's best friends, although Sarah had not known the man personally, had only met Jeff and Cece Baron after Eric accepted the pulpit at Tyler Fellowship.

"Killed?" Something in her tone of voice must have given her away. "Do you mean murdered?"

"Yes. Her body was discovered four years ago, out at Timberlake Lodge. Before that, for forty years, everyone thought she had run away with a lover. Judson Ingalls was accused of the murder. There was a trial and everything."

"Did he do it?"

Sarah shook her head. "No. He was acquitted."

"That only means the jury couldn't agree that he was guilty."

Sarah lifted her head. "Another man killed her. A lover of Margaret's. He came back to Tyler and tried to kill Alyssa before she could remember that, as a little girl, she had seen him in her mother's room the night she died. But there was no more proof than Alyssa's repressed memories, and he couldn't be charged."

"But now the whole town believes Judson Ingalls was innocent."

"He's a good man." Sarah could be as stubborn as he was.

"How come I haven't run into any of these Ingallses before today?" He started taking the lid off the soup bowl, and Sarah could have sworn for a moment, just a moment, that his hands were trembling.

"The rest of the family lives in Milwaukee. At least the ones I know of. But all of Alyssa's children live here in Tyler. Of course they aren't Ingallses, they're Barons. Or they used to be." He was watching her from beneath dark brows that shadowed his eyes and his thoughts. His intensity flustered her. "The girls, I mean. Liza—she's the youngest—is married to Cliff Forrester. Amanda is a lawyer. She was her grandfather's defense attorney. She's married to Ethan Trask. He was the man who prosecuted her grandfather, but they fell in love anyway. He's a judge now and Amanda has a practice here in Tyler. And then there's Jeff. He's the oldest. Dr. Jeffrey Baron…''

"Dr. Jeffrey Baron."

"Yes. He's the chief of staff at Tyler General. He has a private practice, too. A clinic. The Ronald Baron Memorial Clinic. I volunteer there one day a week.'' She didn't add that more than a few of her parishioners took advantage of the clinic's sliding fee-payment scale, or what a blessing it was to them. Somehow the thundercloud darkness of his face made the words stick in her throat.

"Ronald Baron Memorial Clinic.'' There was a sneer in his voice, if not on his face.

She nodded. "It was named for Ronald Baron, Jeff's and Amanda's and Liza's father.''

"Yeah, I heard about him. Good old Ronald. The one who upped and blew his brains out one day some years back.''

"His business went bankrupt. He couldn't face telling all the farmers who had counted on him to sell their grain. It was a terrible time for the family.''

"I'll bet.''

"Cece says it was especially hard on Jeff. He was the oldest. The only son. He and his father were very close. Is your father living, Mr. Kenton?''

"No,'' he said, turning his back on her and signaling an end to the conversation in no uncertain terms. "My father's dead. As a matter of fact, he committed suicide just the way Ronald Baron did.''

CHAPTER THREE

"YOU'RE RIGHT, Lyssa. The twins' costumes were 'udderly' adorable." Edward Wocheck smiled down at the photographs he held in his hands. "And Margaret Alyssa looks absolutely fiendish."

"She'd be thrilled to death to hear you say that. *If* she knew what the word meant."

Alyssa leaned back in her chair and smiled across the table at her husband. It was his first night home, and they were having dinner at Timberlake Lodge so that Edward's father, Phil, could be present at his homecoming. But the old man's arthritis was bothering him this rainy November evening and he'd already retired to his suite in the west wing of the hotel, leaving Edward and Alyssa to finish their meal alone.

"I wish you'd been here to see them trick-or-treating."

"Next year," Edward promised. "Devon's just about got a handle on the restructuring of Addison International. Old Arthur's death hit Nikki pretty hard. She's been difficult about the changes." Nicole, Lady Holmes, was Edward's ex-wife and Devon's mother.

"Is that why you left Kathleen behind in London with Devon?"

Kathleen Kelsey was Edward's executive assistant and the daughter of Alyssa's dearest friends, Anna and Johnny Kelsey.

Edward nodded. "The boy's snowed under with paperwork. She can help him dig his way out."

"And give him a convenient dinner companion on the nights his mother tries to matchmake with some overbred and underfed offshoot of the royal family."

Edward laughed. "Alyssa, your Midwestern prejudices are showing."

Alyssa felt herself blush. "Sorry," she said. She usually didn't let herself be goaded into saying anything negative about Edward's ex-wife. She changed the subject. "I hired someone to fix the porch railing."

"That was good of Joe to work you into his schedule." Edward nodded over the rim of the dessert menu. The menus were newly printed, and he studied his closely, even though he'd okayed the new design before he left for London two weeks before.

Alyssa smiled to herself. Edward's business dealings stretched over half the world, but Timberlake Lodge, which had once belonged to her family, was his pride and joy, and he kept an eagle eye on its management and day to day operations. She couldn't blame him. Even though she had recently hired a manager for the F and M, she still spent several days a week in the office herself.

"You're not listening," Alyssa scolded. "Not Joe Santori. I hired a man that Jeff and Cece told me about. He came into town the day after the storm."

"A drifter?" Edward closed the menu and gave her his full attention. As always, the intensity of his dark gaze traveled along her nerve endings like fire. Even though his hair had turned to silver and the laugh lines had deepened at the corners of his mouth and eyes, he was still a very handsome man—the sexiest man in the world—and she would think that way until the day she died.

"That's kind of an old-fashioned term, but yes, I guess you could call him that," Alyssa admitted. At nine o'clock on a Thursday evening, the dining room was nearly empty. It was a slow time of year at the hotel, a lull between the last of the autumn-color weekends and the start of the busy holiday and cross-country ski season. There were no more than six or eight other diners sharing the wood-paneled, firelit room with them. Of those diners, only two were Tyler residents—police captain Brick Bauer and his wife, Karen Keppler-Bauer.

"I thought you were going to wait until Joe Santori had a chance to take a look at the porch rail."

"I was. But he's so busy with the condos out on Lake Shore Road. And after that storm last week a lot of other people have work for him."

"Pretty bad storm, eh?" Edward had spent his adult life in boardrooms and executive suites all over Europe and the States, but had been born and bred in Tyler and knew the power and scope of a Wisconsin thunderstorm as well as anyone.

"Someone spotted a funnel cloud on the other side of the lake, but no one was hurt."

"That's good to hear."

"Yes. But that's beside the point. I want that porch railing fixed. I worry about the girls. Annie and Belle are forever taking tumbles. And Margaret Alyssa..." She left the rest of the sentence unspoken.

Edward held up his hand in surrender. "I know, I know. She thinks she's a monkey."

"She *is* a monkey. Last week I caught her building a pyramid of chairs and sofa cushions so that she could try swinging from the living-room chandelier.'' Alyssa shuddered at the memory. ''And there are some other things I'd like taken care of. Two of the barn windows were broken out and the garden gazebo needs some floorboards replaced.''

''I guess what I'm really asking is, have you checked this guy out?''

''Well, no. But Cece says that Sarah Fleming...''

Edward was looking over her shoulder at someone approaching their table. He half rose from his chair. ''Brick. Karen. Good to see you.'' Edward held out his hand and Brick shook it enthusiastically.

''I told Karen it was you,'' Brick said, smiling broadly. ''Welcome back.''

''And I told him it was your first night back in town and we shouldn't interrupt.''

''Hello, Karen,'' Alyssa said, smiling up at the younger woman. ''You're not interrupting anything.'' She patted the adjacent chair. ''Sit down. We haven't seen you in a long while.''

''Headquarters is a zoo,'' Karen said. She was a tall woman, slender, with an underlying strength that showed in the self-assured way she handled herself. ''Some days I wish I were back in Tyler.''

Brick had remained standing when Karen sat down beside Alyssa. He leaned over the back of her chair and brushed her hair with his lips. ''No, you don't, honey. You know you love the departmental politics and the policy making that goes on at headquarters.''

''And it's much more convenient to your classes,'' Alyssa added. Karen was working on a master's degree in criminology.

''It really keeps me on my toes.'' Karen had a tendency to be too serious about her work and her life, but Brick was never too serious about anything and he brought out the best in his wife.

"Besides, if she came back to Tyler I'd be out of a job," Brick said with a grin. "She has seniority."

"Oh, Brick. I miss everybody here."

"You'll have a lot more extra time after you graduate in the spring. That's when we've decided to start building the house," he announced.

"That's a lovely piece of property you have out by the lake."

"It is," Karen said, smiling. "I can't wait to start."

"Alyssa was just telling me she hired a man to do some repairs on our place," Edward said.

"Michael Kenton?" Brick moved around the table to settle into the empty seat beside Edward.

"Yes, he's the one." Alyssa looked over at the man who was now Tyler's police captain, a job he'd wanted since he was a boy. "How did you know?"

"Just a guess. Several other people have hired him to do work around their places."

"He seems very competent. Cece said he did a very good job on the roof of Tyler Fellowship. If he hadn't taken the job, Sarah Fleming told them, she would have had to shut down the day-care center until she could find someone else to do the work."

"What do you know about him, Brick?" Edward asked.

"Not much, but if he's going to be staying around town for a while, I think I'll check up on him."

"Is that necessary?" Alyssa asked.

Brick shrugged. "Just routine. I don't expect to find anything. But you have to admit his showing up in Tyler right after that storm was quite a coincidence."

"From what I've heard it sounds more like a blessing." Alyssa felt compelled to defend Michael Kenton, and she wasn't altogether certain why.

"Yeah, well maybe." Brick's tone was noncommittal, but there was a frown between his eyes. "But I'd rather be safe than sorry."

"MR. KENTON?"

He wondered how long he would have to be around before Sarah Fleming used his given name. "It's Michael," he reminded her for at least the third time.

"Michael," she repeated dutifully. "What do you think? Have the shingles sealed properly?" She was looking up at him, her hand shielding her eyes from the last rays of the setting sun. She was dressed in her usual, everyday attire—jeans or a skirt and blouse and a sweater or jacket. Today her blouse was lemon yellow and her sweater a deep forest green. She looked like a flower, and her hair shone copper and gold in the slanting light.

"Your prayer meeting last night did the trick, Reverend Sarah. There was enough sun today to finish the job. Your church roof is good as new."

"Better," she said, ignoring his barb about the prayer meeting.

He shoved his hammer into a loop of his tool belt and moved toward the ladder, watching Sarah from the corner of his eye. He didn't know why he kept needling her that way. He had nothing against religion, any religion. He didn't care one way or the other. There was nothing inside him left to care.

"I wish you would come down from there," she said sharply. "You make me nervous."

He hunkered down, bracing himself against the pitch of the roof. "Are you afraid I'll fall?"

"The thought has crossed my mind," she admitted, flushing slightly. Her skin was so clear and pale that she blushed constantly.

She would blush like that if he kissed her, or put his hands on her breasts, or made love to her. *God, where had that ridiculous thought came from?* Or maybe it wasn't so ridiculous. If the truth were told Sarah Fleming had a damn good body, the kind of woman's body made for love. Angry with himself, he spoke without further thought.

"And then you'd be afraid I'd sue you. If I didn't break my neck in the fall."

"Don't. Don't say that." The cry was torn from her heart.

Michael swung onto the ladder and climbed down. *Dammit, he'd done it again. Opened his mouth and stuck his foot in it.* Her husband had died in a freak accident. He shouldn't have teased her about something like that.

Sarah's hands were curled into fists around the armload of file folders she was carrying. He reached out and laid his hand over one of hers. She drew in her breath sharply and looked into his eyes, focusing on him, on the here and now and not on the terrors of the past.

"You okay?" he asked, lifting his hand away, resisting the urge to rub his palm down the side of his jeans. Her skin was as soft and warm as he'd imagined it to be. What he hadn't expected, was the intensity of the jolt of physical awareness that had streaked along his nerve endings like a live current through a wire when he touched her.

"Yes. I'm—I'm fine."

She didn't look fine. She looked sad and a little

dazed. He amazed himself again by wanting to reach out and wipe that sadness away, make her smile. A real smile, not the practiced gesture he'd come to think of as her "Reverend Sarah" smile. "I didn't mean to frighten you."

"You didn't frighten me, but I admit I don't like heights."

"And you don't like daredevils."

"I don't like people taking foolish chances."

"Did your husband take chances?" Now why had he said that? What business was it of his what kind of man her dead husband had been?

"No," she said. "He was a very careful man."

"But he died anyway."

"Yes. His snowmobile hit a rock buried under the snow and turned over on him. He broke his neck and died instantly."

"Hell." He ran his hand through his hair. "I didn't know that. I'm sorry I made that crack about falling and breaking my neck."

"That's not necessary, Mr.—Michael. Eric's been dead three years. You just caught me off guard, that's all." She changed the subject. "Are you done working for the day?"

He squinted up at the darkening sky. "All done."

"Then it's my turn to apologize. I got so caught up going over my youth group's winter-project suggestions that I forgot to start dinner."

"No problem. I'll grab something at the diner."

"Oh. Okay, if you choose."

Michael looked at her but she had dropped her gaze to the ground between them. Had he imagined it or was she disappointed that he planned to eat out tonight? Did she look forward, as he had come to do, to those short minutes they spent together when he picked up his food or returned the clean dishes every morning?

"Why don't you join me?" he asked.

Her head flew up. "I..."

"Aren't lady preachers allowed to have dinner with a man?"

"Don't be ridiculous." Her hazel eyes flashed gold fire. "I only meant to say I'd have to put the hamburger back in the freezer. I'd intended to make meat loaf for dinner."

"Oh," he said, feeling himself smile. "Meat loaf."

"Yes, but it's Thursday and that means the special at Marge's is meat loaf, and hers is much better than mine."

"I take it that's a yes?"

"Yes." She blushed again. "I mean, I'd be pleased to have dinner with you."

"Michael," he said, wanting to hear his name on her lips again.

She didn't disappoint him. "Michael."

"Good. I'll get cleaned up and pick you up in, say, half an hour?"

"I'll be ready." This time the smile she gave him was full of mischief, and it was his turn to blink in surprise. "We can discuss the final list of repairs the church council okayed. I have them with me somewhere." She fished a typewritten sheet of paper out of one of the file folders. "This should keep you busy as long as you want to stay in town."

Michael held out his hand for the paper. She gave it to him, careful not to touch him, and that was when it hit him that she'd felt that jolt of sexual awareness he'd experienced earlier just as he had. He ignored the immediate physical response of his lower body with willpower born of much practice and concentrated on the words on the paper. He groaned. "I'll be working twenty hours a day if you expect me to get this all done and be out of here before Thanksgiving."

"Is that when you want to be on your way?" Sarah asked softly.

He looked at her, not knowing what to say. Did he want to be gone from this place in three weeks? He didn't know. If he did, he had a lot of things to find out about Tyler in a short amount of time.

A car drove up to the curb. They both turned in that direction. It was a Tyler squad car. Michael's stomach muscles tightened in instinctive response to the sight of the broad-shouldered, dark-haired police officer coming up the walk.

"Brick," Sarah said, walking toward the man who Michael now realized he'd seen a couple of times since he'd been in Tyler. "Is something wrong? Has there been an accident?"

"No, Sarah. Everything's fine." The officer was close enough now for Michael to see that the name stenciled on the plastic tag below his badge was D. Bauer, Chief. Brick was obviously a nickname, and from the size of him, one whose origins weren't hard to figure out.

"Thank goodness. Usually when you show up like this one of my parishioners has had an accident or a heart attack or something bad."

"Everything's fine today. I came to talk to Kenton here."

"Michael?" Bauer gave Sarah a sharp look at the use of his first name, but she didn't pay any attention. "Why do you nccd to talk to him?"

"Just a few routine questions."

"Do you always stop personally to question new-comers to town?" Michael asked, keeping his hands loose at his sides. Cops always looked at your hands, watching for any sudden movements, any threat, any-thing that would give you away. It was second nature to them.

"Sometimes." The cop shifted his stance slightly, as though he expected Michael to bolt and run.

"What's this about, Brick?" Sarah asked.

"It's about what Kenton, here, is doing in Tyler."

"He's working for me. I mean, for the church. You know that as well as I do."

Brick Bauer nodded. "I'm aware of that, Sarah. I mean, what brought you to town in the first place?" His tone was pleasant enough. So was his expression, but that didn't mean a thing.

"The view," Michael said. He'd never had a friendly conversation with a cop in his life. He wasn't about to start now. "I was just driving through and stopped to admire the view."

"Where were you headed when you stopped to enjoy the view?"

Michael shrugged. "Noplace in particular."

Brick nodded toward his pickup. "You own that truck?"

"I imagine you already know the answer to that." Damn, he should have been prepared for this. Tyler might look like a hick town, but this guy was no Barney Fife. He knew what he was doing.

"The truck's registered in Wisconsin. But the De-partment of Motor Vehicles says you're carrying a Florida driver's license. Could I see it?" It was an or-der, not a request.

Michael pulled out his wallet and handed over the

plastic rectangle. ''Florida's my legal place of residence.''

''How'd you end up here?''

''I work on a lake freighter during the season. I left the ship in Milwaukee.''

''How long do you plan to stay?''

''I don't know.''

''Michael B. Kenton.'' The cop handed back his driver's license. ''What's the B. stand for?''

''Bastard,'' Michael said under his breath.

''What?''

''Nothing. The B. doesn't stand for anything. It's just an initial.''

Sarah had been following their exchange in silence. Now she said, ''Brick, what's this third degree all about? I already told you I've hired Michael to do repairs on the church. So have a lot of other people in town.''

''I know. That's why I thought I'd better check him out.''

''Whatever for? If he was a crook or a con man he'd have been long gone by now.'' Sarah took a step toward the cop, crowding him just a little. He stepped back, surprised by her vehemence and her defense of Michael.

Brick gave Michael a sharp look. ''You haven't told her?''

''Would you have?''

''Brick, what are you talking about?'' Sarah demanded. ''Did he tell me what?''

''Kenton, here, is an ex-con. He did three years for arson and insurance fraud in Florida.''

CHAPTER FOUR

"YOU WERE IN PRISON?" Sarah couldn't stop herself from asking the question.

"That's what he said." Michael's face was a mask, his eyes dark pools of obsidian reflecting all the light, giving nothing of his thoughts away.

"Yes, it was." She turned on Brick, taking her anger and her disappointment out on him. She knew Michael Kenton was not a saint; few men would qualify for that title. But a criminal? A convicted felon. She hadn't expected that. Not in a hundred years. "Why did you think it was necessary to check up on Michael's background?"

"I'm a cop, Sarah. That's what I do."

"He hasn't caused any trouble in Tyler."

"No. I agree. But he shows up out of nowhere after a storm that did a lot of damage around here. He's doing business with the townspeople, buying on credit from the local merchants."

"I've paid cash for every damn thing I bought until today. Hell, it was Murphy's idea to open a charge account, not mine." Michael's tone was even, level, but she sensed the tamped-down anger and bitterness underlying his words.

"The church board certainly has no complaints. Mr. Kenton has been doing excellent work for us."

Brick stood his ground. "It's my duty to protect the citizens of Tyler. That's all I was doing."

"I've paid my debt to society, Bauer. I don't have even a speeding-ticket charge against me now. Or didn't you bother to check that far?"

Brick nodded. "I did. You're clean."

"Then why did you come here?" Sarah interjected.

"I told you, it's my job."

"Of course." She looked down at the folders she was carrying and said a quick silent prayer, asking for inspiration that she already knew wouldn't come. She was going to have to work this out on her own. Both men stood without speaking, waiting for her to say something more. "Michael, did you hurt anyone? Did you cause any person pain or suffering?"

"It was a garage full of antique cars that burned. No one was hurt."

"Is that the only crime you committed?"

Brick opened his mouth as if to say something, but Michael held up his hand. "I grew up on the streets in Miami, Sarah. My mother died when I was thirteen. I never knew my dad. My grandmother raised me. She did the best she could, but I was too wild and headstrong to be reined in."

"But you were only a child then."

Michael nodded. "Just a know-it-all kid."

Sarah lifted her chin. She might have doubts sometimes about her spiritual strength, but she didn't have doubts about her ability to read a person's character— at least, not many. Whatever Michael Kenton had done in the past was just that. In the past. For the ten days he'd been living above her garage he'd been a model citizen.

She made herself smile at Brick. "Thanks for coming by. I appreciate your concern, but I don't see any reason to change the way we're doing things here. Michael's paid his debt to society, just like he said. He's not a threat to me or anyone else. He deserves to be left in peace. Now, if you'll excuse me, I have a lot of work to do this evening.''

Brick studied her face for a long moment, then his dark gaze flicked to Michael's hard, set features. ''If that's the way you want it, Reverend Sarah.'' He touched his finger to the brim of his hat. ''Good night, ma'am. Kenton, I'll see you around.'' It wasn't a threat, just a statement. But the warning in Brick's voice was unmistakable.

''Good night, Brick.'' Sarah watched him walk back to his car.

''Did you mean that?'' Michael asked, as the police captain pulled away from the curb.

Sarah lifted her eyes to his, wishing she could read just a fraction of his thoughts so that she could know what he was feeling at this moment. ''Of course I meant it. What you did in the past is none of my business. Or anybody else's in this town, as a matter of fact.''

''I'm an ex-con. A felon,'' he said, emphasizing the word ever so slightly. ''You heard what the cop said.''

''Are you trying to trick me into quoting Scripture here?'' she asked, trying very hard to lighten the darkness in his eyes. ''How about 'he who is without sin, let him cast the first stone'? That's a good one.''

''Does that mean you're not going to throw me out of the apartment?''

''The thought never crossed my mind,'' she said truthfully. ''I told Brick it doesn't matter what you did before you came to Tyler. I'm only concerned with how you conduct yourself now.''

''I could be a danger to you and your flock, Reverend Sarah,'' he said, taking a step closer.

''Don't be ridiculous.'' Sarah held her ground with difficulty. Not because she was frightened of him, of his size and strength, but because during the past ten days she'd discovered she liked his coming near her. Liked the thought of his being close enough for her to feel the warmth of his body and imagine what the work-roughened touch of his hands on her skin, and his mouth on hers, might feel like.

''Do you want to hear my side of the story?''

''If you want to tell me,'' she managed to reply with only the slightest of hesitations. ''I'm not going to force it out of you.''

''I was framed,'' he said bluntly.

''Framed?'' Unbidden, a thought popped into her mind—something she'd read somewhere or heard on TV. *Every man in prison claims he's innocent, a victim of a frame-up or a dishonest cop.*

''Yeah. Framed.'' Michael seemed to be waiting for her to say more. She kept her mouth shut. Let him explain, let him do the talking—that was what a good counselor, a good preacher did. ''Aren't you going to ask why I didn't tell Barney Fife that?''

''He's not Barney Fife. He's a good man and a good cop. And I imagine he's heard that excuse before,'' Sarah said, refusing to back down despite his dark scowl.

Michael stared at her a moment, then the darkness seemed to lessen, just a little. The faintest hint of a smile curled the corners of his mouth. ''Yeah, that's why. Every con in the joint was framed and every cop in the world has heard that sob story a hundred times over.''

''Is it just a story, Michael?''

He ran his hand through his hair. He hadn't had it cut since he'd come to Tyler. It was longer now, just brushing the edge of his collar. ''No, dammit. It's the truth. But it's getting dark and cold out here. Someday I'll buy you a beer and tell you the whole sorry mess, just the way it happened.'' The mockery in his voice was directed at himself, not at her.

''I'm not cold,'' she said, reaching out to touch his arm before she could stop herself. It was only a fleeting touch, feather light, over in a heartbeat, but Michael pulled back as if he'd been burned.

''Yes, you are cold. And probably hungry. Look, would you mind if I give you a rain check on that dinner at Marge's Diner tonight? I don't have much of an appetite anymore.''

''Of course.'' She tried very hard not to let her disappointment show. ''I could bring you some soup and a sandwich. Grilled cheese or fried eggs?'' *Heavens, she sounded like a babbling idiot.*

''Don't bother.'' He turned away, took three steps and then stopped, looking back over his shoulder. ''And Sarah?''

''Yes?''

''Thanks for sticking up for me back there.''

''You're welcome,'' she whispered, but he had already disappeared into the darkness of the backyard.

''No, Margaret Alyssa, you cannot finger-paint with your peanut-butter-and-jelly sandwich.'' Gently but firmly, Glenna McRoberts took the mutilated snack from the little girl's sticky fingers and guided her toward the rest room.

"Why not?"

"Because I said so. And because if you finger-paint a picture for your Grandma Alyssa with peanut butter and jelly, it won't last. It will start to smell funny in a couple of days and your grandma will have to throw it away. If we use paint she can keep it for a long, long time."

"We want to paint, too," Annie Baron piped up.

"Me, too," Belle seconded. The twins, not quite a year younger than their outgoing cousin, were quieter, more reserved, but no less stubborn.

"Babies can't paint," Margaret Alyssa said, sounding superior.

"Momma!" Belle looked at Cece with tears in her gray eyes.

"If Miss Glenna says you can paint, then it's all right with me. Go with Miss Glenna. I'll pick you up when I get done with my work, okay?"

"Okay, Momma."

"Sorry, Angela," Cece muttered, waving her offspring back into the group of preschoolers. "Everything got off on the wrong foot today and the twins aren't in a very good mood."

"Don't worry, Cece. They'll be fine."

"Then I'm off," she said, buttoning her coat. "I'm so sorry I had to cancel our lunch date, Sarah. Maybe tomorrow." She looked distracted. "Or maybe next week would be better. By then I should have this bout of stomach flu at Worthington House under control."

"It's all right, Cece." Sarah smiled. Cece was devoted to her patients at the nursing home. "Give me a call when you have some free time."

"Thanks. I will. Bye, girls." She blew her daughters a kiss. "Be good."

"We will. But we want to paint."

"Then hurry up," Margaret Alyssa warned them. "Or Miss Glenna will change her mind."

Glenna wasn't about to let her small advantage dwindle away. "Exactly. Let's wash your hands and faces and then we can have an apple for a snack before we start to paint, all right?"

"All right," Margaret Alyssa agreed.

"Okay," the twins echoed.

"It's a deal," Glenna said calmly. She was one of Anna and Johnny Kelsey's daughters, whom Sarah was acquainted with from community functions. Recently divorced, she was about Sarah's own age and had the same blue eyes and luxuriant black hair that all the Kelseys possessed, but she was shy and quiet away from the children, and Sarah hadn't gotten to know her very well in the weeks that she'd been working at TylerTots.

"She's doing quite well with the kids," Angela Murphy, the center's director, remarked to Sarah as she guided six toddlers into the quiet room for a story and a nap. "I always like it when we get a clinical student who's got kids of her own and knows how to diffuse a crisis in the making without a fuss."

"The affiliation with Sugar Creek Community College is working out well, isn't it?" Sarah agreed, as she helped settle the toddlers into beanbag chairs and onto cots to listen to the story Angela was selecting from the bookcase.

"It's a godsend. The students get the experience and we get the extra help free of charge. I'm glad the church board agreed to the program. I may even turn a profit this year, and the board can raise my rent.''

''We'll see,'' Sarah said with a smile. She looked around the big, colorful, low-ceilinged room. When she'd come to Tyler with Eric four years earlier, the sanctuary basement had been a dank and dreary place, used only for occasional baby and bridal showers and fellowship breakfasts.

Then she'd met Angela Murphy, the oldest daughter of the owner of Tyler's hardware store, and the idea for TylerTots had been born. Angela had a degree in early childhood education, and Sarah had a dream for a child-care facility that would fill the sanctuary basement with laughing, well-cared-for children.

It had taken nearly a year to acquire the necessary permits and to raise the money to make repairs and alterations to the basement to bring it up to code. But it had been well worth the effort. For a while after Eric's death, getting TylerTots up and running was the only thing that had kept Sarah from giving in to her despair. She still spent as much time as she could manage helping out, but her parish duties were many and varied, and they limited her volunteer time at the center.

''Come on, kids, settle down or no story,'' Angela warned, as the toddlers continued to scoot and wiggle around on their chairs, demanding favorite toys and blankets and drinks of water. ''They're always so wound up on Mondays,'' she lamented, as Sarah retrieved a stuffed dinosaur for one little boy and a much-abused and much-loved baby doll for the little girl beside him.

''Michael Kenton will be over to fix that leaky faucet in the boys' rest room this afternoon,'' Sarah said, tucking up the little girl with the doll.

"Michael Kenton?" Angela's head snapped up. A frown appeared between her eyebrows. "Do you think that's wise?" She signaled one of the aides to take the storybook she was holding and motioned Sarah toward the kitchen, where the smells of lunch preparation made Sarah's stomach growl.

Now it was Sarah's turn to frown. "What are you getting at Angela?" she asked, but she was afraid she already knew.

Angela had the grace to look a bit sheepish. "Well, I mean, do you think it's a good idea having that man here while the children are around? He is an ex-convict, after all."

"Who told you that?" Brick had promised to keep the information under his hat. She'd never known Brick Bauer to go back on his word, but it seemed the only explanation. How else would Angela have learned of Michael's past, if not from the police captain?

"I'd rather not say."

"Who, Angela?"

"Well, it was Betsy Arnold, my friend who's an emergency-squad tech. She overheard a couple of the deputies talking about him when she was down at the police station filling out an accident report the other day. And my dad's been kind of suspicious ever since Brick stopped by to talk about the guy last week."

"Whatever Michael Kenton did in the past is none of our business." No one had confronted her with the information at church yesterday. Perhaps Angela's friend hadn't spread the rumor any farther, although she suspected that was wishful thinking on her part.

"Where my kids are concerned, it is my business," Angela reminded her. "Who knows what kind of man he is? I'd just rather you asked him to fix the faucet after six o'clock, that's all. When the children aren't here. I don't think that's too much to ask.''

Sarah wanted to say that she thought it *was* too much to ask but she knew that Angela's mind was made up. Angela took her responsibilities very seriously. She was in complete charge of the center, and Sarah didn't have the authority to overrule her objection.

"I'll stop by the apartment and speak to him as soon as I leave here.''

"Thanks, Sarah. I have to consider the children's safety first. How do we know this guy isn't some kind of sex pervert or something?''

"He isn't dangerous, Angela. I'm certain of that.''

"I wish I could be certain, too, Sarah. But I can't. And even though it's an old cliché, it's still better to be safe than sorry.''

Angela was the first person to alert Sarah that Michael's past was becoming common knowledge in Tyler, but she wasn't the last. He wasn't in the apartment when she left TylerTots, so she headed for the study in the drafty old parsonage to work on the lesson plan for December's Sunday-school classes and to await his return. She had no more than settled herself behind her desk when the phone rang.

By the time she finally closed the untouched plan book in defeat, she'd heard from two board members and one other concerned parishioner. She'd been right to be worried when Angela told her what she'd learned. The news was spreading like wildfire through the town. She switched on the answering machine so that she wouldn't have to spend any more time on the phone explaining to her startled and suspicious flock that being a Christian meant being tolerant of another's faults, forgiving others their mistakes. She felt as if she were talking to a brick wall.

Her parishioners were good people, but many of them had been tested in life's fires, as well, and they were not as forgiving of weakness as they might be. They lived by a strict code of honor and duty and accepting responsibility. Michael Kenton had failed that high standard. He was now a marked man.

MICHAEL GLANCED at the clock above the chipped and rust-stained kitchen sink as he pulled a can of cola out of the refrigerator and popped the top. He took a long drink of the soda and let the sweet liquid burn its way down his throat. He'd started work on Alyssa Wocheck's porch rail today. Alyssa Ingalls Baron Wocheck. And he'd met her granddaughters, Annie and Belle Baron, and Margaret Alyssa Forrester. Cute kids. Happy and healthy and cherished. It was easy to see that.

Yeah, it had been quite a day. And it was still only a little after four o'clock. He had plenty of time to fix the leaky faucet at the day-care center. Maybe Sarah would be there and he could ask her out on the town. Michael let the corners of his mouth curl in a self-deprecating smile. A burger at Marge's Diner—what a thrill for her.

It had been five days since Brick Bauer had shown up and lowered the boom on him. Five days of watching and waiting to see what would happen next. But telling Sarah about his criminal record seemed to be as far as it had gone. He wasn't used to small-town cops. Maybe they were different; maybe this one was different, a man of his word. A knock at the door interrupted his musing.

It was Sarah, as he knew it would be, looking cool and calm in a soft beige sweater and brown cotton skirt, her hair pulled up into a soft knot on top of her head, small gold hearts gleaming in her ears.

"Hi," he said, opening the door a little wider. He hadn't lighted the stove and the room was cold. It was cold and gloomy outside, too, with a hint of snow in the air. He'd been twenty-two years old when he first saw snow—through the window of his cell in the Tennessee prison where he'd spent the last six months of his sentence.

"Hi." She wrapped her arms around herself, pushing her breasts upward, highlighting the creamy expanse of skin visible at the V neck of her sweater.

"I've been working at the Wocheck place this afternoon, but I was just coming down to start on that leaky faucet at the day-care center."

"I thought that might be what you planned to do."

"After I'm done I'd like to take you to dinner at Marge's. To make up for backing out on you the other night."

"I—I'd like that," she said.

"What's wrong?" Something was bothering her, that was obvious. Her emotions were always close to the surface and easy to read.

"I just wanted to tell you that Angela Murphy thought it might be less disruptive for the kids if you fixed the faucet after the center closes at six."

"She didn't seem to think it would be a problem if I worked around the kids when I was over there Friday afternoon."

"That was Friday. This is Monday. The kids are pretty rambunctious today."

"Rambunctious?"

She gave him a wan little smile. "It's one of my mother's favorite words for the way my brothers and I behaved when we were acting up."

"That's not the only reason you're here, is it?" A cold finger of apprehension skittered up and down his spine. There was only one thing he could think of that she would have to tell him that would make her this uneasy.

"I—"

"A bunch of hyperactive kids is just an excuse. This Angela Murphy doesn't want me working on the sink right now, isn't that it?"

"No. Yes." Sarah took a step forward, as though to put her hand on his arm, and then stopped with the table still between them. Instead, she reached out to curl her hands around the back of one of the mismatched wooden chairs. "Angela is concerned—"

He leaned forward abruptly, making the salt and pepper shakers jump as he spread both hands flat on the table. "Your cop friend ratted on me, didn't he?"

"No." She was quick to jump to Brick Bauer's defense. "It was an accident. Someone overheard two of Brick's deputies discussing you. That person told someone else—"

"Who told someone else, who passed it along to their Aunt Tillie and half the free world."

She shrugged. "That's the way small towns work."

"Well," he said, "I guess it's time for me to move on."

Something in his tone must have alerted Sarah to what he was feeling. "Why?" she asked, tilting her head just a little in a mannerism he was coming to know meant that she was zeroing in on the emotions underlying a conversation. "Why should you leave?"

"C'mon, you've seen the movies. Ex-con comes to town. People find out. The good citizens of the place ride him out of town on a rail."

"This has never happened to you before, has it?"

God, she was fast on the uptake. Him, the guy who'd gotten the nickname "Stoneface" in the joint because he kept his emotions so well hidden from them all. She took one look at him and knew what he was thinking, or thought she knew. If being ostracized by the citizenry was what she thought had upset him, he wasn't going to disabuse her of the notion.

"I've never stayed in one place long enough for anyone to find out," he replied.

"Then you have no idea how people will react."

"I've got a damn good idea. And so do you." She didn't have an answer for that and looked down at her hands. "We know what Angela Murphy thinks. How many others have you heard from?"

"One or two," she admitted. "But they just wanted to—"

"Warn you?"

Her head came up. Her chin jutted out. "Inform me," she insisted. "And even if they did want to *warn* me about you, don't you think I can take care of myself? You're not a murderer or a rapist, after all."

He wondered if she would be so certain of his essential harmlessness if she became aware of how prominently she had figured in his dreams—hot, hard and totally erotic dreams—these past few nights.

"No, I'm not a murderer or a rapist. I'm just a dumb guy who let someone he trusted make a damn jackass of him. It cost me my business, my reputation and three years of my life."

"You really were framed?"

"I told you I was."

"What happened, Michael?" She leaned forward and the empathy and compassion in her gold-and-green eyes were almost his undoing. He sucked in his breath and took a step backward, away from her heat and her scent, away from temptation.

"I'll tell you all about it sometime. But not tonight, okay." He felt like crawling into a deep hole and dragging it in on top of him.

"Do you still want to take me to Marge's? Or are you going to stand me up again?" she asked unexpectedly.

Michael jerked his head up, his eyes drawn to hers. Their gazes met and held. "I..." Maybe he should tell her now. It was nothing so terrible, after all.

"You can't stay holed up in here, Michael. Unless you're going to pack up in the dead of night and leave town, you'll have to face them all sooner or later."

"I'm not going to leave town."

She nodded. "Good. I knew you didn't mean that when you said it earlier."

"But I still don't feel like eating out in public tonight, do you understand?"

"I understand."

"And you don't have to be my champion, Sarah." He amazed himself by saying that. It had been a long time since he'd thought of anyone but himself first. He wasn't ready to tell her everything there was to know about him. And he didn't want her drawn into any controversy he might arouse.

"I know," she said and smiled, a quick, almost-mischievous twist of her lips. "You want to fight your own battles. But don't be surprised if I do start acting like your knight in shining armor." She laughed and threw up her hands, blushing a little. "Sometimes I can't help myself. I'm good at it."

The door closed softly behind her. Michael stood rooted to the cold linoleum floor for five seconds longer, then padded to the window behind his bed so that he could watch her walk into her house. What was it about this small, shy woman that drew him so irresistibly? She was nothing like the women who had always attracted him.

And he sure as hell must be nothing like the man that she had loved and lost. But it was there—something in the air between them. The shy and chaste Reverend Sarah might not recognize it for what it was, but he did. It was sex, the basic primordial attraction of male to female. It was lust. And he had it bad. It was that more than uneasiness about meeting a Tyler gossip in Marge's that prompted him to stand her up yet again. Or fear that he might weaken and tell her the real reason he didn't want to leave Tyler.

Difficult as it was, he could put Sarah out of his mind if he had to. He wasn't that much of a slave to his hormones. And he had other fish to fry tonight. Having the townspeople know about his past was a blow, but not a knockout punch. He still had his secrets, and with any luck they'd stay just that—secret. He wasn't ready to leave Tyler, not yet. There were still too many questions he didn't have the answers to, too many people he wanted to meet, too many things about the Barons and the Ingallses that he still wanted to learn.

CHAPTER FIVE

"AND THAT CONCLUDES the sports-awards portion of our ceremony." The public-address system suddenly decided to become temperamental, and the voice of Tyler High's principal, Clint Stafford, was drowned out by a series of clicks and squeals that had half the three hundred or so parents and students in attendance covering their ears and frowning in discomfort.

Clint signaled the students who were manning the sound system's controls, and adjustments were made, then he lifted his hands and grinned. "Sorry about that, folks. Can you hear me okay now?" He was a tall man, strong and sturdy looking with dark hair and eyes. He'd been hired as vice-principal eighteen months earlier. He was a tough disciplinarian and an innovative teacher and administrator, just what Tyler High needed.

Sarah found herself nodding in answer to his jovial question and felt foolish for doing so. She shifted on the hard bleacher seat and tried to get comfortable. The ceremony had lasted more than an hour already. Two teens from her Scripture-study group were receiving awards tonight, one for English and one for music, and she'd promised weeks ago to be in attendance. But with all that had happened regarding Michael Kenton in the past few days, she wished she could have stayed home. She wasn't in the mood to defend her decision to allow him to remain in the garage apartment to any more of the members of Tyler Fellowship, or the townspeople at large, for that matter.

"Ladies and gentlemen and Tyler students, it's now my pleasure to introduce Dr. Jeffrey Baron, who will announce the candidates chosen to enter the Ingalls F and M apprenticeship program for the current school year. As you know, each semester two students are invited to work in the Ingalls lab on a project they've submitted to the screening committee. Tonight two juniors will join the students already enrolled in the program. Dr. Baron will present the award on behalf of his grandfather, Judson Ingalls."

Jeff Baron rose from his seat beside his mother on the stage and came to the microphone. He was a very good-looking man, with old Judson Ingalls's commanding profile and the chestnut hair and dark blue eyes that must have come from the Baron side of his family.

"Tonight I'd like to honor two young people for their initiative and hard work by giving them a chance to develop further in the lab at Ingalls F and M science projects they've planned. Matt Hansen will be working on hormone production in dairy goats." There was a polite round of applause as the tall, slender young man rose from his seat on the gym floor and climbed the steps to the stage. Jeff presented him with a plaque and shook his hand. There was more polite applause.

Sarah's bottom was getting numb. She glanced down at her program and noted there were only two more awards after this one. Thank goodness. In a few more minutes she could go home.

"And our second winner is Jonathan Weiss, who will be studying the effects of ultraviolet radiation on single-celled plant life." A tall, rangy sixteen-year-old sitting two rows below Sarah, ordinary looking except for his devastatingly sexy smile, unfolded himself from his seat and headed toward the stage. The woman sitting beside him must be his mother. Marina, Sarah thought her name was. If there was a Mr. Weiss, Sarah had never met him. The family was new in town and didn't attend Tyler Fellowship, so her contact with them had been limited. She had met Jon a few months earlier, when he'd stopped by the parsonage one afternoon with a friend who was a member of her teen group. She had invited him to return and join the group if he liked and his mother approved, but he never had.

"Congratulations, Jon," Jeff Baron said. The boy took the plaque Jeff handed him, shook hands, mumbled his thanks and returned to his seat as the awards ceremony continued.

Fifteen minutes later it was all over. Sarah stayed in her place until the gymnasium had started to empty. If she got caught up in the milling throng of proud, camera-toting parents and their embarrassed offspring, she was sure to be stopped and questioned by someone else with an opinion on how the problem of an ex-convict in her garage should be handled.

Finally she saw a clear path down the bleacher steps to the double doors that led to the parking lot behind the school. Looking neither right nor left, she made a beeline in that direction, only to be caught up in a small traffic jam of people directly in front of the door as they stopped to zip up jackets and fumble for scarves and gloves.

"It's snowing," someone called out. There were moans from the adults and whistles and whoops from the kids.

"The first snowfall," Alyssa Wocheck said, coming

up behind Sarah. "When I was a child I couldn't wait for it to happen so I could get out my sled and have my father sharpen my skates."

"Hello, Alyssa." Here, at least, was one person who wouldn't lecture her about the possible dangers of harboring an ex-convict on her property. Alyssa had been keeping Michael busy with repairs to the big old house on Elm Street. "You sound as if it isn't such an exciting event for you anymore."

"Well," she said, and laughed as she smoothed her gloves over her hands, "that was more than forty winters ago. Now I think how long the winters will be, but inside I'm still that same wide-eyed little girl. Yes, I do get excited by the first snow."

"So do I," Sarah confessed. "I feel just like those kids. Right up until I have to wrestle the snowblower out of the garage and tackle my driveway."

The knot of people in front of the door began moving forward once more. Outside it had indeed begun to snow, big fluffy white flakes coming straight down out of a charcoal-gray sky that seemed low enough to reach up and touch. They walked in silence for a minute or so, adjusting to the cold wet air in their lungs and the slippery snow underfoot.

A woman waved at them from behind the first row of cars. "Sarah! Reverend Fleming! Wait, please."

"Oh dear," Sarah said, half under her breath. "It's Myra Allen. And we were so close to making a clean getaway. Hello, Myra."

"I would like to talk to you for a moment. It's about that man. Hello, Alyssa," she said, bobbing her head in the birdlike manner that annoyed Sarah so. "That convict that you have staying in the apartment over the parsonage garage."

"He's not a convict, Myra."

"Well, ex-convict. Why split hairs? I'm just worried about you. A woman alone…"

Sarah was tired of defending her decision to let Michael Kenton remain in the garage apartment. The man had done nothing wrong. But Myra was a member of her congregation. She'd been attending services faithfully for the past fourteen months, and Sarah couldn't tell her to her face that she thought she was out of line. "What are you trying to say, Myra? That I'm not safe in my own home?"

"Well, we really don't know anything about that man, and you are all alone in the pars—"

"Your concern is admirable," Alyssa broke in, her voice unruffled. "But Sarah is perfectly capable of taking care of herself. And really, Myra, as Christians, we should be more tolerant of the mistakes of others. As Sarah said, Michael Kenton is a free man. Whatever crimes he committed in the past he's made restitution for."

"I suppose you're right."

"I couldn't have said it better myself, Myra." Sarah smiled again, this time without any effort. "And don't forget, the church board is aware of Michael Kenton's record. They have voted to allow him to stay on. That should carry some weight with you." She closed her eyes for a moment and said a quick, silent prayer of thanksgiving for Jonas and Randy Phillips. Their solid, unwavering support had helped convince the other three board members not to send Michael packing. "Don't worry, Myra. And don't rush to judge him. He's been a godsend for the church."

"And a real help for the rest of us who have availed ourselves of his services," Alyssa prompted.

"When you put it that way..." Myra wasn't a mean or vindictive person, but she was easily swayed. Sarah just hoped they had nudged her far enough in the right direction that she didn't slide back again.

"I knew you would understand, Myra. Now I really must be going. I'll see you at choir practice Thursday evening, won't I?"

"I'll be there with bells on. Goodbye, Sarah. Goodbye, Alyssa."

"I take it this isn't the first heart-to-heart you've had with one of your flock?" Alyssa asked as they started walking again.

"No, and it probably won't be the last. I may have to start behaving like the old-time fire-and-brimstone preachers and harangue them from the pulpit Sunday morning."

"I think you would be very good at it," Alyssa said unexpectedly.

Sarah laughed, half embarrassed, half pleased by the remark. "I usually try to get my point across a little more subtly than that. You catch more flies with honey than vinegar doing the Lord's work, too."

"I imagine that's true. May I offer you a ride home?" Alyssa asked. "I'll be going past the parsonage on my way out to Timberlake." She pushed up the sleeve of her coat to look at her watch. "Devon's finally returned from Europe, and if I hurry I can be there in time to say good-night to my father-in-law before he goes to bed."

"Thank you, but no. I think I'll walk."

"I'll walk with you partway then, if you don't mind. I was lucky and found a parking space right by the sidewalk."

"Thanks," Sarah said. "I'd like the company."

Alyssa smiled as though she had read her thoughts. "We don't have to make small talk, you know. And I certainly won't lecture you about Michael Kenton the way Myra did."

"What do you think of him, Alyssa?"

"I don't know him well enough to venture an opinion," she said cautiously. Her tone was neutral, but there was a slight frown between the older woman's eyebrows as Sarah glanced over at her. "He's punctual, neat, a hard worker. And I don't believe he's said more than a dozen words to me over the past three days. I don't think I'm going out on a limb if I say he's a very hard man to get to know. Although…" She laughed a little and shook her head. "It's odd. I can't get him to string more than a dozen words together at one time, but the little ones think he's wonderful."

"Your grandchildren have met him?"

"Yes. They were all three running around the house the other afternoon. They were fascinated by what he was doing to the porch. They pestered him with questions for a good fifteen minutes, and he answered each and every one as if he were talking to the three most important young women on earth."

Sarah liked hearing that about Michael Kenton—that he was good with children.

Alyssa opened her purse and began looking for her car keys. "Are you sure I can't drop you at home?"

"No, thanks. I like walking in the snow. Good night, Alyssa."

"Good night, Sarah. And stick to your guns where Michael Kenton is concerned."

"I will." She had no choice. Already she was aware that her interest in him had gone far beyond her role as pastor of her flock. She was interested in Michael Kenton the man as well as Michael Kenton the lost soul.

HE WAS LIKE A KID when it came to snow. He couldn't get enough of it. Of course, he'd never spent the entire winter in a place like Tyler, never stuck around for the short, dark February days and braved the cold, biting winds of March. Before today the longest he'd lingered along the shores of the Great Lakes had been when the weather was unusually mild and the shipping season dragged on into late November.

He turned his collar up around his ears and stuck his hands in the pockets of his old navy peacoat. He wasn't wearing a hat but he'd grabbed his gloves on the way out of the apartment and now he was standing under the branches of the crippled maple near the driveway, his face lifted to the sky, letting the big, wet snowflakes melt on his skin and tongue just like a ten-year-old.

He wondered if the tree would make it through the winter, as Sarah insisted it would, or whether it would have to be cut down in the spring. He smiled a little to himself. If anyone could will the old maple into good health, it was Sarah. She believed in miracles even if he didn't.

Michael heard Sarah coming before he saw her, the heels of her boots tap-tapping along the sidewalk, loud in the quiet that was settling over Tyler with the first snowfall. He spoke as soon as she turned onto the sidewalk that paralleled the driveway so that she wouldn't be frightened when she spotted his dark figure under the tree.

"Do you think the snow will stick around or will the sun come out and melt it all tomorrow?"

"Michael?" She didn't sound in the least startled. "What are you doing standing under that tree?"

"Playing in the snow."

She laughed, and he thought that must be how sleigh bells sounded. She settled the strap of her purse higher on her shoulder in a purely feminine gesture he found surprisingly erotic—but then, for him, just about any movement Sarah made was erotic. "I forgot you're from Florida. Have you seen snow before?"

"Yes," he said, knowing he was frowning and glad she couldn't see his face. "I've seen snow before, but not often enough to be bored by it."

"When I was growing up in Brazil I always used to dream of seeing snow," Sarah said, coming closer to join him in the lacy shadows cast by the branches of the great tree. "The first time I saw it was when I was sent to boarding school in Ohio."

"You were born in Brazil?"

She laughed again. "No. I was born in North Carolina, but I lived in Brazil until I was twelve. My parents were missionaries." Something in her tone told him she didn't want to talk about her parents, but he asked anyway. His own childhood had been so fragmented, so unsettled due to an alcoholic mother and absent father, that he was always curious how other people lived.

"Are your parents still alive?"

"Yes. They're officially retired, but they're doing outreach work in Arizona. Serving others through the church is what gives meaning to their life." He didn't have to ask what that meant. Sarah would have a hard time competing with her parents' devotion to their life's work, so he suspected that in her own mind she'd never quite measured up, never been quite good enough for them to love with all their heart and soul. He'd learned a lot from the shrinks they'd made him talk to in prison.

"No brothers or sisters?"

"Two brothers," she said, leaning against the tree trunk to watch the snowflakes fall through the branches. One stuck on her long, dark lashes, and he longed to reach out and brush it away. "Both of them are older. One is a teacher in Nebraska and the other the programming manager of a religious radio station in Chicago."

"Do you see them often?"

"They're busy. I'm busy," she hedged.

"But you followed Mom and Dad into the family business."

It was her turn to frown. "Actually, I have a teaching certificate. But I met Eric one summer at a mission retreat and we fell in love. He did want to follow the path my parents had chosen as their way to serve the Lord, and I wanted to follow him. To help people. He had a true calling." She hesitated, then looked straight at him. "I struggle," she said simply.

"Does that mean you wish you weren't Reverend Sarah?"

Her smile was a little crooked. "No. It just means I wish I were better at what I do."

"You *are* very good at what you do."

"Thank you for saying so." She held out her hand to catch a snowflake on her glove and changed the subject. "I'm sorry to say this snow won't last. But be patient. You'll see more than you care to if you hang around Tyler long enough."

"Will I be hanging around Tyler?" He thought of seeing the maple tree put out leaves in the spring, of

Sarah standing beneath its shade, and he realized he wanted very much to be there with her.

"I told you the church board is very satisfied with your work."

"Then I'm definitely not going to be ridden out of town on a rail?"

"Stop saying that. No one's out to lynch you. We're not that kind of people here." Her eyes flashed and he smiled to himself. He liked getting a rise out of her. There was so much spirit, so much fire bottled up inside the Reverend Sarah Fleming, heat and passion to rival the sun.

He propped one hand against the tree, so close to her that the silky tendrils of her hair brushed the inside of his wrist. "Then you think it's safe for me to stay?"

"It's safe," she said, lifting her eyes to his. Her gaze was steady but guarded. "Are you staying?"

"For a while." He shouldn't be talking to her this way. He wasn't telling her the whole truth, couldn't tell her the whole truth, and he didn't like lying to her. But she was so close and so warm and she smelled so good. She was the woman who haunted his dreams every night and filled his waking hours with fantasies he wondered if she might not like to share.

"Then you'll be here for Thanksgiving next week?"

"Thanksgiving? It is coming up, isn't it? Are you going to Chicago or Nebraska or Arizona for the weekend?"

She shook her head, and her hair brushed like cool fire across his skin. "No," she said, her voice barely above a whisper. "I'm staying here. And I'm fixing a turkey with all the trimmings even if I have to eat the whole bird myself."

"Then I'll stay here, too."

"Isn't there anyone you want to be with?"

You, he thought but knew enough not to say it out loud.

"There was only my grandmother, and she died last spring. And she wasn't a turkey-and-stuffing-and-pumpkin-pie kind of grandmother when she was alive." He thought of the rough-spoken, wisecracking woman who had been the only source of love in his youth and he mourned her loss, as he did every time he thought of her.

"I'm sorry."

"Don't be," he said, and lowered his mouth to hers. Her lips were cold and she stiffened instinctively at his touch. For a moment he thought she would continue to resist, that he had read her all wrong, that she wasn't interested in him at all.

Then her lips warmed beneath his, flowered open as he leaned closer so that their bodies almost touched. She lifted her arms, circled his neck and erased that small distance between them. He could only guess at her softness beneath the clothes she wore, but it was enough to send a rush of heated blood through his veins. Her breath sifted out in a sigh that warmed his cheeks. *God, she felt good, held against his body. Not just man-and-woman good, but right. As though their bodies were meant to fit together just this way.*

He probed her open mouth with his tongue, letting the rhythm of their kiss substitute for a more intimate joining. For a moment she allowed him that liberty, kissed him back with a passion that matched his own. Then she made a small, urgent sound in the back of her throat and pushed at his shoulders. For another moment Michael resisted her efforts to separate them. He knew the way a woman's body reacted. Sarah wanted this as much as he did. And if he persisted she would not deny him.

Reluctantly he stepped away. He didn't want it to be like that. He wanted Sarah to come to him with open arms—and an open heart. To stay with him.

Stay with him? What did that mean? An affair? Not with Sarah. With Sarah it would mean commitment.

He took two steps backward, so quickly he almost stumbled over his own feet. "It's getting late," he said, his voice hoarse with the cold and with the passion that still streaked through his veins. "And it's freezing out here. You should be inside."

"Yes." She didn't sound like herself either. She lifted her fingers to her mouth. "I—"

He reached out and laid his fingers over hers. "Don't say anything. It was just a kiss." If that was just a kiss, he couldn't begin to imagine what making love to her would be like.

"Just a kiss," Sarah repeated. She closed her eyes, took a deep breath and opened them again. "Just a kiss," she said more firmly. "Good night, Michael."

"Good night, Sarah."

She turned to go, then looked back over her shoulder. It had stopped snowing a few minutes ago. It was still and quiet, with only the rustling of bare branches as the ancient maple settled into sleep overhead. Her face was a pale oval in the faint glow of the streetlight on the corner. "I'd like it very much if you'd share Thanksgiving dinner with me."

"I'd like that," he said. *And maybe by then I'll be able to tell you why I'm really here.*

"Good," she said and smiled. Her real smile, her Sarah-from-the-heart smile. "We'll eat at two."

CHAPTER SIX

"IT'S DARK AS HADES in here. There's a light switch beside the workbench if you need help finding anything."

Michael didn't let it show that Edward Wocheck's entrance into the small barn behind the Ingalls house had startled him. He'd been so intent on studying the vintage Bentley, whose innards were spread out on that same workbench, that he hadn't heard the other man approach. He turned slowly, schooling his expression into one of only ordinary interest, even though he knew Edward couldn't see his face.

"It doesn't matter. I don't need the light. I'm only here to check the windows on the west side. Mrs. Wocheck thinks they need replacing before winter." That was the truth. Checking out the Bentley under its thin sheet of protective plastic—ordinary, throwaway painter's drop cloths like those he used every day—was an unexpected bonus. It had been years, almost six altogether, since he'd been this close to a classic automobile.

"They do," Edward agreed. "But it's four o'clock on the day before Thanksgiving. Can't it wait until Friday? Or Monday?"

"I've got nothing better to do this afternoon."

"I thought you were doing some work for Liza and Cliff today."

Michael tensed. Edward Wocheck was an important man. Not just in Tyler, but any damn place you wanted to name. Not the kind of man who went out of his way to keep track of the hired help's schedule, unless there was a damn good reason for doing so. It had been a week since the word had gotten out about his past. A quiet seven days without any problems. It seemed after the first flurry of phone calls and nervous speculation that the townsfolk had decided he wasn't going to murder them in their beds. And if they hadn't actually accepted him as one of their own, they had left him alone. That was the way he liked it. That was the way he wanted it to stay.

"I replaced some floorboards on the deck at Mrs. Forrester's place this morning. It's too cold to stain them, though. That'll probably have to wait until spring. The winter will be hard on them. I explained all that, but your daughter-in-law wanted the repairs done today, regardless."

Edward Wocheck smiled and shook his head. "And what Liza wants, Liza usually gets."

"That's what I figured." Liza Baron Forrester was the youngest of Alyssa Wocheck's offspring—maybe a year or so older than Michael was. She was slender and blond, a little flamboyant, but friendly, with a happy laugh and a ready smile. She didn't look all that much like her brother and sister, or at least not as much as Jeff Baron and Amanda Trask resembled each other. He knew because he'd seen pictures of both of them while he'd been working at the Ingalls house.

But she did look a lot like the woman in the portrait that he'd glimpsed in her living room. Her grandmother, Margaret Ingalls, she'd told him when she saw where his eyes had strayed. The woman whose body had lain buried beneath a tree at Timberlake Lodge for forty years before being discovered.

He hadn't said anything about the murder, of course, although he'd read about it in back copies of the *Tyler Citizen* at the library one rainy afternoon when he didn't have anything else to do. He'd learned a lot about the Barons and the Ingallses from the printed accounts of what went on during that year in their lives. But there was still more he needed to know.

"I'm glad there's someone to help her out while Cliff—that's her husband—is settling into his new job with the Department of Natural Resources."

"She mentioned something about that." Michael stuck his hands in his pockets. He wasn't wearing gloves and the barn wasn't heated. Edward, not seeming to notice the cold, switched on the lights and began to uncover the Bentley. Michael's hands curled into fists inside his pockets. His palms itched to feel the satiny finish of her paint. She was a beauty. In mint condition. One of the best he'd ever seen. And worth a small fortune on the open market.

"Cliff comes from an old Rhode Island family. They've been in the publishing business for more than a hundred years. His brother, Byron, married a Tyler woman, too—Nora Gates. Have you met her?"

"Gates Department Store?" Michael asked, just to keep the older man talking. "I've been in there. But I've never met the woman."

Edward merely grunted in reply. His mind wasn't on their conversation; Michael could see that. He was staring at the engine of the Bentley as if it were a snake. "This damn car," he said under his breath. "I don't know why in hell Nikki had it shipped over here.

Devon despises the thing. And I can't make head nor tail of it.''

"Bentleys are pretty temperamental machines," Michael said before he could stop himself.

"You know classic cars?"

Michael felt the muscles of his neck and shoulders tighten with the tension of old, unresolved anger and betrayal. He made himself relax, forced his words to remain neutral. "Restoring them is what I'm trained to do. It's what I figured I'd spend my life doing. They're also the reason I went to prison."

Edward Wocheck raised his head, the Bentley's idiosyncrasies forgotten. "Want to tell me about it?"

"It's in the past. Better forgotten."

"Okay, if that's the way you want it."

This time Michael made no attempt to keep the bitterness out of his voice. "That's the way it is."

He heard the small door located next to the barn's big sliding doors open and someone come inside. It was late afternoon now, almost dark, and it wasn't until she entered the circle of light around the Bentley that Michael could be certain it was Alyssa Wocheck.

"I thought you might both be out here," she said in her pleasant voice. Her scent was pleasant, too. Wildflowers and summer meadows instead of dust and mildew and motor oil. "Edward, you aren't still trying to get this monstrosity to run, are you?"

"It's not a monstrosity, Alyssa. It's one of the most beautiful cars ever built."

"Even if you would rather be driving Liza's Thunderbird?"

Michael had seen that car, too. An American dream machine if ever there was one, parked carelessly beneath a pine tree behind the boathouse where the Forresters lived. Alyssa came closer and peered under the Bentley's hood. "Devon won't thank you for trying to get it to run. He doesn't like it any better than you do."

"I know that." Edward smiled at Alyssa, wiped his hands on a shop rag and rolled down his sleeves. They were standing very close together but he didn't reach out to kiss his wife, or even hug her; yet something passed between them, a bonding, a connection, that even Michael couldn't ignore.

"What are we going to do with it?" she asked. "Devon won't drive it, you know. He wouldn't be caught dead in that car in Tyler. He's worked too hard to be accepted for himself in this town to be seen in an anachronism like that."

"What do you think, Kenton?" Edward Wocheck asked unexpectedly. "You and my stepson are about the same age. What would you think about being seen tooling around town in an automobile like this one?"

"It's an incredible car. But I think I know where Devon's coming from. Fitting in someplace that means a lot to you is more important than just about anything else. Even being able to own and drive a classic like this baby."

Alyssa smiled warmly, and Michael caught himself smiling back.

"You're absolutely right," she said. "I hope you stay in Tyler long enough to meet Devon. I think you'd find you have a lot in common."

There were any number of things Michael could have said to that, like what in hell would a guy like this Devon Addison have in common with an ex-con like him, but he didn't. He accepted the compliment at face value.

Alyssa went right on talking. "We're expecting him

Friday. He's going to miss Thanksgiving dinner, but he'll be here in time for the first round of leftovers. Would you care to join us for the holiday, Michael?''

He'd been surreptitiously studying Edward Wocheck's face as he watched his wife, wondering what it took for a man to love a woman as he must love her. Alyssa's invitation caught him by surprise, and Edward, too, from the quick, slight frown that pulled his dark brows together.

''Thanks. No. I'm—I'm going to have Thanksgiving dinner with Sarah Fleming.''

''That's nice,'' Alyssa said. ''Of course, you'd both be welcome here. Would you like me to call Sarah and invite her, too?''

Michael didn't know what to say. He didn't want to eat with the Barons and the Wochecks. He didn't belong in this house, with his feet underneath their dining room table.

''I think she's already bought the turkey,'' he said lamely. Somehow his breath seemed caught in his throat. He swallowed hard. ''But I appreciate the invitation.''

''Of course. Will we see you Friday? Or are you going to take the day off to start your Christmas shopping?''

Christmas shopping? He'd never really been Christmas shopping. There had only been his grandmother to buy for, and now there was no one.

''I'll be here,'' he said. ''Eight o'clock. Is that okay?''

''I'll see that there's a space heater here for you,'' Edward said, pulling the plastic sheeting back over the Bentley's roof. ''Make it more comfortable.''

''Thanks.'' Edward's words were friendly, but he

was still frowning. His look was assessing, evaluating. Michael wondered what he was thinking about. "It'll only take me a day or so to do the windows. That should just about finish up the job."

"Yes," Alyssa said. "Everything's shipshape. You do very good work."

He nodded in acknowledgment, anxious now to get away from this kind, unsuspecting woman.

"There are some repairs I'd like made to the inside of the house." She paused. "Are you planning to stay in Tyler much longer?"

"I don't know," he said. He hadn't planned on staying this long. But then again, he hadn't considered how hard it would be to learn what he needed to know without coming right out and asking questions of people point-blank. "I haven't thought much about it. But maybe I will. I'll let you know."

"I LIKE that young man," Alyssa said softly, watching as Michael Kenton headed toward the door. After it closed behind him, she turned to her husband. "I like him very much."

Edward was still frowning as he adjusted the plastic covering over the big green car. "We don't know anything about him."

Alyssa leaned both hands against the high fender. "It's not like you to prejudge someone, Edward."

He shrugged. "But it is like you to pick up strays."

She was quiet for a moment. She couldn't deny that statement. Edward knew as well as she did that it was true. A fleeting image of Liza's husband, Cliff Forrester, as he'd been years ago when he first came to Tyler—alone, friendless, hurting inside—skittered across her mind's eye. She could no more have turned her back on him than she could have ignored an injured puppy or kitten on her doorstep. She felt the same way about Michael Kenton, although she was certain he wouldn't thank her for it.

"I'm not judging him, Lyssa," Edward said when she didn't answer. "I'm only saying it would be prudent to remember where he's been."

"I haven't forgotten that. I'm also aware that his childhood couldn't have been a happy one."

"Why do you think that?"

"Oh, bits and pieces of his background that he's told to Sarah Fleming and Cece passed on to me. Liza was very impressed with him, by the way," she added, hoping to blunt his arguments. "And he was very patient with the girls when they were pestering him that day last week."

Edward wasn't about to be sidetracked by the fact that Michael Kenton was good with children. "A lot of people have had less-than-idyllic childhoods. That doesn't excuse his committing a crime."

Alyssa stiffened. "You mean you would have objected to having Michael Kenton join us for Thanksgiving because of something that happened years ago?"

Edward reached out and touched her cheek. "No, Lyssa. I'm only saying I think we should be cautious of Michael Kenton because of what he's hiding from us in the here and now."

THERE WAS A MAN in her kitchen.

It seemed odd—strange, somehow. There hadn't been anyone to help her with dinner preparations or cleaning up afterward since Eric died. And even then they had lived in this house for such a short time before the accident that it had always seemed like hers alone.

And Michael Kenton was definitely a man who seemed out of place in a kitchen. Not because he didn't know one end of a saucepan from another. He did, and he moved with smooth efficiency and a peculiar masculine grace from one task to the next. But it was as though eating, and the preparation of food, were for him necessary evils, not the soothing, satisfying routines they had always been for her. Nurturing, life-affirming rituals, her father called them—a universal language of love and sharing.

She was a little bit surprised that Michael had accepted her invitation to help in the preparations of their Thanksgiving dinner. But he had, and she was grateful for the company. More than grateful. Pleased and excited. *Aroused.* She cut that thought off short, but the truth was she hadn't been able to get Michael Kenton completely out of her mind since the night of the high-school-awards ceremony. The night he'd kissed her.

And now he was here, standing beside her at the sink, cleaning celery and carrots for the relish plate.

Sleet beat against the glass, glazing the panes with a translucent layer of ice. The bad weather was expected to last only a few hours, according to the National Weather Service. A warm front was moving up from the south and the sleet would turn to rain before nightfall. But Sarah worried anyway. A lot of her congregation would be on the move today, coming and going to and from family dinners all over the state. It would be dangerous driving. She said a quick, silent prayer for the safety of everyone on the roads.

"What a lousy day." Michael's thoughts were following the same path as her own. He leaned his fists on the edge of the sink and peered out the window.

"I don't mind snow," Sarah said, aware of the sound of her own voice, overloud in the quiet room. "But I hate ice." She wiped her hands on a towel and turned on the radio on the counter. The Detroit Lions were playing the Green Bay Packers. The sounds of a football game underscoring their words seemed less intimate, somehow, than music might have been. She didn't change the station.

"I should have gotten snow tires for the truck." He stabbed a celery stalk into the dill-and-chive dip that she'd made from a recipe in the cookbook the Tyler Quilting Circle had published as a fund-raiser the year before. "This stuff's pretty good."

"Thank you," she said, laughing. "I know raw vegetables are good for you. But they're better when they've got something cool and fattening sticking to them."

He tried a carrot next. "Real good."

She turned away from the window and opened the oven door, The aroma of roasted turkey filled the warm air. She didn't want to talk about vegetables. She wanted to know why he'd brought up the subject of snow tires for his truck. A man who intended to head for Florida anytime soon wouldn't be thinking about buying snow tires, would he?

"Snow tires are an absolute necessity around here." Sarah held her breath, waiting for what he would say next. She didn't have the nerve to come right out and ask him if talking about snow tires meant he intended to spend the winter in Tyler. Spend the winter above her garage, where she could look out of her bedroom window and see the light beside his bed go off when she couldn't sleep, or when she got up early in the morning while all of Tyler was still in bed, to find that he was awake before her.

"Yeah, I'm beginning to realize that. I think I'll stop by Carl's Garage Monday and buy a set."

Sarah laid down the basting spoon and closed the oven door. "That's a good idea." It was all she could manage to say. *He was going to stay. At least for a little while longer.* And knowing him, as she had come to over these past weeks, she knew it would be the last thing he said about his plans for the future.

Michael swirled a celery stick in the dip and raised it to her lips. "How much longer until that bird's done? I'm starving."

Sarah was smiling when she looked up at him. She couldn't help it. *He was going to stay. He wasn't going to leave her alone and lonely as she'd been for so long.* "You're not starving," she scolded, not wanting him to see how much his words had affected her. The smile faded away as his knuckles brushed her mouth and her heart lurched into a rapid staccato beat.

"I'm starving, Sarah," he said, his voice as low and dark as the storm clouds overhead. She opened her mouth and he touched the celery to her lips. She swallowed convulsively, almost choking on the cool, tart taste of the dip. He was so close. She had only to take a half step forward, reach up on tiptoe and their mouths would meet. She remembered the last time he had kissed her, experienced again the chaos it had produced in her heart and in her mind. She wasn't certain she was ready to deal with that kind of emotional upheaval again. She reached out and took the celery stick from his hand, careful not to touch him. Her heart was beating like a snare drum in her chest.

"We'll eat soon," she said, heat coursing through her body, every inch of her alive to his nearness, every nerve ending alert to the anticipation of his touch. "Very soon."

THEY SAT DOWN in the small, wainscoted dining room at a quarter past two. It had stopped sleeting a little while earlier, just as the weather forecast had predicted. Now it was raining, a soft, steady rain that pattered against the windows, melting the sheet of ice that had clung to the glass since morning.

Sarah said grace with bowed head and folded hands, conscious even as she asked the Savior's blessing on them and the food they ate of Michael's dark gaze on her. They ate quietly for a while, only the sounds of the radio, now tuned to an easy-listening channel, and the scrape of silver against china intruding on the silence of the dark November day.

"More turkey?" Sarah asked when Michael had emptied his plate for the second time.

"I couldn't eat another bite." He leaned back and rested his hand on his flat stomach. "Turkey and dressing and all the fixings. You're too good a cook. I'm getting fat."

Sarah shook her head. "I'm not that good a cook. You just aren't used to sitting down to real meals."

"You're wrong. They feed you great on a lake freighter. The work's hard and out in the weather, so they don't stint on the mess." She didn't think they had fed him so well in prison, but he didn't mention it and neither did she. He pushed his chair back from the table and stood when she did.

"You're going to have to force yourself to eat a few more bites. I baked a pumpkin pie. It wouldn't be

Thanksgiving without pumpkin pie. I thought we'd have dessert and coffee in the living room. Is that all right with you?''

She thought for a moment he might refuse the invitation, but then he smiled. ''I'd like that. I'll help clear the table.''

He didn't smile often, and when he did it always unnerved her, dazzled her eyes and her heart, like the sun suddenly coming out from behind a dark cloud. ''I can manage.''

''I know. But I want to help.''

She nodded. ''The tray is right behind you on the sideboard.''

He gathered up dishes and silverware, glasses and serving dishes still half-full of food. Sarah sighed when she looked at them. ''We're going to be eating leftovers all weekend. I hope you don't mind. I just can't seem to get the knack of putting only enough food for one or two people in bowls meant to feed a family.''

''No problem.''

By the time he'd stacked the last of the dirty dishes in the sink, she had cut the pie, added dollops of real whipped cream and poured the coffee. She carried the tray into the living room and placed it on the coffee table in front of the small, tiled fireplace that was one of the house's chief charms. She turned on the stereo and joined him on the couch.

Again they ate in silence, savoring the food and the strong black coffee. Sarah watched from the corner of her eye as Michael made a face and added cream to his for the second time.

''I'm sorry. I learned how to make coffee from one of our lay teachers at the mission in São Roberto. And in Brazil this is how they drink it.''

"I'll get used to it," he said with a shiver.

Sarah laughed again. "No wonder you make your own coffee every morning."

A hint of color darkened his neck and cheeks. He was blushing. Sarah was entranced. She curled her feet up under her on the couch and sipped her coffee, watching his strong, angular features through the screen of her lashes. Behind her on the stereo, a latin samba was playing—an old record, a favorite from her childhood that she had bought with her own allowance money in Brazil and carried with her ever since.

Michael set his cup and saucer on the tray and leaned back against the couch cushions, his legs crossed carelessly at the ankles. He was gentled, at peace, lulled by the food and the music and the warmth of the fire.

Sarah relaxed as she finished her coffee. The sexual tension that had sizzled between them had dissipated as they ate, lulling her into a sense of contentment. This was what Thanksgiving had always meant to her—not so much the number of people gathered around her table for the meal, but the feelings behind it. Fellowship and the sharing of God's bounty and blessing. If she were alone, she might have gone to her desk and jotted down those thoughts to be expanded into a sermon she could use on an appropriate Sunday. But not today. Today she wanted to stay right where she was.

She set her cup aside to take up her quilting, a wall hanging in a riot of spring colors, appliqúed with appropriate liturgical symbols. She hoped to finish it in time to hang it on the bare wall behind the altar at Easter.

She wondered how her congregation would react to seeing it for the first time. A few of the older members, raised in a more rigid evangelical framework, might think it not in the best of taste, but she was pretty sure the rest of the members would rejoice in its color and warmth. It was one of the good things about the denomination that Tyler Fellowship was affiliated with. They were too small and struggling to be hidebound. As far as possible they allowed their member churches to be autonomous, and their pastors were allowed to guide their flocks as they saw fit.

"Don't you ever just sit quietly and rest?" Michael asked.

Sarah jumped, pricking herself slightly with her needle. She'd been lost in her stitching and her thoughts, and she hadn't realized he was watching her. "I've never been able to sit still and do nothing."

"What have you been thinking about?"

"I've been thinking that I'm a very lucky woman."

He reached out one big brown hand and ran his fingers over the soft cotton surface of the quilt. "The kind of thoughts you're supposed to have on Thanksgiving?"

She felt herself blushing. "I suppose so." He made her feel gauche and naive. She sat a little straighter in her corner of the couch. She wasn't ashamed of how she felt. She wasn't going to let him make her think she was. "That's what today's for, after all, not just watching football games and overeating."

"And it might do me good to contemplate my own blessings a little more closely, eh?"

"It wouldn't hurt," she said tartly, then caught the faint smile on his lips and in his eyes. He was teasing her again, and she'd risen to the bait as she always did. What was it about this man that kept her off balance so?

The smile was gone. He was serious now. "How are you a lucky woman, Sarah Fleming?"

"I have a home and friends and a job I love. What more can anyone ask?"

"You could ask for love itself. A husband. A family. Children."

A sharp shaft of pain pierced her heart. She looked down at the quilt, refusing to meet his eye. Her stitches were becoming too large and ragged, she noticed. She was going to have to take them all out again.

"Of course I want those things. I had love. My husband was a wonderful man. One of the things I mourned the most after his death was that we had no children."

"But your having a child wasn't God's will?" The angry edge was back in his voice. He hadn't set foot in the church, except to do repairs, in the almost four weeks he'd been in Tyler. One or two of the congregation had brought it to her attention, but she had reminded them that attending services was not one of the restrictions put on the use of the garage apartment, and nothing further had been said.

"Possibly. If it was, I accept it."

"You just folded your hands and bowed your head and said, 'His will be done'?"

"No," she said, catching and holding his dark, shadowed gaze. "I cried and ranted and beat my fists against the wall. I *hated* God for a long time. I hated Him for taking my husband from me. I hated Him for leaving me alone to shepherd my flock. I hated what I was doing. I hated lying to everyone, saying that I was all right. That my faith was all right. It wasn't. Some days it still isn't." She shut her mouth with a snap. She had never, *never* spoken to anyone of what she had just told Michael Kenton. "But those days don't come very often anymore. And I've accepted that Eric is dead and I may never have children. But there are other children to love. And I can be happy that I have TylerTots and my youth groups to guide and counsel."

His fingers had stopped stroking the quilt. Slowly, carefully, he lifted his hand to her cheek. "I don't believe in God," he said quietly. "I never have."

"He exists," she whispered, struggling to remain Reverend Sarah and not just plain Sarah, a woman who had not been touched like this by a man for a long, long time. "He is real."

"I didn't say He doesn't exist. I just said I don't believe in Him. But if I did, Sarah, it would be because I can see the truth of what you say in your eyes and in your voice."

"I—"

"Shh, Sarah. Be quiet. I don't want to talk theology. I don't want to argue about how many angels can dance on the head of a pin. I want to think about much more elemental, more human and ordinary things."

"Like what?"

"Like I am a man. And you, Sarah Fleming, are very much a woman." He leaned closer, his lips tracing the path across her lips and cheeks that his fingers had blazed just moments before. She leaned into his kiss, and his mouth covered hers in a rush of fiery heat. There was nothing timid or shy about the contact. It was completely, totally sexual and exactly what she wanted from this man—to be a woman, desired and desiring, no more and no less. For this small space of time it didn't matter that they were completely unsuited to each other. That he was a convicted criminal, a man whose past was as murky as his future was uncertain, a man who was openly skeptical of all she held most dear.

Her quilting had fallen to the floor unnoticed. Michael pulled her into his arms and she went willingly, twining her arms around his neck, holding him as close and as tightly as he held her. He was the man she wanted. The man who made her feel whole and human, and female again, and nothing else mattered beyond that fact.

He moved his hands to her breasts and her breath sifted out against his lips. His fingers moved to the buttons of her blouse, parted the fabric and slipped it off her shoulders. His mouth hovered just above the lace edge of her bra and his tongue flicked out to taste her skin, brand her with its heat and warmth. The passion that had simmered between them all day threatened to boil over again. Michael nuzzled the valley between her breasts, molded her with his hand, brushed his thumb tantalizingly over her pebbled nipple. He held her close against him, searching for the bra clasp between her shoulder blades, and undid it with long clever fingers, freeing her to spill into his waiting embrace.

He shifted his weight to lie closer to her, his arousal hard and heavy against her. He moved his hand between them, to the juncture of her thighs, to the softness at the very center of her being, kneading slowly, with a tantalizing rhythm that drove rational thought from her head. His mouth claimed hers again.

But this kiss was different, no longer questioning, questing. She could feel it in the tension that tightened muscle and tendon beneath her hands. Michael was a man, fully aroused, and she was a woman. He wanted her. And she wanted him. Her body moved with a mind of its own, her stomach clenched in desire…and fear. Soon there would be no turning back, no retreat. Sarah closed her eyes against the sudden unreasoning spurt of apprehension that slipped along her nerve endings and cooled her blood.

What was wrong with her?

Michael had done nothing she hadn't wanted him to do, hadn't welcomed. Why, now, did she feel as if there were no air to fill her lungs, as if she might burst into tears?

He sensed the change in her immediately, and his hands stilled. He moved slightly, shifting position so that their bodies were no longer one.

"What's wrong, Sarah?" he asked, gruffly but with an odd gentle note to his words. He frowned, tracing the track of one wayward teardrop.

"Nothing," she said, blinking desperately to hold back more tears of frustration and embarrassment. "Nothing's wrong."

"Yes, there is." He stroked her hair. "I frighten you."

"No!" She struggled to sit up. *No. He mustn't think it was his fault.* Michael pulled her up against him and helped her refasten her clothes while the color rushed into her cheeks again. How could she tell him that she wasn't frightened of him? That she was frightened of herself, of her response to him, a stranger, a man she barely knew. "No. It's nothing you did. I…I frightened myself," she finally managed to say.

He didn't contradict her. "How long has Eric been dead?" he asked.

She bit down on her bottom lip, and then looked up from fastening the buttons of her blouse. "Three years."

"That's a long time to be alone." Michael brushed a strand of hair away from her cheek. "And you have been alone, haven't you?"

Sarah nodded. "A very long time. I...there hasn't been anyone since Eric died." *And, God help her, she'd never felt like this when Eric was alive.*

"I would never hurt you, Sarah," Michael said tenderly.

She couldn't let him think the realization of the depth of her feelings, or the sudden unreasoning fear of her own inadequacy was his fault. She reached out and covered his hand with hers. "I know that, Michael. It wasn't your fault. It's mine. All mine. I...I just..." She wanted him, needed him, but how could she come right out and say it?

He gave a harsh, grating laugh. "I guess I should have asked you this question before we got where we are. Are you still in love with your husband?"

Sarah looked down at her hands. *Was she?* She shook her head, raising her eyes to his. "No. I loved Eric, but he's dead and I've accepted that. It has nothing to do with what I felt for Eric. It has everything to do with me. You see..." She knew she was going to be hurt by what she intended to say. She knew he didn't share her feelings, might never share her feelings, but she couldn't stop herself from speaking the words aloud.

"Don't, Sarah." Michael sounded almost desperate. He reached out and placed the tip of his finger against her lips. "Don't say something we'll both regret."

She brushed his hand away. "I can't help it, Michael. I have to say it. I'm afraid because of how much I already care. I'm afraid of how deeply I already feel. You see, I think I'm falling in love with you."

I THINK I'M FALLING in love with you. God, would he never get the words out of his head? Michael slammed the half-empty bottle of whiskey down on the table. It was the first drink he'd had since the night he'd moved into this place, but it wasn't going to be the last. *I think I'm falling in love with you.*

He bolted down the liquor in his glass and scraped his chair back from the table. The sound was loud in the cold, quiet room. He should have turned on the old portable TV on the counter, or at least the radio by the bed. Anything so that he didn't have to sit here alone with his thoughts. He poured another drink, swallowed it and shuddered. He'd lost his taste for whiskey. Another thing that had changed for him since he'd come to Tyler, Wisconsin.

He shouldn't have stayed so long. He shouldn't have been so hell-bent on finding his roots. He'd let himself be drawn into the silken web of caring and commitment that Sarah spun so effortlessly and so innocently. *Sarah.* Soft and sweet and eager to please, but with a sense of duty and purpose that gave her softness the underlying strength of tempered steel.

He walked to the window, resting both hands on the curved iron of the old bedstead where he slept, alone and aching, every night. He looked out the window. The kitchen light was off. The house was dark except for the gold rectangle of light shining on the wet grass around the corner of the house that he knew held her bedroom. Was she working on Sunday's sermon, or reading in bed? Had she fallen asleep with the light on? What did she look like as she slept?

Michael banged his fist on the bed frame and turned back toward the kitchen. He needed another drink, but he stopped himself before he got that far. There wasn't enough whiskey in the state to stop his thoughts from following their forbidden path.

God, he wanted to know what it felt like to have Sarah in his bed. But not for just a one-night stand. Sarah wasn't that kind of woman. Sarah was a woman for a lifetime. That was what made it all so impossible. Sarah was forever, and Michael Baron Kenton's life plans, such as they were, had no place for forever.

CHAPTER SEVEN

"MAY THE PEACE of the Lord and of this blessed season be with you and yours."

"Amen."

Sarah lifted her head and smiled out over the congregation. It was a good turnout for the first Sunday in December, when warm beds and early holiday-shopping sprees to Madison or Milwaukee were temptations sometimes too great to ignore. But it was the man in the second-to-last pew that she was really smiling for.

For the first time since coming to Tyler, Michael Kenton had chosen to attend the worship service. She'd been aware of him from the moment he'd set foot inside the door. She'd watched with apprehension as heads swiveled to mark his entrance. A few mouths were pursed in disapproval, she noted, but there were smiles of welcome, too. She'd watched him from her seat at the left of the pulpit as he listened to the children's choir and joined in the singing of hymns. She'd never heard him sing, she realized. She wondered what his singing voice was like. Low and rich, probably, judging from the way he spoke. A baritone, or perhaps even a bass.

She'd even made eye contact with him—once, at the beginning of her sermon, after which she'd almost forgot what she wanted to say. From then on, she'd made a point not to look his way, to keep her mind on her duties and on the celebration of God's word.

The strains of the recessional came from the wheezing old organ behind the pulpit. As clever as Michael was at repairing things, there was nothing he could do about the organ. It was simply worn-out. She would love to start a fund drive for a new one, Sarah thought with a sigh. But there were so many other, more pressing needs in the parish. The organ, like so much else, would have to wait.

People were beginning to hunt for gloves and purses; murmurs of conversation began to float into the aisles. Sarah held up her hands and pitched her voice to carry over the others. "Remember, rehearsal for the Christmas pageant will be Tuesday night at seven, downstairs at TylerTots. Mothers who have volunteered to make costumes please see Miriam Phillips about getting together to work on the wise men's crowns." She looked down at the notes she'd made for herself. "Oh, yes. Don't forget the community tree-lighting ceremony tonight at seven in the town square. I hope I'll see you all there."

"With bells on, Reverend Sarah," the choir director said as she herded her young singers into the classroom to the right of the dais.

"I'll look for you," Sarah said, making her way quickly to the vestibule. She was glad she'd worn a heavy turtleneck with her navy suit instead of the silk blouse she usually chose for Sunday morning. The cold air from the open doors made her shiver. She curled her left hand inside the wide sleeve of her black robe and began shaking hands and making small talk with the departing congregation.

This was the best part of her work. This was where

she could touch base with her people, take soundings of their health and happiness. She saw that Nellie Phillips, Jonas's eighty-seven-year-old mother, was having trouble with her arthritis again. She also knew that the old woman would almost certainly be confined to her bed before Christmas by the severity of the condition. She would have to make certain she found time in her schedule to visit at least once a week. Nellie was the last living charter member of the congregation. Her large and close-knit family was still the most active and dedicated in the congregation.

"Take it easy going down the steps, Nellie," Sarah cautioned. "They might be a little slippery this morning." There was a side-door ramp leading to the sanctuary for the use of handicapped members, but Nellie had been coming to church through the front door all her life and wasn't about to change that habit now, no matter how painful climbing the steps might be. Sarah admired her courage and determination.

"I'll be careful." The old lady chortled. "Don't want to fall and break my hip now. Too close to Christmas. I've got too much baking to do to be laid up."

"I hope that means I can expect a plate of your sugar cookies before too many more days?" Sarah asked hopefully, licking her lips in anticipation as she held the old woman's gnarled hand between her own.

"I expect it does," Nellie said and began her slow, laborious way down the steps, a sturdy grandchild on each side. "God bless, Reverend Sarah. I'll see you next Sunday if I'm still among the living."

"God bless, Nellie."

When Sarah looked back again Michael Kenton was at her side. "Good morning, Reverend Sarah," he said. He'd had his hair trimmed, but not by much. It fell in a heavy, dark wave over his forehead. His eyes were nearly as dark, except when they caught the light and turned the deepest hue of sapphire.

"Welcome, Michael," she said, aware that one or two of her congregants were still visiting on the church steps, despite the misty drizzle that seeped out of the December sky. "We're glad you could join us this morning. Have you met Nathan Beckman and Riley Owens?"

Michael shook hands with the two men. "Welcome to Tyler Fellowship," Riley intoned, the small frown between his gray eyebrows alerting Sarah to the fact that he wasn't one hundred percent in favor of the visitor.

"Good to meet you." Nathan Beckman's smile was broad and genuine. "We need some new blood in this church. Come back next week."

"I will," Michael said. The two men nodded and turned away.

"Why did you come this morning?" Sarah asked in a low voice.

It was almost the first conversation they'd had since Thanksgiving afternoon. She felt awkward and shy. *Why, oh why, had she told him she might be falling in love with him?*

Because it was the truth, and she could no more have stopped herself from speaking than she could have halted the sun in its journey across the sky.

Michael shrugged. "I decided it was time I made an appearance. I've been living on church property for almost six weeks. I figured you'd start catching flak, sooner or later, if I didn't toe the line."

"We don't force our beliefs on others—" she protested.

"Your nose is red," he interrupted, with just a hint of a smile curving the strong line of his mouth.

Sarah gave up. When Michael didn't want to talk about himself, he changed the subject, just as he'd done now. "I'm freezing," she whispered, taking her cue, nodding at Myra Allen and her husband as they passed behind Michael. They nodded at Michael, too, and Myra smiled, a reluctant smile but a good sign.

Michael returned the nod and smile. "I'm making progress," he said.

"They're good people."

"I didn't say they weren't. Just prune-faced and hidebound."

Since that described Myra and her husband exactly, Sarah couldn't come up with a reply. He hadn't been around much since Thanksgiving. And perhaps that was a good thing. She had needed this past week to get her feelings under control again. "I hope you're not too hungry. I haven't got anything planned for dinner yet."

He shook his head. "No cooking today."

"Oh. Have you made other plans?" Sarah nodded at Darryl Phillips, Jonas's brother, so that he knew she was leaving and he could close up the church behind her. He had most likely already turned down the thermostat and locked the doors leading to the basement stairway, so that none of the children could wander away from Angela before she got things under control in the morning. As Sarah started down the steps with Michael, Darryl began turning off the lights, and before they reached the bottom of the flight she heard the heavy, carved-walnut doors slam shut behind them.

"Nothing spectacular." Michael pointed to a big green car, very old and foreign looking, that sat in the driveway. "I'm taking the Bentley out to Timberlake

Lodge for Edward Wocheck. I've been working on it this week."

"You didn't tell me you were doing more work for the Wochecks." She watched him looking at the big car and knew how much he had missed doing the work he loved. She looked away quickly so he wouldn't catch her gazing at him.

"It was Alyssa—Mrs. Wocheck's doing, I imagine. I don't think her husband would have given me the commission without some prodding on her part. But I'm not going to look a gift horse in the mouth. It's been too long." Abruptly he changed the subject. "I was wondering if you'd follow me out in your car. We could have Sunday brunch at the lodge. My treat."

Sarah hesitated, her heart beating like a drum in her chest. She ought to say no. She'd made a big-enough fool of herself in his arms Thanksgiving day. But she wasn't strong enough to deny herself the bittersweet pleasure of his company. He looked so good in khaki pants, dark shirt and a rather carelessly knotted tie, visible beneath his familiar pcacoat. She'd never seen him wear a tie before, but she liked the way he looked in one. "I'd like that. Let me change my clothes and I'll be right with you."

"Take your time. I have a couple of errands to run."

"On Sunday? In that thing?"

Michael dropped his eyes a moment, then looked up again. "Okay. I want to take her out for a spin, open her up. These cars were built for speed."

She could see the suppressed excitement in his glance, hear the rough edge of it in his voice, and she blessed Alyssa Wocheck for providing the opportunity for him to work on the car. "Okay. I'll meet you at Timberlake in, say, an hour?"

Michael nodded. "An hour's fine."

Sarah ran her hand across the high fender. The finish was cold and smooth beneath her fingers. "I've never ridden in a car like this. What kind did you say it was?"

A shadow crossed his features for a moment and was quickly gone. "It's a Bentley. Bentleys were famous English racing cars in the twenties. But this is a newer model. From when the company was taken over by Rolls-Royce. It's a rich man's car. A beauty, a touring car not a racing machine, but she can still leave a lot of cars on the road today in her dust."

"It's huge."

"And it's heavy. Built like a tank. We could take a spin around the block if you'd like. I'm sure Edward Wocheck wouldn't mind."

She laughed. "No thanks. That car is definitely out of my league."

"Then I'll see you at Timberlake."

She hesitated a moment, still uncertain where she stood with this enigmatic man. "Are you sure you want to do this?"

"I'm positive," he said, leaning so close his warm breath touched her cheek.

"It—it will only take me a moment to change."

They were hidden from the street by the high bulk of the old car. Michael reached out very quickly and touched her hair, smoothing a flyaway strand away from her face. For a moment she thought he was as uncertain as herself. "Sarah—"

Darryl Phillips appeared from the back of the church and got into his car. Michael dropped his hand and stepped back. "Hurry," he said gruffly. "I'm starved."

TIMBERLAKE LODGE was quite a place. Michael stood beneath the huge antler chandelier that crowned the wood-paneled lobby and surveyed the big room. A cavernous fieldstone fireplace dominated the far wall. It was flanked by long, comfortable-looking chairs and sofas, and its heat drew him like a magnet. He skirted the big plank table, massed with pots of multicolored poinsettias, and the magnificent Oriental rug it was centered on, intent on warming his hands before the blaze.

Down a short hallway he could hear the sounds of cutlery and muted conversation. That must be where the restaurant was located. He ought to see about reserving a table before Sarah arrived, but he decided against it. He didn't want to keep Edward Wocheck waiting, and the woman at the desk had said the lodge owner would be with him very shortly. He'd better wait. He settled himself into a high-backed wing chair at the edge of the grouping around the fireplace and continued to study his surroundings.

Two couples were drinking coffee in front of the fireplace, discussing plans for the afternoon. They were well dressed and looked well fed and pleased with themselves. Behind the reception desk, a young woman with raven-dark hair and blue eyes conferred with two more members of the staff. A sweeping staircase led to the second floor and a discreet sign pointed the way to meeting rooms and the bar.

Michael was aware that Timberlake had originally belonged to the Ingalls family. That Edward Wocheck, Tyler's hometown boy made good, had bought it and enlarged it into what it was today. It was a beautiful place, big and sprawling. The wings that Addison International had added to the building were so well integrated that, for a stranger like him, it was impossible to tell what was old and what was new.

A stranger like him.

Was he really a stranger to this place? Was there something of it in his blood?

Restless, he rose from the chair and stood before one of the big glass windows that looked out over the lake. He knew that somewhere in this building Margaret Ingalls had died, and that somewhere on the landscaped grounds, her body had been buried for over forty years. Maybe he had more in common with the Ingallses and the Barons than he had first thought. At least he had more in common with Alyssa Ingalls Baron Wocheck. Like him, she'd grown up without a mother. She knew how it felt to be abandoned by the one person you should be able to count on above all others. But at least she had had her father to love and care for her. He'd been denied even that....

Disgusted with the maudlin turn of his thoughts, Michael spun away from the window to come face-to-face with Edward Wocheck.

"Good morning, Kenton," the older man said, holding out his hand.

"Good morning, sir."

"Call me Edward." His grip was firm and strong, his gaze direct.

"Thank you, Edward."

"So you've got the Bentley up and running."

"Like a top."

"Good. Devon should be right... There he is. Devon, over here. I'd like you to meet Michael Kenton. This is my stepson, Devon Addison. The Bentley is his."

"I don't know if I should thank you or not," Devon said, holding out his hand. He looked four or five years older than Michael, blond and tanned. His grip was strong and steady, his smile genuine. He was wearing jeans and a plaid shirt, and except for the solid gold watch on his arm and the confidence only money and breeding could bring to a man his age, he didn't look or act like the head of a multimillion-dollar business conglomerate.

"It's a beautiful machine."

"An anachronism, and temperamental as hell, but it was my grandfather Addison's first car, and my mother wants me to have it for sentimental reasons. Beats me why, though. The old robber baron didn't have a sentimental bone in his body. Neither does my mother."

Michael held out the keys. "I enjoyed working on it." He was anxious to get this over with. Sarah would be arriving any minute. For a fleeting moment he felt like tossing the keys in Addison's direction and turning tail. He didn't want Sarah seeing him with these self-assured, successful men. He didn't want her comparing him to them and finding him wanting.

"Let's take a look at her," Devon was saying. "Jeff, come here. We're going check out the Bentley."

"Jeff, have you met Michael Kenton?" Edward asked.

"No. I don't believe I have."

Michael's breath stuck in his throat. It was the first time he'd come face-to-face with this man. *His brother.*

"Michael Kenton, this is Alyssa's son, Dr. Jeff Baron. I think you've met his daughters, Annie and Belle?"

"Great kids." It was all Michael could manage to get past the lump in his throat as he returned Jeff Baron's greeting.

"We think so," Jeff said with a grin.

They didn't look alike, not really. They were about the same height and probably the same weight, Michael guessed. Jeff's hair was lighter, with a definite auburn cast, while his only looked that way in certain lights. Michael favored his mother and grandmother, people had always said, so he guessed now that there wasn't much of his Baron heritage that showed on the surface. To look at him and Jeff together, you wouldn't know they shared the same father. Except for their eyes. Jeff's, like his own, were a dark, deep blue, and in this light they looked almost black.

Michael continued to look into his half brother's face. What was different about Jeff Baron? Why had their father, Ronald, chosen him and his sisters over Michael? What kind of man could he have been to have seduced a young girl and then abandoned her when he found out she was pregnant? Yet he'd been the kind of father to Jeff that would prompt him to name a clinic—a clinic he had fought to keep up and running for more than five years—after him.

Jeff Baron was saying something. "I'm sorry? I didn't hear you," Michael said, dropping the other man's hand.

Jeff smiled. Michael wondered if it was their father's smile. "I said, did you have any trouble getting parts for that relic?"

They were already moving toward the big double doors leading to the long porch that fronted the hotel. Michael had no choice but to follow them when Devon Addison held open the door. "Surprisingly, apart from one or two minor repairs, she mainly needed a good tune-up. But there's an excellent source for antique and foreign car parts in Milwaukee. I—" He'd been about to say he'd used them in his business before, but he stopped himself short. The supplier would remember him, all right. The world of classic cars was a small one. Anyone who'd been accused and convicted of destroying not only a Rolls-Royce Silver Ghost, but a 1930 Duesenberg, as well, wouldn't be forgotten. Not for a lifetime.

"The Bentley has drawn a crowd," Devon remarked. "I wonder if it would be worth the expense to bring the rest of Grandfather's cars over here."

"There are more like this?" Jeff asked, spreading his hands to frame the big green car.

"Six or eight. Grandfather collected cars. There's a Daimler and a Bugatti, I remember. A Jaguar and a sweet old Caddy. And of course, the Rolls. I suppose they'll have to be sold, or donated to some museum somewhere."

Michael had left the car parked on the circular drive that fronted the hotel, and now one or two of the guests were giving it the once-over. As Michael handed Devon Addison the keys, a couple approached from a path that led down to the lake. The woman carried an umbrella, but the man was bareheaded, the collar of his raincoat turned up around his ears.

"Amanda. Ethan." Jeff Baron lifted his hand and waved. "Didn't expect to see you out here this morning." The guests who had been examining the car wandered away, preferring the warmth and comfort of the hotel to the cold, raw, December day.

"We're having brunch with Liza and Cliff," the man said, nodding to Michael, the only stranger. "Devon, good to see you," he said, offering his hand.

"Good to be back in Tyler, Ethan."

Edward Wocheck made the introductions. "Michael Kenton, this is my stepdaughter Amanda and her husband Ethan Trask. Amanda is Jeff's sister. This is Michael Kenton. He's been working on the Bentley."

The man shook hands, but Michael hardly noticed his face. *Amanda, his sister.* He hadn't expected to meet her and Jeff both like this, at the same time. He'd thought he could pick the time and place, if he ever wanted it to happen, the way it had been with Liza at her house that day.

"Nice meeting you," he croaked.

"We've heard a lot about you from Mom," Amanda said, smiling. "She's very pleased with your work around the house." She had the same auburn hair and straight white teeth that Jeff had. It was obvious she'd never wanted for anything in her life, never known the humiliation of standing in line for food or rent money.

"And the girls think he's great," Jeff added, pulling his head out of the open window of the Bentley, where he'd been studying the dashboard. "Let's take this thing for a spin. Want to join us, Michael?"

From the corner of his eye he saw Sarah's small, red car turn into the driveway.

"No, thanks." His hands were shaking so hard he had to stick them in the pockets of his pants to hide the trembling. "Here's my ride."

"Your ride?" Amanda Trask followed the direction of his gaze. "Oh, it's Sarah Fleming." She looked back at him again, and even though her expression was still pleasant, the smile still in place, Michael couldn't help but recall that she was a lawyer and trained to see beneath the surface. How many other people in Tyler were beginning to speculate about his relationship with the woman preacher?

"You don't have to rush off," Devon said, but there was something in his voice that gave Michael pause, the slightest flicker in the glance he sent in his stepfather's direction. You learned to listen for undertones and nuances in another's speech in the joint, just as you watched body language, in case—just in case.

"Yes, join us for brunch," Jeff said. "Mom and Phil are probably already in the dining room. Cece and the girls should be here any minute."

"No," Michael said. He could feel sweat break out under his arms and in the small of his back. "Sarah and I have plans. Thanks, anyway. Good to meet all of you." He had to force himself to walk, not run toward the sanctuary of Sarah's car.

She had her hand on the key, ready to turn off the engine, when he jerked open the door and climbed into the seat beside her. "Hi," she said. "I'm sorry it took so long. The phone rang just as I was going out the door."

He put his hand over hers on the steering column. "Don't stop the car. I—" he shook his head in disgust "—I'm doing it to you again."

"Doing what?"

"Reneging on my invitation."

"I don't understand."

"I gotta get out of here."

"All right." She glanced at the group gathered around the Bentley, then at him. He leaned his head against the back of the seat and closed his eyes. He couldn't look her in the eye. She saw too much, too clearly.

Sarah put the car in reverse and backed out of the parking space she'd just pulled into. "Want to tell me about it?"

He shook his head. "There's nothing to tell. I just don't belong in a place like Timberlake. I should have thought of that before I asked you out here." He didn't belong with people like Devon Addison and the Barons.

"Bull—feathers," Sarah said. He opened his eyes. She was looking in the rearview mirror. "What happened? Did they say something about your being in prison? I—I find that hard to believe. I've never known Alyssa Wocheck's family to be unkind, or judgmental."

"It's nothing," he lied. What would she say if he told her the truth? That he was the illegitimate son of the sainted Ronald Baron and a naive seventeen-year-old baby-sitter from Milwaukee Ronald had seduced by the lake one summer day thirty years ago? That Michael had panicked back there when he thought about saying the words aloud in front of his half brother and sister?

"I don't think you're telling the truth," she replied, as though she could read his mind. She reached out and covered his hand with hers. "Please, Michael. Tell me what's wrong. Tell me what I can do to help."

"Sarah, don't. Not yet. I...haven't worked it all out in my own mind yet." At least that much was the truth. He didn't know what the hell to do next.

"Do you want to go home?" she asked, as she stopped outside the gates of Timberlake, waiting for his reply before heading the car back into town.

Home. Funny but he *was* beginning to think of that cold, dreary apartment as home.

"No." The word came out too loud and too harsh. "No. Not yet."

"Then where do you want to go?" Her voice was soft but strained. She was biting her lower lip, the way she did when she was nervous. *God, what a jackass he was, treating her this way.* He looked over at her and longed to reach out and smooth his hand across her silken hair. She was like the calm center at the eye of the storm that raged inside him.

"Anywhere," he said simply. "As long as it's with you."

CHAPTER EIGHT

SARAH RESTED her head against the car seat. The short, December twilight had long ago faded away. It was dark here under the trees at the side of the road, intensifying the silence of a country night beyond the window. It was very late. They should have been home hours ago, but Sarah made no move to suggest they leave this deserted spot. She was very conscious of the man beside her in the driver's seat. She turned her head and studied him as he looked down on Tyler. The moon was a bright silver sliver in the night sky just above the horizon. It gave little light, and Michael's face was in shadow. All she could see of him was his profile and his strong, brown hands resting on the steering wheel. The same strong, brown hands that had held her when he kissed her and that she longed to feel touching her again.

Abruptly, Sarah turned her head. That kind of thoughts would only bring her further pain. Michael Kenton enjoyed her company. He would enjoy her body if she gave herself to him, but that was all. Perhaps it was all he was capable of. She blinked back the threat of tears.

Below them, Tyler was spread out against the mirrored brightness of the frozen lake. From this vantage point, the colored lights strung across Main Street and festooning the trees in the square twinkled like fairy stars.

"I'm sorry we missed the tree-lighting ceremony." Michael's voice was gruff in the darkness.

"It's all right. I'm sure no one missed us." She would have liked to be there when the hundreds of strings of lights on the big evergreen had been turned on, but she had wanted even more to be with Michael.

They had spent the day in Madison, one of Sarah's favorite places. She liked the combination of small-town charm and academic sophistication. The drizzle of the morning had turned into a light, fluffy snow just after noon. They had strolled the paths along the edge of Lake Mendota, on the campus of the University of Wisconsin, where Sarah had taken some courses in family- and teen-counseling the summer before. It was a beautiful place, quiet and serene on this snowy Sunday. The rest of the day they had whiled away doing a little early Christmas shopping and sharing a huge pizza at a noisy family restaurant near the campus.

Michael hadn't referred to what had happened at Timberlake to upset him so, and Sarah had not pressed him. A good counselor never pushed too hard for disclosure. People had to learn to trust before they could share the pain in their life and in their heart, and Michael Kenton had never learned such trust.

"What happens at the tree-lightning ceremony?" Michael asked, his voice warming her with its roughness.

This was a much safer path than the one her thoughts had been following. Sarah answered eagerly. "When it gets dark, the community band plays Christmas carols. There's hot chocolate and popcorn. Santa and Mrs. Santa arrive in a sleigh, if there's snow, and on a fire engine if there isn't. Santa always throws the switch on the big tree. That's the signal that in Tyler, at least, the Christmas season has officially begun.'' She leaned forward a little, her hands clasped, as she recalled the excitement of the youngest members of the crowd when that long-awaited moment arrived. ''And in keeping with the true Christmas spirit, there are donation areas for all kinds of worthy charities. There's a food-donation barrel for the weekly free dinners that each church in town sponsors for the needy during the winter. There's a booth to donate good used or new coats for children whose parents can't afford them. There's a Toys for Tots drop-off staffed by local members of the Marine Corps Reserve. And of course we start canvassing for donations for the bazaar at TylerTots. That's our major fund-raising event of the year—''

Michael reached out and laid his hand over hers. ''Slow down, Sarah,'' he said with a chuckle. ''You're starting to hyperventilate.''

She made herself relax against the seat, grateful he couldn't see her blush. What an innocent she must seem to him, getting so excited about a small-town tree-lighting ceremony. But she loved living in Tyler. It was here she'd discovered the sense of community, of belonging, that she'd longed for as a child—a foundation of stability she'd always found lacking in her parents' vagabond and ascetic life-style. It was home.

''I get carried away with Christmas. I always have.''

''Yeah, Christmas.''

Something in his voice alerted her. She turned toward him. ''I'm sorry. I forget, sometimes, that other people have Christmas memories that aren't as happy as mine.''

"I have happy memories," he said, still not quite convincingly.

"Just not enough of them?"

He shifted restlessly in his seat. "Yeah, Reverend Sarah. Just not quite enough of them."

"I'm sorry, Michael. I can't seem to stop myself. Trying to help, I mean," she said, feeling unsure of herself, as she so often did in his company, but determined to learn all there was to know about him. "It's what I do."

He pulled her into his arms, cursing the steering wheel and the size of her car under his breath. "I know it's what you do, Sarah. And you're good at it. Too damn good. You make me want to say things I'm not ready to talk about." He lifted his hand and smoothed her hair away from her face. The timbre of his voice changed, becoming low and arousing, flowing across her skin like warm honey. "You make me want to do things that you've never dreamed about."

Sarah didn't stop to think about the consequences. She had loved and lost. She knew how fragile and how precious that feeling could be. The pain of Eric's death had been devastating, but loneliness and the fear of taking a chance on love again were more devastating still. "You'd be surprised what I dream about, Michael Kenton," she said, and lifted her face for his kiss. For a moment he hesitated, then covered her mouth with his. Sarah pushed against him, heedless of the steering wheel digging into her side. The doubts that had assailed her Thanksgiving day were purged by desire. She wanted only to be close to him, as close as two humans could possibly be. She wrapped her arms around his neck and let the kiss go on and on, feeling the heat of their passion spreading through her veins to ignite the very center of her being.

His coat was unbuttoned, and she could feel the pulse at the base of his throat beating against her wrist. His hands were busy unzipping her coat, thrusting it aside, so that he could lift her higher, nuzzle the skin of her throat, mold his hands to the softness of her breasts. His arousal pushed against her thigh, hot and hard. It was a devastatingly sexual kiss, a joining on an elemental level. This time there was no fear in her, no apprehension. Each day that passed made her more aware of herself as a woman, more attuned to her wants and needs. Intellectually Sarah knew she should hold back, temper her response, keep herself from hurt. But it had been so long since she'd felt this desirable. It had been so long since she'd wanted a man to make love to her that she put all logical thought aside and reveled in the return of passion.

She felt his fingers brush against her skin as he unbuttoned her shirt. She twisted in his arms, trying to get comfortable, wanting him to deal with the last barrier of cotton and lace that separated her breasts from his mouth. She felt his hands on her back, and her bra fell away. His breath caressed her nipples and he hesitated, remembering, no doubt, what had happened before. Sarah bracketed his face with her hands, pressing him to her. He sucked gently, sending white-hot spasms of pleasure along the pathway between her womb and her heart.

"Michael." She didn't know if she whispered his name or shouted it aloud. She wanted to feel his skin against hers. She wanted to lie naked beside him, feel him with her, in her. It no longer mattered that he had never said he cared, never said he loved her. None of the things she had deemed important all of her life could stand beside her need for this man. She had not thought herself capable of such passion, such wanton behavior.

She tugged at his belt, the zipper of his pants. He reached down and covered her hands with his, held them tightly. "Sarah," he said, his voice rough and dark with passion. "Stop."

"I don't want to stop." She pushed against him. She didn't want him bringing her back to a sense of herself, a sense of restraint.

"I'm not going to make love to you, Sarah. Not after what happened at Thanksgiving." She recognized the effort it took for him to speak so firmly, but she ignored it.

"I was off guard that day. I…I wasn't sure I would be a good lover to you." She struggled to find the right words.

Michael groaned. "You're not ready for this." His voice was rough, wary. She could feel him pulling back, sealing himself away.

"I'm ready."

She meant what she was saying with all her heart and soul or she would never have found the courage to speak the words aloud, to be this aggressive, to fight this hard for what she knew was meant to be. "You aren't the first man who's been attracted to me since Eric died, but you're the first, the only one, who's attracted me in return. I believe in love at first sight, Michael. That's how it was with Eric. That's how it was with you." She could admit it now. Indeed, she had no other choice.

He cupped her face in his hands and took a deep, shuddering breath. "I can't take what you're offering me. I don't love you, Sarah. Not the way you want me to.''

She thought she'd been prepared to hear those words. She thought it didn't matter, that it wouldn't hurt as if he'd driven a stake through her heart. ''I don't care,'' she lied. She knew the words sounded as desolate as she felt.

''Yes, you do.'' He hesitated, then pulled her close, stroked her hair. His heart was beating as hard and as quickly as hers was. Was it only physical passion? Did he truly feel none of the connection that bound her so strongly, even in the face of his seeming indifference?

''I don't care,'' she insisted, blinking back betraying, hateful tears of weakness and need. The rush of words that had sustained her argument moments before deserted her. She could barely speak at all, and when she did, she knew she sounded like a child, lost and forlorn. ''I want you. That's all that matters.''

''I'm not worth it.'' His voice broke. ''Believe me.''

''I can make you love me,'' she whispered. It was a cry as old as womankind.

He closed his eyes as though she'd delivered a blow straight to his heart. ''I don't think I'm capable of loving anyone. Not the way you deserve to be loved. Not the way you want to be loved.''

''You don't mean that, Michael.'' The catch in her voice made it sound as if she were pleading with him. Sarah bit her lip to still its trembling.

''Don't try to analyze me, Sarah.'' He reached up and touched the tip of her nose. ''I want you to respect me in the morning,'' he said, almost hitting the right, light note. Almost, but not quite.

The fight went out of her. She began to tremble. Sanity returned in a icy rush. She had come so close to betraying everything she believed in, and he had stopped her. He had kept his head, held back. He might not admit it, but for Sarah, for the moment, that was enough. Michael might believe he was selfish and self-centered, but if he truly did think only of his own wants and needs, he would have taken what she offered without a moment's hesitation. He was a good man, whether he believed in himself or not.

"What happened to you, Michael? Why are you so afraid of your feelings?" He didn't answer immediately, just buttoned her blouse with fingers that were rough and gentle at the same time. They were trembling, but so was she, with cold and frustration and deep, deep sorrow for the pain she saw reflected by the starlight in his eyes.

"God, Sarah. You don't pull any punches, do you?"

"Not when I know I'm right." He shifted her in his arms, leaning against the door as he held her against him. It was still a cramped and uncomfortable arrangement, but Sarah wouldn't have moved away if her life depended on it.

"Maybe I ought to get out of this town. It's changing me," he said, his voice rumbling in his chest beneath her ear.

"How, Michael?" Her body still thrummed with passion, with need but she ignored it, concentrated on listening, or hearing what he said and, more importantly, what he didn't say. If she could understand him, she could help him heal, help him become the man he was meant to be, and then, God willing, he could love her, would love her as she was coming to love him.

"It's making me think too much. It's making me start to consider putting down roots. I've never wanted roots."

And he'd never wanted love. He might as well have spoken the words aloud. "There's no place you can call home? Nowhere else in the world?"

"Not since my grandmother died. And then all there was was a two-bedroom apartment in the worst part of Miami. But it was clean and she always had something in the refrigerator to eat. It may not have been much, but it was more than most of the neighbors had. God, that place. A government housing project. A hellhole. I'll never forget the sights and the sounds and the smells. Prison was better. It's a wonder I stayed out of real trouble as long as I did."

"Who framed you, Michael? Who was responsible for your going to prison?"

He didn't answer for so long that she was afraid he was going to ignore her question. The windows had steamed over, sealing out the world. The moon had disappeared and it had started to snow again. It was dark and cold and there was only the wind and the scrape of branches against the side of the car to keep them company.

"I'd better get you home. It's getting late," he said at last.

"No, Michael. Don't change the subject."

"It was my business partner," he said flatly.

"Was he a friend?"

"I thought so." His tone warned her not to pursue that subject further.

"And your business was restoring classic cars?"

"Yeah. *Kenton and Carnelli Classic Cars.*"

"How did you learn to do that?"

"When I was on probation from juvenile hall the second time, my case worker got me a job through one of the rehab programs. Giuseppe Carnelli was a great old guy. He knew cars. He had worked for Ettore Bugatti before the Second World War. I liked the work. I was good with my hands. Mechanical. The old man taught me everything I know. He taught me where to find parts. He introduced me to his clients—rich men, powerful men. I thought I'd found my niche in life.''

''What happened?'' Sarah could feel the tension in him—not sexual any longer, but angry, old and familiar.

''Rick Carnelli was Giuseppe's nephew. He was about ten years older than I was. A real mover and shaker, I thought. He'd been to one of the big Ivy League schools back East. He had the connections we needed to expand the business. I knew the cars. He knew the people who could afford to own them.''

''You went into business together.''

''Giuseppe turned it over to us. We were the sons he never had, he said. For two more years everything went along pretty well. I was twenty-two and earning a good living. I found a nice apartment for my grandmother in a good part of town. I fixed up the loft above the garage. Rick bought a condo on the ocean. We were going to buy Giuseppe out in a couple more years so he could retire to Italy.''

''Your business was doing that well?''

''We were doing okay,'' he said. ''But Rick had a taste for the good life. Once in a while a check would bounce. They shouldn't have. I let it slide. God, what a jackass I was. I should have seen the signs from the beginning, but I didn't. I was just a kid. Making it on my own, working on cars that were works of art, some of them practically handmade, worth hundreds of thousands of dollars. And movie stars and politicians and people with names you saw on TV every day were in my shop, peering over my shoulder, asking my advice.'' He laughed, a low, mocking rumble beneath her ear. "I had the world by the throat. I had it made.''

"Rick Carnelli was the man who framed you?''

"Yeah. It was Rick.''

"Why couldn't you prove it?''

"He's dead.''

"Dead.'' She couldn't help herself. She shivered, and Michael's arms tightened around her.

"I didn't kill him, if that's what you're thinking.''

She shook her head. "No. I'm thinking that if he's dead you'll never be able to prove your innocence.''

"Bingo,'' he said, but there was no bitterness in his voice, only resignation that she knew had been forged in the furnace of despair.

"How did it happen?''

"Rick loved to play the ponies. That's what I thought was wrong when the checks bounced. But it wasn't only the ponies he was into. It was gambling. Big-time. And the guys he owed money to weren't the kind to back off just because he told them the check was in the mail. He got desperate, I guess. He might have gone to Harvard, but he wasn't too bright. We'd made an investment, on our own. A Rolls-Royce Silver Ghost and a Duesenberg. They were in pretty bad shape, but a hell of a find, anyway. Rick had insured them for a bundle without telling me. He forged my name to the insurance papers. Then one night he set fire to the garage. But he didn't do a very good job of it. The insurance company wouldn't pay up. I got nabbed, the kid with the record a mile long. And Rick disappeared.''

"But you were a juvenile when you were in trouble. I thought those records couldn't be used in court.''

"Believe me, that's not always the case. Especially when one of the dumb things you did as a kid was set fires."

Sarah's heart ached for him. It was no wonder that he thought the world was against him sometimes. "Then who killed Rick?"

Michael shrugged. "The guys he owed money to, I suppose. I told you they played rough. I was already in prison when they found the body. He'd been shot, but the coroner said it looked like he'd been buried alive."

"My God," Sarah said, shutting her eyes to block out the horrific image.

"Yeah, a fitting end for the bastard, but with Rick dead there was no way left to prove I hadn't set the fire. I figured I was lucky they didn't try to pin the murder on me, too. I served my time and headed north. Got a job on a lake freighter where no one cared who I was or where I'd been."

"What about your grandmother and Giuseppe?"

"Giuseppe went back to Italy. He died right after they found Rick's body. He never spoke to me again after the trial. When I got out of prison, Gram tried her damnedest to get my case reopened. She never quit believing in me. But it was too hard on her. She had a series of strokes and I had to put her in a nursing home, a nice place. The nicest I could find. She died there, last spring."

"And now you're alone?"

He hesitated. Sarah lifted her head. He looked at her for a long moment, searching her face. Sarah held her breath. She had the impression he had something important to say.

But all he said was "I'm alone." He moved her gently away from him. "It's time to go home, Sarah."

She didn't argue with him. He looked drained, the way she felt. His profile was a stark outline against the frosted windowpane. She sat in silence, watching the windshield wiper scrape away at the frost. For a private, untrusting man like Michael to unburden himself to her as he just had was an act more intimate than sex.

He had to care, she told herself over and over in rhythm with the windshield wipers. He hadn't told her all those things just because she was here, available, a convenient listener. *He had to care.*

MICHAEL WRESTLED with the warped wooden garage door. It was the old-fashioned kind that folded up into sections like an accordion, heavy as hell. Damn that penny-pinching church counsel. How did they expect a tiny little thing like Sarah to manage this relic? "I'm going to replace this door," he said gruffly. "I'll get Jonas Phillips to okay the expense."

Sarah laid a hand on his arm. "No, you won't. I don't want a new garage door. There are too many other things the parish needs." He could have sworn he felt the silkiness of her fingers on his skin, even through the layers of cloth that separated them, even though she was wearing mittens that looked as if they'd been knitted from yarn as thick as his finger. But then he didn't have any trouble imagining all kinds of things where Sarah was concerned—how it would feel to hold her naked in his arms, to thrust himself inside her and feel her tighten with pleasure around him.

"It's stopped snowing," she said, lifting her face to the sky. "Jonas will probably be around early to clear the walks. I hope the snowblower doesn't wake you."

"You know I'm always up before the sun."

"I know," she said, dropping her gaze to her shoes.

"But Jonas has cows to milk and he gets up even earlier than you do. He might turn up here before sunrise." She lifted her face and smiled at him, and his body tightened and hardened again. Did she know what she did to him, smiling like that?

The shock of it hit him right in the gut. He could barely catch his breath, order his thoughts. *God,* was she right? Did he *love* her? Was that what was wrong with him? Was that why his insides churned when he thought about leaving this place, leaving Sarah?

There was sure as hell something wrong with him. He'd never before put a woman's needs ahead of his own. He'd never even thought about it. Sex was sex and he was good at it—that was all there was to it. But love was different. When you loved someone, you cared, you thought about that person first and yourself last.

Was that what it was then—love? Was that why he'd pulled back, refused the gift of herself she'd offered so trustingly? He wanted Sarah. He wanted her more than any woman he'd ever known. And he'd waited longer to have her. He was still waiting. Waiting for everything to be just right. He didn't want her to leave him, not tonight, not yet, but he couldn't find the words to make her stay. He had come as close as he dared, as close as he could, back there in her car, when he'd said he was starting to put down roots.

"Good night, Michael." She was walking away.

He didn't want her to go.

"Sarah, wait." What could he say? *I think I love you but I don't know for sure. And oh, by the way, my real name is Michael Baron Kenton. I'm Ronald Baron's bastard son.*

"Yes?" She waited, patient, beautiful in the snowy starlight.

He took a step forward, another one; took her in his arms. He looked down into her face. Her nose and cheeks were red with cold. He pulled her hat off so that he could feel her hair tangled around his fingers, smell its flowery scent.

"Sarah, don't go." *Take the chance, Kenton,* a voice inside his head kept whispering over and over. *Take the chance. You must be falling in love with her or you could let her go, turn around and walk away from her and never look back.* With any other woman he'd known he could have done just that without a second thought. But not Sarah. Not this small, determined, passionate creature who had become as necessary to him as the air he breathed. "I don't know how to say it...." He was going about it all wrong. Damn, if he could just come out and say it, tell her everything. But he wasn't ready to do that, not right now. He didn't like keeping secrets from her, but his feelings were all mixed up with his secrets. Better to leave things unsaid than to lose her.

She reached up and touched her mittened fingers to his lips. A tear slipped from beneath her lashes and slid down her cheek. "Don't, Michael. Don't say something you aren't ready to say. Let me go, Michael. It's late. Very late, and it's been a long day."

He could feel her slipping away, emotionally as well as physically. *Just say it,* the voice screamed. *Damn it, man, tell her you love her.* The rest would come in time, when he understood his heritage, himself. The urgency in that voice, his voice, scared him, galvanized him. "Sarah, no. Wait. I love you. I've been falling in love with you for weeks. I just didn't know what it was. I—''

The explosion rattled the windows in the garage door and set the branches of the dying maple chattering overhead. Sarah spun out of his arms as an orange fireball lit the sky behind them.

''My God,'' Sarah said, her hands to her mouth. ''What is it? What happened?'' Already the fire siren on top of the city hall had begun to wail. All around them lights were going on in bedroom windows up and down the street.

Michael narrowed his eyes against the blinding light of the fireball. ''Something sure as hell blew up.''

Sarah grabbed his arm. ''It's the F and M. It has to be coming from that direction.'' She was already hurrying down the driveway.

Michael reached out to grab her arm. ''I'll get the car.''

''Yes, get the car. They might need help. Thank God this was Sunday, and no one should be in there. What in God's name could have happened?''

''Come on,'' he said, his voice grim. ''We'll find out.''

CHAPTER NINE

THE FIRE WAS finally out. Sarah's eyes felt as dry and as gritty as the soot-darkened snow and ice around the blackened shell of the F and M. She held her fingers before her face for a moment to relieve the strain, then looked out of the window of the shelter house at Sugar Creek Park and saw with a small jolt of surprise that the sun was fully above the horizon. She had been here all night. She blinked in the red-gold light glinting off the layers of ice that glazed the cinder-block walls and made the area around the building a danger to life and limb, but she didn't look away.

Only the Tyler fire crew remained at the scene. During the hours when the fire had been at its height, Sugar Creek and Belton engines had been called in to help fight the blaze, but they had returned to their stations just before dawn. When she saw them leave, Sarah had finally let herself believe the worst was over. For one terrifying hour, soon after the first explosion, it had seemed they would have to evacuate the Green Woods Motel next door, and several houses that were downwind, because of the chemicals stored in the back portion of the building. But fast thinking and coordination among the fire units had prevented that from happening.

Much of the factory, the main source of income for a large number of Tyler residents, was in ruins, but

Sarah could only be thankful that it had not been worse. As incredible as it seemed, no one had been seriously injured or killed in the blast. The night watchman, the only person in the building, had been at the other end of the factory from where the fire apparently started.

He was still here, holding court—a plump, middle-aged man Sarah didn't know very well, sitting on one of the hard, wooden bench seats beside his tearful wife, talking to the weary fire fighters and concerned towns-people gathered round eating sandwiches and drinking strong, black coffee. Talk was always the best therapy, Sarah had found, and even though she'd heard his story twice already, she turned away from the window to listen again.

"I'd have been a goner for sure if I'd been in the part of the building where old Judson's lab's located," he said, shaking his head, wincing as the bandage pulled across a cut on his forehead. "I always make a round of the offices and lab just about two every night. But tonight? Well, tonight I guess the Good Lord was looking out for me. I thought I heard something out on the work floor and I went that way 'round. Saved my life for sure. I'd a been smack in the middle of the old man's lab when it blew sky-high. I'd probably still be coming down in pieces all over the place."

"William Benson, that is enough! Don't talk like that," his wife said, but she squeezed his arm and laid her head on his shoulder. "Let's go home, honey. You need some rest."

"Couldn't sleep," William returned. "Too wound up." He signaled for another cup of coffee. "The vet, young Dr. Phelps, driving by just then sure didn't hurt. I didn't know what direction was up when I crawled out that door. I could just as easy have turned around and gone back inside, that's how shook up I was. He helped me away from the building. Lucky for me, one of Myron Hansen's cows decided to go and have a breech calf in the middle of the night. Phelps called in the alarm on the phone in his truck.''

''Everyone in town was awake by then, Will,'' Murphy reminded him. ''Fire dispatcher got half-a-dozen calls. Jolted me right out of my bed.''

''How do you think it started?'' Will asked Gabe Atwood, one of Tyler's firefighters, who had just entered the building for a cup of coffee.

Gabe pulled off his helmet. His eyes were red-rimmed and his face smudged with soot and smoke. ''Don't know yet, Will. It's still too hot to get inside the lab, but that looks like where it started.''

''Find any trace of that guy I told you I saw running through the park?'' Several heads swiveled in the direction Will indicated, although from where they were sitting there was nothing to see but plank walls. ''I know I wasn't dreaming. Roger Phelps saw him, too.''

''Half the town's been tramping around out here tonight, Will,'' Murphy stated. ''There are forty cars parked out front of this building right now. There were ten more here an hour ago. If there was any trace of this guy you say you saw, it's long gone.''

''Murphy's right about that.'' The whole room smelled strongly of smoke from the fire, but when Gabe stepped closer, Sarah wrinkled her nose at the combination of smoke and chemicals and burned oil that came from his turnout coat.

She filled a cup with hot coffee and handed it over. ''Cream or sugar?'' she asked.

''Black's fine. I'll drink this outside if the smell bothers you,'' Gabe offered with a tired smile.

"Don't be ridiculous," Sarah said. "My nose just has a mind of its own."

He smiled more broadly. "I know what you mean."

"Have a seat. How about a sandwich? We've plenty here."

"No," he said, the smile disappearing as quickly as it had come. "I can only stay a minute." He lowered his voice. "The chief's talking to Brick now."

"Then it's true? They're going to call in the state fire marshal's office to investigate?" The news of Will and Roger Phelps spotting a figure running away from the fire and the rumor that it might have been deliberately set had started circulating not long after Sarah and Michael arrived on the scene.

"I don't think we have any other choice. A fire like this one just doesn't start by itself."

Sarah couldn't help herself. She looked past Gabe's shoulder to where she had last seen Michael, helping two other men clear debris from the parking lot. He was gone. She wondered where he was. She had seen him only off and on after they arrived at the fire scene. She hadn't thought anything of it at the time. It had been all chaos and confusion. There had been food to fetch and prepare, coffee to brew, hungry, tired people to feed and comfort. But now that the hectic pace had slowed, she missed him. What was he thinking? What was he feeling? Surely, what had happened tonight had recalled painful memories of the fire that had sent him to prison.

"Do you think we need to make another pot of coffee, Sarah?"

"What did you say, Moira? My mind wandered for a moment." Turning toward the speaker, Sarah wrapped her arms beneath her breasts and hugged herself against the chill of the unheated room.

"I said, do you think we need to brew another pot of coffee?"

"I don't think so," she said, managing a tired smile. "Almost everyone's gone home to try and catch a few hours' sleep."

Moira Schweinhagen looked almost as tired as Sarah felt. Her husband worked at the F and M. It had been a long, hard night for her, too. Her face crumpled and she sniffed back tears. "I feel just like Will. I'm too worked up to sleep. All I can think of is what is Pat going to do for a job? How are we going to make the mortgage payment or buy groceries for next week? I don't make enough at the Hair Affair to support us all."

"Oh, Moira, I know that's a terrible worry. But don't borrow trouble." Sarah hated mouthing platitudes, but sometimes the old way still worked the best. "You know the Ingallses will do everything they can for their employees. And the government. There are loans you can get. Pat will be eligible for unemployment, and—"

"I'm still worried, Sarah." Her eyes swept past Sarah's shoulder. "Look at that place. It's a wreck. I wouldn't blame Alyssa Wocheck if she threw up her hands and said forget it, called in the bulldozers and razed it to the ground."

"Alyssa won't give up that easily," Sarah said, forcing herself to sound far more convincing than she felt. "She's Judson Ingalls's daughter, isn't she?"

Moira put her hand to her mouth to hold back a sob. "That poor old man. He's had too much trouble these past years. And now this. He loved this place. He built it up from nothing. He fought to keep from having to sell out to the Japanese. I wonder who's going to tell him it's burned to the ground?''

ALYSSA PUSHED a strand of hair from her eyes and bent to lift a desk drawer full of soggy papers into the back of someone's pickup, which had been driven as close to the office entrance as Chief Sorenson would allow. The cold morning air was finally free of smoke, but the smell of fire was still strong in her nostrils. There was nothing she could do for the time being but supervise the loading of salvaged materials. The firefighters wouldn't let her inside the building until it could be evaluated for structural damage, but those who weren't needed elsewhere to keep hot spots under control had volunteered to remove records and computer equipment from the building.

"Let me help you with that, Mrs. Wocheck."

Michael Kenton appeared at her shoulder and took the heavy drawer from her hands. "Where do you want it?"

"It doesn't matter," she said wearily. "It belongs to my secretary's desk. I don't even know if there's anything worth salvaging in there."

"It's a big job." He placed the drawer next to two others that had already been loaded.

"I don't know how we'll ever sort this all out," Alyssa said. "The one thing I'm thankful for is that Jeff was able to move the clinic to the hospital last year. I don't think I could bear to see him have to start his father's clinic over from scratch again. He's worked so hard…" She turned just in time to see her new computer being carried through the doorway. "Oh no," she said, as close to tears as she'd been all night. "It's ruined."

Michael spoke quietly from behind her. "If your backup disks were someplace safe you can always run the program on another computer."

Alyssa nodded and looked up at him, managing a smile. "You're right. We keep the disks in the safe. It's older than the building, and practically impregnable. Gabe Atwood said it looks as if it hasn't been touched, thank God. And the accountant has copies of everything else. Thanks for reminding me. It just looks so bad."

"There's a lot of heavy machinery in there. It's pretty hard to put out of commission." Michael Kenton looked as tired as she felt. There were sharp lines etched at the corners of his mouth and his hair was grayed with ash. Had he been here all night? A lot of townspeople had—employees, old friends, strangers. Their faces had all begun to blur together.

"Thank you for your help," she said. She'd tried to thank everyone she could, but it was hard to keep it all straight.

"Chief Sorenson told me they'll be able to get inside and inspect the production area in another hour or so," a male voice interjected. Alyssa turned at the welcome sound and greeted her husband.

"How bad is it? Do they know how it started? Did he say?"

Edward shook his head. "They don't know anything for certain yet, Lyssa."

"What am I going to tell Dad?"

He ran his hand through his tousled hair, steel-gray now, but just as thick and fine as it had been when he was a boy. "Don't think of that just yet. It's still too early to call Arizona. When you call him, you'll want to have all the facts that are available. It's not fair to upset him otherwise.''

''I suppose you're right.'' She watched as Gabe Atwood, with the help of Nate Cummings, the assistant manager she'd hired the year before, carried out a set of half-melted file cabinets. ''Oh, Edward.'' Alyssa couldn't stand it anymore. The enormity of what had happened almost overwhelmed her. She was tired and dirty and sick at heart. ''What will we do?'' She let herself be pulled against his chest, drawing ¬trength from the warmth of his body and the security of his arms around her.

''Why don't you go home, take a hot shower, have a good breakfast and get some sleep?'' Michael Kenton was standing directly in front of her now, the newly risen sun at his back. His breath made smoke clouds in the frosty morning air and his nose was red from the cold.

''That's a good idea,'' Edward said, but Alyssa sensed a sudden tenseness in his arms and heard a note of restraint in his voice. Michael Kenton noticed, too. His eyes, so blue they were almost black—eyes the same color as Jeff's, she noticed for the first time— narrowed. ''Liza and Cece are at the house with the girls. Jeff just told me,'' Edward continued. ''Why don't you go home, fill them in on what we know and then take young Kenton's advice—get something to eat and some rest? We can cope here. Amanda and Devon are still around, if any decisions have to be made. And Cliff's somewhere on the scene.''

''Your husband's plan makes sense, Mrs. Wocheck.''

''Alyssa,'' she said automatically. He nodded. She felt Edward still watching the younger man, although she didn't look up to see her husband's face. "I—I don't know." She was tired and confused, and she couldn't begin to understand the tension radiating between the two men.

"Go home, Lyssa," Edward said more gently than he had before. "Let Cece and Liza fuss over you. It will do them good, make them feel useful. Look, here comes Anna. She can take you home."

"But Dad... And someone will have to inform the insurance company."

"Let me handle the insurance people, and we'll call Judson together as soon as I get home. Hi, Anna," he said, greeting Alyssa's lifelong best friend. "Lyssa's about had it. Would you take her home?"

"That's what I'm here for. Johnny's going to be busy with Chief Sorenson and the investigators from the fire marshal's office."

Alyssa lifted her head, although the sun's rays hurt her burning eyes. The words struck like tiny daggers in her heart. "Why does there have to be an investigation? Just because Will Benson thinks he saw someone running away from the building? He was half-unconscious, in shock."

"It's just routine," Edward said, too quickly to be convincing.

"It's not routine."

"It's a big fire, Alyssa," Anna Kelsey soothed. She put her arm around her friend's shoulders. "There has to be an investigation. Johnny's going to be here. And Edward. There's nothing you can tell them. You were asleep in your bed just like I was when it started. C'mon. Let's go home."

"All right," she said, giving up because she was just

too tired to fight with all of them. "Did I thank Michael—?" She looked around, but he was gone.

"You thanked him, Lyssa," Edward said, brushing his hand across her cheek. "Go home."

"Yes," she said. "But come as soon as you can. I want you there when I call Dad."

"I COULDN'T FIND YOU anywhere," Sarah said from behind him. "So I came home."

He turned away from the stove in her kitchen, where he'd been heating water for oatmeal. She liked oatmeal for breakfast. She ate it nearly every day and always brought him a bowl on his breakfast tray. "I was getting in the way," he said. She came toward him, the smell of smoke and fire strong in her hair. Michael swallowed hard, took a deep breath to control the nausea that threatened to rise up and choke him.

"No," she said, stopping an arm's length away. "You weren't in the way. You were helping. Other people noticed, too. I heard them talking."

"Sweeping up broken glass and moving furniture is no big deal."

"Yes, it is. It shows you care."

"It shows I have a strong back."

She took another step closer. "You left because of the fire. The fire your partner set. You left because of the memories."

He felt trapped. He could brush her aside like a fly and take off for his apartment, but she'd probably just come after him. She was stubborn like that—wonderfully, gloriously stubborn when she felt she was in the right. She *was* right, of course, but that didn't make it any easier to think about, to remember. He couldn't let himself weaken.... "For God's sake, Sarah. Not now.

Go take a shower, get into something comfortable. I'll fix us breakfast and then we can crash, sleep this off like a bad hangover.''

She stared into his eyes, her own gold-green, like the soft, new grass in a spring meadow. "All right. I'll go take a shower. I'm sick of the smell of smoke and fire, too. But I won't be pushed away, Michael. Last night you told me you loved me. That means something.'' She pulled her lower lip between her teeth and bit down hard. "Even if I have to battle your memories every inch of the way to get you to say it again.''

He rested his forehead on hers, fighting to regain control of his emotions. It was the only way he knew how to survive, to shut down, to think and not feel. "Go take a shower,'' he repeated. "We'll talk when you get back.'' By then maybe he would be able to deal with the past, and with the secrets.

Fifteen minutes later she was back, dressed in a sweatshirt the color of honey that barely outlined the tips of her breasts but still made his heart pound and his gut tighten, and stirrup pants that molded themselves to the curves of her hips and bottom. Michael set a dish of steaming oatmeal in front of her with a thud that made her look up at him from beneath spiky lashes.

"There's brown sugar in the cupboard to the right of the stove.''

He found it without any trouble. The inside of her cupboards were as neat as she was.

"Aren't you eating anything?'' she asked, stirring sugar into the cereal.

"I'm not hungry.'' He began running water into the sink. He squirted soap into the water and watched the bubbles build for a long minute. Then he pushed up his sleeve and reached for the oatmeal pan.

"Michael!" She was beside him in a heartbeat. "What happened to your arm?" He looked down in surprise, to where a scratch about three inches long oozed blood. It was raw and nasty looking but not serious.

"I must have cut it on something at the fire."

"What something? Metal? Glass?"

"Honestly, Sarah, I don't remember."

"I'll call Jeff Baron." Sarah frowned as she realized he wouldn't be at the clinic. "No, he's probably still at the fire. Get your coat. We'll go to the emergency room at Tyler General and get it looked at."

"Sarah, it's just a scratch."

"Okay. Maybe. But you'll need a tetanus shot—"

He reached out and lifted her chin with his hand, holding her still with only the most gentle pressure of his fingers. "Sarah. I don't need a tetanus shot. I've been in prison and working on a lake freighter. My shots are up-to-date. All of them."

She smiled, a quirky little smile that ended in a slight frown. "You're sure?"

"I'm sure."

"Does it need stitches?"

"No, little mother hen. It does not need stitches."

"Then a bandage. I'll get one from the bathroom."

He circled her waist with his hands, stopped her from moving away. "Later. I'll put one on it later."

Her frown grew wider, pulling her eyebrows together, wrinkling her forehead. "Do you think I'm a mother hen?"

He groaned, fighting the familiar urge to shut down, pull away, keep himself closed off and his emotions out of danger. He pulled her close against his heart. "I think you're the sexiest woman I've ever met."

She tilted her head back to see his face. "Really?"

"Cross my heart."

"Thank you," she said. "No one's ever said that to me before. It's not true, of course. But thank you, anyway."

He might have his neurosis under control, but not his libido. Her skin was dewy and fresh. Her hair, pulled up in a loose knot on top of her head, smelled of wildflowers and sunshine. There were pale violet circles under her eyes and tiny lines etched from nose to chin that attested to her fatigue, but she was, for him, the most beautiful and desirable woman in the world. He bent his head to kiss her. She tasted of toothpaste and oatmeal and passion. For a long moment he lost himself in the honeyed sweetness of her mouth. He molded her body to his, felt her arms go around his waist to pull him just as closely to her.

"God, Sarah, you make me want to drag you down on the floor and make love to you here and now."

"What's so awful about that?" she asked, her face pressed against his chest, her voice breathless and hurried.

He groaned. "It sounds like some kind of damned porno flick. Reverend Sarah making it with the hired man on the kitchen floor." He said it to shock himself as much as her.

She pulled away from him, lifted her face to his. "If that's all it would mean to you, then it does sound sordid and tawdry. But for me it wouldn't be any of those things."

"What would it be?"

"Making love with the man I love."

"The ex-con who's got the hots for the preacher lady?"

"The man who loves me."

He loved her. The realization of it still shocked him, still made him want to run for cover. Loving meant commitment and constancy, words that had meant little or nothing to him before Sarah came into his life. Words that still scared the hell out of him.

"What if I want to go back to Florida and live on the beach somewhere? And I say come with me or it's over? What if I decide to work the lake freighters and be gone for six months out of the year and leave you here to fend for yourself?"

Her smile was serene. "I've been fending for myself for more than three years now. I can't say I approve of your being a beach bum—you're much too talented for that. But if you want to continue working on the lake freighters, I would understand."

"You're being damned obliging this morning."

"Is this a test, Michael?"

"No." His laugh was harsh and sharp, because he was so amazed at himself and so scared. "I think it's a proposal."

CHAPTER TEN

"A PROPOSAL?"

"Marry me, Sarah. Marry me and make me the luckiest man on earth."

They were the words she'd wanted to hear for days, longed to hear. But they were words she'd convinced herself would never be spoken. "I love you. But..." She lifted her eyes, searching his face. "Am I rushing you? Is this what you really want?"

"Sarah, you're not making this any easier." He smiled. "I'm thirty years old. I know what I want. It's just taken me so damned long to get my nerve up to say it."

She cupped his face with her hands. The pulse in his throat beat against her palm. "I would be honored to be your wife." She searched his eyes. They were dark as a midnight sky and reflected her face like the surface of the lake on a moonlight night. "Are you sure—"

"I'm positive, Sarah," he said, squeezing her shoulders so hard she winced. He shook his head, loosened his grip immediately. He spoke quickly, hurrying his words. "I love you. I want to marry you. I'll turn myself into the perfect preacher's husband. I'll be down front, first pew, every Sunday. I'll wear a tie. I'll sing the hymns. I'll even stand beside you at the door and shake hands and make small talk."

She laughed, a shaky little laugh that hid her elation

and her excitement. *He meant it.* She could feel it in the tension in his body, hear it in the roughness of his voice. "You don't have to do all that."

"Yes, I do." He pulled her back into his arms. "I love you, Sarah." His voice was rough with emotions that he usually tried to hide. "I want to be with you. All day. All night. Every day for the rest of our lives."

"But, Michael, do you want to settle down in Tyler?" She thought a shadow passed across his face, but he dropped his head to nuzzle the curve of her throat, and she let the wonder of it all push her doubts to the back of her mind. *He loved her. He wanted to be with her. They could make it work despite the differences in their background and their outlook on life. He loved her, that was all that mattered.*

"I want to be where you are."

"How will you earn a living?"

He shrugged, smoothing wisps of hair away from her face. "I don't know yet. Does it matter?"

"Yes, it matters. Not because of the money," she said, wrapping her arms around his waist. "It matters because I want you to be happy here."

"I'll be happy wherever we're together."

Sarah let her breath sift out between her lips. She guessed Michael had never been truly happy anywhere he'd lived. She knew so little about him, really—who his family was, what his childhood had been like. She wanted him to trust her, to tell her all those things, and he hadn't as yet. But for him to make this one, simple statement was a beginning, and it meant more to her than all the flowers and candy and love poems in the world.

"We can make a good life for ourselves here," she

said, raising her lips to his. "We can put down roots, raise a family."

"Kids?" He drew back a little and stared into her eyes. "Do you think I can do it? Be a father? A good father?" Now she wasn't imagining a shadow on his face. It was there, doubt and anxiety and some other emotion she couldn't decipher.

"Yes," she said, and smiled. "I think you can do it very well."

"Then I'll try my damnedest." His fingers tightened on her arms again, but there was no pain. "Sarah?"

"Yes?" She swayed toward him. She couldn't help it. It felt so good to be in his arms. She was aroused and exhausted all at the same time. It was a heady, intoxicating feeling.

Michael sucked in his breath. His mouth came down on hers. His kiss was rough at first, hungry for the taste of her, then gentled when she slipped her arms around his neck and kissed him back. "God, Sarah, you make it hard to do what's right."

"This is right," she said, losing herself as always in the power of his attraction for her. "This is most wonderfully right." She moved against him without conscious thought, naturally, but the effect on him was immediate and incendiary. He slid his hands down her back and swept her into his arms. He turned on his heel and carried her into her bedroom without a moment's hesitation.

"How did you know which room is my bedroom?" she asked, her face pillowed on the hard curve of his shoulder.

"I've watched you turn on your bedroom light nearly every damn night since I came to this town." His voice was smoke-roughened and dark with passion, with a need as great as her own.

"I do the same thing," she said, feeling his arousal hard and hot against her thigh as he set her feet on the floor. The back of the bed pressed against her legs. Her heart hammered in her chest. "Michael." She could barely form his name.

"I should go," he said, and turned as if to leave the room.

"No!" Sarah reached out and grabbed his arm, holding as tightly as she could. He stood still but she knew he could have broken her hold with a flick of his wrist. "Don't go. Stay with me. Please."

He groaned deep in his throat and pulled her down onto the bed beside him. He took her in his arms, rolled onto his side and pulled her close against him. "You make it so hard to do what's right, love."

"This is what's right, Michael," Sarah replied, ignoring the small but insistent voice of her conscience echoing inside her head. *It was not right.* Lovemaking was a privilege and celebration of marriage, reserved for couples who had made that ultimate commitment to each other. She had believed that all her life, practiced that belief, taught it to others. But that was before Michael. Before her need for him.

He closed his eyes as though the plea had been an arrow aimed straight for his heart. "Sarah, we've been through this before."

Fear blossomed inside her, not fear of physical lovemaking, not fear of her own desirability, but fear of losing him, of watching him retreat into himself where she could not follow. And that fear was strong enough to cause her to risk everything, even her soul, to keep him with her. "I want to be with you, Michael."

"And God, I want to be with you." He eased her onto her back, his leg riding between hers. His sex, outlined sharply beneath the fabric of his jeans, was heavy against her leg. His body moved against hers in concert with his kiss, a dance of love, a simulation of a joining even more intimate than the embrace they now shared. Sarah moved beneath him, her hips answering each thrust of his, her body suspended between heaven and hell.

Michael slid his hands beneath her sweatshirt, brushed aside the thin lace of her bra and caressed her nipple with the pad of his thumb. She arched against him, longing for more, wanting to touch him in return, pleasure him as he pleasured her.

"Michael," she said breathlessly. "I want you to make love to me. I want you."

He went still a moment, then moved against her again, slower, less demanding. "Damn it, Sarah." He kissed her mouth, her cheek, her eyelids. "You make it harder than hell for me to be the knight in shining armor."

"Michael?" Her body ached for his touch. Her heart ached for the lost look in his eyes.

He kissed her again. "I'm trying to do the noble thing." He smiled, a smile that was off-center and a little grim, but still a smile. She loved his smile, so rare and so precious. She closed her eyes against a surge of emotion so intense the pleasure of it was nearly pain.

"I don't understand." He still held her tight against him, but he made no move to take their lovemaking further. His kisses grew slower, less passionate, feather-light caresses that soothed and gentled, brought her back from the brink. Sarah's eyelids fluttered open. Her breath came in short little pants. She could feel Michael's heartbeat thunder against her breast.

He laid his forehead against hers, fighting to catch his breath just as she was. "We're not going to make love. Not here. Not now."

"Michael, it's all right. I'm not frightened of the thought of making love to a man again. I'm not frightened of myself. I want you. I love you. Let me prove it."

"Thank you, Sarah. I'll cherish the offer of that gift for the rest of my days. But I'm talking about your soul now. Not your body. I'm talking about giving up everything you believe is right to prove your love." He laughed, a harsh, grating chuckle that held no mirth. "Listen to me. Mr. Agnostic getting philosophical."

"Love isn't wrong." She couldn't go on. Tears filled her eyes. She was torn, torn as she had never been before in her life.

"Maybe I don't believe what your church teaches about these things, about lovemaking and marriage and all the rest of it, but that's not the point. *You* believe it."

"I don't care," she said. Michael brushed the hair from her face, leaning over her, pinning her with his blue-black gaze so that she could not look away. "You care very much. You told me how much when you talked about your congregation and your work with kids. With teenagers who feel the same damn way I do when I take you in my arms, who do what we've been doing, and then have to face the consequences."

She squirmed to get away, but he held her face between his hands. *Dear Lord,* what he said was true. How could she sit in front of her teens every week, seeing the trust in their eyes, and tell them not to let their feelings override their sense of right and wrong, when she was doing exactly that? How could she stand before her congregation and urge them to do their utmost to live by standards that she was not capable of upholding herself? Tears threatened at the back of her eyes. She blinked them away, made herself look straight into his eyes. "I'm human, Michael. I'm a woman. I'm not a plaster saint."

"Yes," he said, smoothing his finger over her cheek. "You are every inch a woman. My woman. The woman I want to be my wife, the mother of my children." He shook his head, as if marveling at some wondrous revelation. "And when it's right, it's worth waiting for. Don't ask me how I know, but I do. Let me be the hero. Let me make the noble sacrifice. Go to sleep, Sarah." He tucked her against his side and kissed her temple. "Go to sleep."

Her body still ached with frustration, with unfulfilled desire but her heart was suddenly at peace. "You're a good man, Michael Kenton. Don't let anyone tell you otherwise." She rested her hand on his chest, over the strong, steady beat of his heart. He covered her hand with his and closed his eyes.

Sarah was content. He had opened up to her. He had spoken to her from his heart. She closed her eyes and murmured a silent prayer of thanksgiving. She had just learned something as well. Once in a while, perhaps only once in a lifetime, two people came together in a moment, in a joining, more precious, more intimate, than sex.

"SARAH, WAKE UP. There's someone at the door."

"What?" Sarah sat up, feeling fuzzy headed and confused. Anxiety swept over her, dissolving the lingering sweetness of her dreams—dreams of Michael beside her, laughing, content, with no shadows darkening his eyes, a child, their child, in her arms. Her bedroom was dark. The last of the short winter daylight was fading away outside the window just like the euphoria of her dream. She fought to hang on to the warmth and the sweetness, but the room was chilly and she shivered when Michael moved away from her side. "What time is it? Have we slept the day away?"

"It's a few minutes after five." Michael swung his feet off the bed, sounding amused. "Yes, we did sleep the day away. But I think after last night you can be forgiven that one little sin."

There was a slight wariness in his tone. Sarah heard and was sad, but not discouraged. She would have to be patient, as patient as Job, to bring this complicated, enigmatic man all the way out of his shell.

"Very funny," she said, sliding her feet around on the floor, searching for her shoes. She switched on the bedside lamp. "My hair is a mess. I can't believe we did this."

He caught her shoulder. "Sarah, don't worry. I'll slip out the back door. No one will know we've been together."

"No." She reached out and wrapped her hand around his wrist. She wasn't aware she'd spoken so fiercely until she saw the look of surprise on his face. "You won't go sneaking anywhere. We haven't done anything to be ashamed of."

"It's a small town, Sarah. We've spent the day together in a house with the shades drawn. Someone's always ready to think the worst."

"No." She stood up so quickly the room spun in a slow circle. She still felt groggy and out of focus, but the ringing of the doorbell, interspersed with the sound of determined knocking, was a summons too insistent to ignore. "Someone might need me."

"Okay. I'll stay out of sight."

Sarah hurried toward the living room, turning on lights as she went. She pulled open the heavy paneled door to find Brick Bauer standing on her porch. He was wearing a heavy, dark coat, open over his uniform. His badge gleamed silver in the glow of the porch light and his breath made white clouds around his head. It had warmed above freezing during the day. The snow was nearly gone, and fog and mist shrouded the trees and dampened the evening sounds from the street.

"Brick? Is something wrong?" All kinds of thoughts crowded through Sarah's mind. *Had there been an accident? Was one of her flock hurt, or dying? Was it one of the children?*

"I need to talk to Kenton," Brick said, looking past her. "I know he's here."

Sarah was aware of Michael's presence at her back, his solid strength, the warmth of his body. *The man she loved. The man she was going to marry.* "Yes, he's here," she said, stepping aside. "Come in. It's too cold to stand in the doorway talking."

"Edward Wocheck and Jeff Baron are with me," Brick said, moving away from the door.

Sarah heard Michael's sudden, sharp intake of breath. She took a step backward, brushed against him and felt the tension radiating through him like live current. Brick's broad shoulders had been blocking her view of the porch. She hadn't realized he wasn't alone. "Edward Wocheck? Jeff? I don't understand."

"This won't take long, Sarah," Brick said. "We'll all be more comfortable inside."

"Oh. Of course." Feeling more confused than ever, she opened the door wider and motioned for him to enter. "Please, come in. All of you."

"Kenton. I have some questions I'd like answered." Brick took off his hat, held it between his hands. His voice was carefully neutral. So was his expression. Sarah gave up trying to read his purpose from the look on his face and turned her attention to the other two men. Edward Wocheck's expression was even more noncommittal than Brick's, but Jeff Baron's emotions were less well schooled. He looked as confused and off balance as she was. A cold chill slithered up and down her spine. What was going on? Why were they here?

"Do I need a lawyer, Bauer?"

"It's nothing official, Kenton. You don't need an attorney."

Michael let his gaze shift to Edward and Jeff. "I'm not so sure."

Something in his voice made the short hairs at the back of Sarah's neck stand on end. "Brick, what is going on?"

"The investigator from the state fire marshal's office was here earlier today," Brick said, dropping his eyes to her face.

"So soon?" Somehow, she had imagined it would take days or weeks to discover the cause of the fire.

"They don't waste any time, Sarah. The fire at the F and M was definitely not an accident. We won't have a full report for a couple of weeks, but he suspects it was arson."

"Arson? But who? Why?" She turned to Edward Wocheck, as though he might have an explanation.

His tone was surprisingly gentle. "We don't know,

Sarah. The only clue anyone has is that Will Benson saw someone running away from the building.''

''But surely—''

Michael stepped forward before she could say any more. ''Are you implying it was me?''

''No one's saying anything like that.'' Brick's voice was steel. ''But Edward has brought me some interesting information about you that puts a whole new slant on things. I'd just like to know where you were yesterday afternoon and last night.''

''Here,'' Michael said shortly.

''Here with Reverend Sarah?''

''No, damn it. Here on the property.''

''Michael?''

''Not now, Sarah.'' The look he gave her was so charged that she closed her mouth automatically. There was more going on here than she understood, currents below the surface that were strong and dangerous. Michael turned to Edward Wocheck. ''Does Alyssa know?'' he asked the older man.

''Not yet. I just found out myself, late this afternoon.''

''How long have you suspected?''

''Long enough to have my stepson, Devon, look into your background.''

''Michael.'' Sarah fought down the twinges of fear that tugged at her heart. ''Explain this to me.''

''Kenton hasn't been totally honest with us about his past,'' Brick said. ''In light of that, I think it would be a good idea if he could come up with an alibi for yesterday. And last night.''

''He was with me.'' Sarah couldn't let this go on.

''All day and all night, Reverend Sarah?'' Brick's question was innocuous, but the implication was clear.

Her face flamed. She tried to think back over the long, eventful day. Had they been together every moment? Yes, Except for the hours between worship and when she had picked him up at Timberlake Lodge. "Almost all of the time." She sounded defensive, a little desperate, even to herself.

"We were together during the day," Michael said bluntly, before she could explain further. "We weren't together when the fire started, if that's what you're asking. I don't have an alibi."

Brick looked at her, but she was watching Michael's dark, set face. He was lying and she didn't know why.

"Then I'm going to advise you not to leave town, Kenton, until this matter is cleared up."

"Are you saying I'm a suspect?"

"I'm saying, in light of your past record and the fact that you're Ronald Baron's illegitimate son, it'll look real suspicious if you leave Tyler."

Sarah felt as if the floor had dropped out from under her. *Ronald Baron's illegitimate son.* She put her hand out blindly and curled her fingers around the back of a chair, holding on for dear life. *Michael, why didn't you tell me?*

"What the hell kind of scam are you trying to pull?" It was the first time Jeff Baron had spoken since he'd entered her house. His face was contorted with anger, disbelief and sorrow. He looked like a man betrayed.

"It's no scam. Ronald Baron was my father, too."

"I don't believe you. My father was a good man. He wouldn't have betrayed my mother that way."

"Maybe he was a good man. I don't know. I never met him. All I know is that his name is on my birth certificate." Michael's hands curled into fists at his sides, but he didn't say anything more. Sarah made herself look at the two men, really look at them. The physical resemblance was slight. They were about the same height and build. They shared the same proud nose and jaw, and eyes so dark a blue they were nearly black. Superficial traits only, but there was something more—something in their stance, in the way they held themselves, in the way they spoke and responded—that convinced Sarah that Michael spoke the truth. Michael Kenton and Jeff Baron were, indeed, brothers.

"I have proof, Jeff," Edward said patiently, as though it was not the first time he'd repeated those words. "Ronald Baron was this man's father. How long have you known, Kenton?"

"Four or five years." Michael spoke as though the information meant nothing to him, but the tenseness in his neck and shoulders belied the careless pose.

"Who was your mother?" Jeff demanded.

"It doesn't matter."

"It does to me."

"Her name was Ellen Kenton. She was from Milwaukee. You don't have to worry. No one from Tyler knew who she was."

"And it better stay that way." Jeff took a step forward. "I don't know what your sordid little story is and I don't want to hear it. I won't have my mother and my sisters upset by this."

"Jeff." Edward Wocheck put a hand on his son-in-law's arm. "Alyssa has to be told."

"No."

"Yes, she does. But I'll do it. Like Jeff said, Kenton, I don't want my wife or her daughters upset. Do you understand?"

"Yeah," Michael responded, his face wiped clean of emotion. "I understand."

"I know you have tools and equipment still in the old Ingalls barn. I'd appreciate it if you'd get them out of there as soon as possible."

"Aren't you afraid I'll steal everything else that isn't nailed down?"

"Don't push me," Edward warned.

Jeff leaned forward from the hips, shoulders braced, hands knotted into fists. "Listen to him, Kenton. That goes double for me." The threat was unmistakable. Sarah had never seen Jeff Baron so upset. She had always considered him her friend, but now he looked and sounded like a stranger.

"Let's go, Jeff." Edward took Jeff by the arm and steered him out the door. "I'm sorry this had to happen in your house, Sarah," he said as they left.

"Don't leave town, Kenton," Brick reminded Michael, as he, too, took his leave. He touched his finger to the brim of his hat. "Good night, Reverend Sarah."

She nodded automatically and shut the door in his face. She leaned her head against the cold wood, her mind a whirlpool of conflicting thoughts and emotions.

Michael had been keeping his identity from her all this time. Even though he'd told her he loved her, wanted to marry her and spend his life with her, he hadn't trusted her enough to tell her who he was. He didn't trust her. That was what hurt most of all.

"Sarah."

She resisted turning around. She didn't want to look at Michael, didn't want to see the stranger that he'd become reflected on his face, in his eyes. "Why didn't you let me tell Brick we were together all of last night?"

"Cops only hear what they want to hear."

"That's no answer, Michael."

"Sarah. For God's sake, turn around." She felt him step closer, but he didn't touch her. Sarah gathered her resolve and turned to face him. It was even harder than she'd imagined. He wasn't a stranger. He was Michael, but ringed with emotional barricades, the way he'd been when he first came into her life. Sarah sucked in her lower lip and bit back a sob. There was a tremendous pain in her chest, as though her heart had cracked completely in two.

"Brick would believe me."

"Maybe," Michael said. He lifted his hand as though to touch her hair, then dropped it to his side. "But the rest of the town would have a field day with the news. Reverend Sarah is shacking up with the ex-con, hired help—the prime suspect in the biggest fire around these parts in a hundred years."

"No. Tyler isn't like that."

"Every place is like that, Sarah." There was a hint of sorrow in his voice, or was she only imagining it? Sarah hardened her aching heart. She didn't know this man well enough to read the nuances in his speech or body language. Hadn't he just proved that? "And if they didn't condemn you, they'd pity you. Poor Reverend Sarah, taken in by that crook, that bastard—"

"Stop it! My friends aren't like that."

"Yeah, prove it."

"I can't prove it." She was angry now. It felt good. Better than the pain. She refused to see the same pain flare briefly in his blue-black eyes. "I don't have to prove it. I believe it."

"And I can't believe it. That's our problem, isn't it?"

She nodded, suddenly unable to trust her voice.

"Yes," she said simply. "I'm sorry, Michael. I can't marry you."

He jerked backward, as if she'd struck him a blow. "You said you love me."

The tears were very close to the surface now. "I do love you."

"But you can't marry me. Why, Sarah?" He reached out, took her by the shoulders so that she had to face him, couldn't look away. She closed her eyes for a long moment, then raised her gaze to his.

"It's not about love or sex or lies and half truths. It's much more simple than that. And more important. You don't trust me, Michael."

"Trust you?" He gave her a little shake. "What does that mean?"

She reached up and put her hands on his chest. His heart was beating like a drum. "Why didn't you tell me you were Ronald Baron's son? Why didn't you tell me you came here looking for your father? For your roots?" His eyes flickered away from hers, and when he looked back they were dark mirrors, hiding everything he felt behind them. He didn't speak, and his silence was more condemning than words. "You didn't tell me because you don't trust me. Love is a very fragile emotion, Michael. Trust and honor are what you must surround love with so it can flourish and grow strong and lasting. Without—"

"Sarah, don't."

She shook her head. "Without trust there's nothing, Michael. Nothing that will last."

She thought for a moment he would erupt in anger but he only shook his head and tightened his grip on her shoulders. "I wouldn't know, Sarah. You see, you're the first woman I've ever loved."

She had thought the pain had been bad before. Now it was devastating, breathtaking. "I'm sorry, Michael. I can't change the way I feel."

"Then it's over? Just like that?"

She nodded. "If you can't understand what I'm trying to say then it's over. It has to be, for both our sakes."

He dropped his hands from her shoulders. Sarah stumbled backward a step, came up against the back of the couch and leaned against it for support.

"Okay. It's over. I'll clear my stuff out of the garage in the morning."

He didn't fight, didn't argue so that she could argue back, get him to open up to her as he had that morning in her bed. He had slammed shut the cell doors of his own emotional prison and locked her outside. And he couldn't help her, she had no way to find the key.

She opened her mouth to tell him he didn't have to go, but shut it again. He couldn't stay here; they both knew that. She meant every word she had just said with all her heart and soul. But she still loved him, and possibly always would. And having him so close would only bring them both further heartache and sorrow.

"Yes," she said, unable to meet his eyes again, her gaze focused on the pulse beating above the collar of his shirt. "I think it's best if you go."

CHAPTER ELEVEN

ALYSSA WONDERED if Michael Kenton thought he could escape this meeting by coming to take his tools from the barn long before the sun had risen. She had watched for him each morning since Edward had told her who he was. She had checked the barn each evening, when she returned from her temporary office next to Amanda's, to see if he had been there to remove his things during the day. This frosty morning her vigilance had paid off.

He was avoiding her, of course. And if the truth were told, she was just as reluctant to face him. But Judson and Tisha had arrived home late the night before, and now she had no other choice but to confront the man who was Ronald Baron's son.

Her father would have to be told who Michael Kenton was—soon, before the word spread around town. And the knowledge would spread. No matter how much she and her family wanted it to be kept secret, his connection to her dead first husband would soon be the talk of Tyler. It was the way things were in small towns, something you accepted if you lived in one. If she put it off, it would only make things worse.

Alyssa turned the collar of her fleece coat up around her ears and pushed open the door. One small light bulb burned above the old workbench. Michael Kenton was carefully placing tools in a red metal toolbox, intent on what he was doing, oblivious of her presence until the creaking of the door hinges gave her away.

Belatedly, Alyssa realized she had hoped she would have a few more moments to study this young man who had now become important in her life. Not because she suspected him of being involved in the fire at the F and M; she trusted her instincts, and she did not believe he was guilty of that crime, regardless of what she had been told of his background. Important, rather, because Ronald Baron, the man she had married and spent twenty years of her life with, had fathered him. *And she had never suspected his existence.*

Michael straightened as he realized who she was. Alyssa sucked in her breath. With his face in shadow and only his profile visible, he had the look of his father. Ronald had been a handsome man, and Michael had the same set to his jaw, the jut of his nose, characteristics that he shared with her son, Jeff. *His brother.*

Alyssa lifted her hand to her throat, feeling a swift, sharp pain of loss and disillusionment that she had thought she'd put behind her fifteen years before when Ronald died. Her husband had deceived her and betrayed their marriage vows, just as she had so long suspected, and this man standing before her was the proof.

"Mrs. Wocheck, don't be alarmed. I'm just packing up my things." His face was still in shadow, his voice level, but the tautness of his neck and shoulders betrayed something of the strain he must be under.

"I can see that. And I'm not in the least alarmed to find you here."

He nodded curtly and returned to his task. "Thanks. I'll finish cleaning up the mess right away. I was going to work on Liza's T-bird in here or I'd have cleaned it up before this.''

''Aren't you still going to work on Liza's car?''

He shrugged. ''I don't know. Maybe, but not here.'' He dropped a wrench into the toolbox. The clatter was loud in the silent barn. ''I'll be gone in half an hour.''

''Take your time.'' She moved closer, wishing she could see his face, study his features with a new, more-discerning eye.

''Sweeping the floor is going to stir up a lot of dust,'' he observed.

Alyssa smiled; she couldn't help herself. It was much the same thing Jeff would have said if he wanted her to leave. ''I'm not going to be turned away so easily. We have to talk, Michael.''

Another wrench joined its fellows in the box. ''I wouldn't think you'd want to be alone with the man who's the prime suspect in burning down your business.''

''You're not a suspect, that I know of.''

His reply was a snort of disgusted laughter. ''I stand corrected. The way Brick Bauer has his men keeping an eye on me, you'll have to forgive me if I think otherwise.''

''I don't want to talk about the fire, Michael. I want to talk about you.''

His head came up. The sun was above the horizon now. His features were resolving themselves into a whole. Her eyes hadn't played tricks on her before. He was a good-looking man. As Jeff was. As Ronald had been. ''What do you want to know?''

Alyssa laughed a little nervously and shook her head. ''Nothing.'' She lifted her hand. ''Everything. How old are you?''

"I'll be thirty on my next birthday."

"When were you born?"

"May eighteenth."

"You're fifteen months younger than Liza, then."

"I wouldn't know. My mother didn't know anything about your family." He wiped his hands on a red shop rag. "At least she never told me anything about any of you. I never knew who my father was until long after she died."

"How old were you when that happened?"

"Thirteen." A fleeting look of sorrow passed over his features, but it was gone as quickly as it came.

"Who was your mother, Michael?" Alyssa found she could disassociate herself from the worst of the pain her questions invoked. Ronald's betrayal was so long in the past. She was happy now, happier than she had ever been, despite the fire and her worries about the F and M's future. The love she'd found with Edward Wocheck had made her strong.

"Her name was Ellen Kenton."

"Kenton? Of course. But I don't recall ever knowing anyone by that name."

"You wouldn't have known her. She was from Milwaukee. She never came to Tyler that I'm aware of."

"Then how did my husband meet her?"

"She lived with a family on Willow Lake the summer before I was born. My grandmother told me that's where she met my father. The family's name was Selton."

Alyssa sucked in her breath. Willow Lake was a summer resort town only a few miles from Tyler. "Marjorie and Harrison Selton. Yes, I remember them. Mr. Selton was a commodities trader. My husband...your father was in the grain business. He owned the Tyler Cooperative Elevator. But I don't...I don't remember ever seeing your mother.''

"I doubt she was invited to cocktail parties or country-club dances much.''

Alyssa took no offense at the words, although it saddened her to recall those wasted years. Her world had revolved around such affairs at that time. She had thought that was what Ronald wanted of her. But, obviously, it had not been enough. "No, of course, you're right. Still, when one's husband has an affair with a woman...'' She lifted her eyes to his. "No,'' she whispered, suddenly sickened by the thought. "She wasn't a woman, was she? Not really. How old was your mother when you were born?''

"Just eighteen.''

Alyssa was suddenly very cold. She pulled the collar of her coat tight around her throat. *Oh Ronald, how could you have done such a thing to her? To me? To our children?* "So, she was seventeen when my husband seduced her.''

"Yes.''

"I'm sorry." How could she explain this news to Jeff? He had worshiped Ronald Baron. He was convinced that Michael's mother had been a mature woman on the make who had seduced his father. It would be hard to make him believe otherwise.

This time Michael waved off her words. "It's not your fault.''

"Did you come to Tyler to find out about your father?''

"I don't know why I came and that's the truth.''

"Did you know that Ronald was dead? That he killed himself?'' She spoke gently. She couldn't bring herself to harden her heart toward this man. He was even more a victim of Ronald's weaknesses than she and her children. She had liked Michael Kenton from their first meeting. She felt no different now.

"My grandmother knew. I found the newspaper clippings in her things after she died last spring."

"Do you have any other family?"

"No."

"You said your mother died when you were thirteen." That would have been shortly after Ronald took his life. Alyssa hoped there wasn't a connection, but she was afraid there might be. "How did she die?"

"She took an overdose of cocaine. As close as I can figure it was about three weeks after your husband shot himself."

"I am sorry. I know what it's like to lose your mother when you're young." She took a step forward before she could stop herself, her heart touched by his loneliness, his aloneness. But while she ached for him, she sensed he would not welcome her touch. And if the truth were told, her own emotions were still too chaotic, too confused for her to reach out to him just yet.

"I know," he said gruffly. "I've read about what happened to your mother in the *Tyler Citizen*."

"Yes." Most of the time Alyssa could put those memories out of mind, but not always. "It was a long time to believe that she had deserted me. That she didn't love me. I'm glad I was able to finally learn the truth about why she left me and my father alone."

Michael nodded again. He threw the rag he'd been holding into the toolbox and shut the lid. "I'll sweep up now."

"You have another job you're going to today?"

He gave her a tight smile. "Since the fire, most people have decided the work they wanted done can wait until after Christmas. I figure they think I'll be gone by then. Or in jail.''

"Oh,'' Alyssa said, refusing to rise to the bait. "I see.''

"It might be better if I'm out of here before traffic picks up and people see my truck out on the street in front of the house.''

"Yes,'' Alyssa said with a twist of her lips that she knew missed being a smile. "I don't think my son would understand our talking this way.''

"I don't think your husband would much appreciate seeing me here, either.''

"Edward wants what's best for me, but he's a fair man. When he hears your story—''

"You believe what I've told you?''

She blinked in surprise. "Of course,'' she said. "Ronald Baron was my husband. I suspected for a long time…'' She swallowed hard to keep tears from choking her voice. "He hurt me as much as he hurt you.''

"What was he—''

"Lyssa? Lyssa, are you out here?''

The barn door opened again. Michael Kenton shut his mouth with a snap. Alyssa sensed he had been going to ask her about Ronald, and she almost welcomed the interruption her father's entrance offered, even though it meant she must now tell him who Michael was. She didn't know what she would have said about Ronald. She wasn't sure she was ready to stir up all those old feelings again.

"I'm here, Dad.''

Michael Kenton straightened, his eyes going to the figure approaching them. Alyssa tried to see her father with a stranger's eyes. Still straight and unstooped, although he would soon be eighty-three years old, Judson Ingalls was a tall man with a full head of white hair and alert, blue eyes.

"What are you doing out here on this damnable cold morning?"

Judson blinked in the bright sunlight coming through the dusty windows that Michael had never gotten around to replacing. "My blood's gotten thin out there in Arizona. I'm almost frozen to death just walking out here from the house." He shoved his hands into the pockets of the disreputable old cardigan he always kept hanging by the kitchen door.

"I didn't think you'd be awake this early, Dad," Alyssa said, smiling past the tight constriction in her chest.

"I never could sleep once the sun was up, no matter what damned time zone I'm in. Who's this young man?" Judson asked, cocking his head to give Michael the once-over.

Alyssa took a deep breath. "This is Michael Kenton," she said, reaching out to wrap her cold hands around her father's arm. "He's new to Tyler and he's…he's Ronald's son."

THE SUN, BLOODRED and without heat, was beginning to dip low on the horizon. A cloud bank was moving in from the west, bringing the smell of snow with the cold wind that blew before it. Funny. He'd only been here about a month. He'd never spent a winter this far north in his entire life, but he could smell the snow, icy and metallic, just as Sarah had told him he would if he put his mind to it.

God, it hurt even to think about her. Michael stood on the bluff overlooking Timber Lake and watched a small flock of Canada geese settle for the night in the open water at the center, honking a greeting for those of their company still airborne overhead. The weather was supposed to turn cold again, and in another day or two the lake would be frozen solid, the geese forced to move south into Illinois and Kentucky to find food and shelter.

Without quite knowing why, he picked his way down the steep slope to the path at the water's edge. To his right was the fancy wrought-iron gate that marked the entrance to the grounds of Timberlake Lodge. To his left, around a bend, was the boathouse where Liza Forrester lived, but the pathway where he now stood was deserted. He'd been at Timberlake to pick up the check Devon Addison had left there for his work on the Bentley. He'd timed his arrival carefully, just before the business office closed, when he figured there would be little chance of his meeting up with Edward Wocheck or his stepson. He'd been lucky, and neither of them appeared in the few minutes he was there.

He shoved his hands into the pockets of his coat and turned up the collar. Grabbing a pair of gloves when he got out of the truck wasn't second nature to him yet. Neither was wearing a hat. He was cold and tired, but the sights and sounds of the winter countryside spread out before him were too tempting to ignore.

He stared out over the water, his gaze drawn to the low hills on the far side. Beyond that rise lay Willow Lake. He wondered if there was anyone there who might remember his mother. Probably not. Like Alyssa, who would remember a young city girl brought along as a live-in baby-sitter? And he doubted Ronald Baron had been indiscreet enough to single his mother out in public. No one would remember her there. She had passed through life making barely a ripple, important to no one but him and his grandmother.

"Hey. Hi. I know you."

Michael looked up in surprise. He hadn't heard her approach, the small, blond-haired girl who was Liza Forrester's daughter, his niece.

"Hello, Margaret Alyssa." She was wearing a bright pink coat, zipped about halfway up, and a funny little hat with a tassel bobbing on top, pulled down so low on her forehead it hid her eyebrows. She wasn't wearing boots or gloves, and Michael had the distinct impression the child wasn't supposed to be where she was.

"What are you doing here?" she demanded. "Are you coming to my house to build something? It's almost dark. Too late for work. My mom's fixing supper and my dad's trying to get her car started. It's broken and the man who's supposed to fix it..." She poked her finger at him. "Hey, is that you?"

"I guess it is."

"Well, you're late and my dad's plenty mad. He doesn't like to work on my mom's car. He says it's a pickle."

"A pickle?"

"Or a relish."

"A relic?"

"Or something." She shrugged. "He told me to go inside and let him work..." She realized she'd said too much. She narrowed her eyes. "You're not supposed to be here, I bet. This is my special place to feed the geese and you aren't supposed to leave town. I heard my mommy tell my daddy that's what Uncle Brick said. He's the police," she added, puffing out her cheeks proudly. "I'm his helper."

"I should have guessed that from the third degree you're giving me." Michael dropped to a crouch. "What are you doing out here by yourself, Margaret Alyssa?"

A crafty look came into her eyes. "I'm allowed," she said too forcefully. "I'm four and I'm allowed." She stuck her hands in her pockets. "I came to feed the geese." She pulled out a handful of cracked corn. "See? They're hungry. There's nothing left for them to eat. I always feed them here, but now there's ice and they can't come close to me." She eyed the lake with a determined look.

Michael had no idea how deep the water was at the lake's edge, a few inches or many feet, but it didn't matter. The ice that rimmed the lake didn't look thick enough to support the weight of even a small child, and regardless of Margaret Alyssa's insistence that she "was allowed," he had no intention of letting her test its strength.

"Why don't you just sprinkle the corn here on the path? The geese will find it in the morning." There was ample evidence all around them that the geese used the pathway, just as humans did.

"It's going to snow tonight. My dad said so. It will cover up the corn. I need to get it far out there so they can find it now." She took a step toward the water's edge.

"Wait," Michael said. "I'll do it."

"Can you get it out there?"

"Sure," he said. "I used to play baseball in school." Basketball, too. He'd been pretty good at both sports. It was the only reason he'd stayed in high school and made any attempt to keep up his grades. "Here, give me the corn."

"Well..." The four-year-old considered his suggestion, her eyes downcast. "Okay, I guess." She opened
her hand into his, smiling into his eyes. "I suppose you
can throw farther than me. But just because you're big-
ger. Not because you're a boy and I'm a girl. My mom
says girls can do anything boys can do."

"Margaret Alyssa! Maggie! Where are you? Answer
me!" Liza Forrester's voice was shrill with concern.
Michael could hear her running along the frozen path
before he saw her. He stood up.

"She's over here, Mrs. Forrester," he called, so that
his sister wouldn't be alarmed when she saw him with
the child.

"Margaret Alyssa! Thank God." Liza skidded to a
halt, her turquoise coat flapping open over a bright red
sweater and slacks, a brilliant purple scarf looped
around her neck. She pressed a hand over her stomach
while she caught her breath. Her nose and cheeks were
pink from the cold, her face pinched from worry.
"Oh," she said, looking surprised to see him. "It's
you."

"I stopped by the lodge to get my paycheck," Michael explained. "I walked down here to admire the
view. Margaret Alyssa came along a few minutes later.
She told me she wants to feed the geese." He opened
his hand to show Liza the corn.

"That's what I was afraid of," Liza said, relief
flooding her face as she stooped to gather her daughter
into her arms. She gave the child a little shake, causing
her own yellow sunburst earrings to dance below her
ears, then hugged her daughter tight again. "Margaret
Alyssa Forrester, how many times have I told you not
to come down to the lake by yourself? You scared
Mommy nearly out of her wits. I think you are going

to have to spend a lot of time in the 'time out' chair for this.''

"But my favorite TV show is on tonight,'' Margaret Alyssa wailed. ''I have to see 'Unsolved Mysteries.' I have to.''

"No, you don't. If you miss your program, maybe you'll remember next time not to come down to the water by yourself. It's too dangerous. What if you fell in?''

"But I can swim. You and Grandma Lyssa taught me how, remember?''

"But the water is ice-cold now. Your arms and legs would get stiff right away. You might drown and Mommy would be sad for the rest of her life.''

"I didn't think about that,'' Margaret Alyssa said, hanging her head. ''But I can swim real good.''

"Your mother's right,'' Michael added. It was apparent the child still felt she had been in no danger. ''If something happened to you, your mommy would think it was her fault and be sad forever.'' He shut his mouth with a snap. *Who in hell was he to be teaching life lessons to someone else's child? Then it hit him again, like a blow between the shoulder blades. This wasn't just any child. This was his niece, his blood.*

"Would you, Mommy?''

"Yes, pumpkin. I'd be sad forever without you.''

"Would you be too sad to want to have another little baby?''

Liza's color deepened slightly. She glanced at Michael and shrugged. ''Yes,'' she said. ''I think I would be too sad to have another baby.''

"Then I'll be good,'' Margaret Alyssa said with a dazzling smile. ''I want a baby brother or sister and you promised me you would try and get one real soon.''

Liza rose, with Margaret Alyssa in her arms. ''Thank you, Michael,'' she said simply. ''You might have saved her life.''

''Throw the corn,'' Margaret Alyssa demanded, saving *him* from a reply. ''Throw the corn. It's getting dark. The geese won't be able to see it if you don't throw it now.''

''Okay,'' Michael said, winding up. ''Here goes.'' He gave it all he had and was relieved to see the corn sail far enough out toward the open water to satisfy even Margaret Alyssa's exacting standards. ''How's that?''

''Okay,'' she said.

''Just okay?'' Liza asked with a trilling laugh. She wasn't looking at her daughter, however. She was watching him.

''Really okay. Can he come home to eat dinner with us?'' she asked unexpectedly. Or perhaps not so unexpectedly, Michael decided. He was fast losing all his preconceptions, few as they might be, of how a four-year-old should act and talk.

''Would you like that, Michael?''

He shook his head. ''I'm surprised you'd ask.''

Liza laughed again, shifting Margaret Alyssa in her arms. ''I admit Jeff's news set me on my ear. But you shouldn't be surprised I'd ask. I'm the black sheep of the family.'' She tilted her head, her smile growing a little wider. ''Only now I guess there are two of us, Brother. And besides, I want you to look at the T-bird. It definitely needs work. And Cliff, sweetheart that he is, is no mechanic.''

Michael shoved his hands deep in the pockets of his

coat. He wanted to reach out and take the child from her mother's arms, feel her slim, strong arms wrap around his neck, her warmth cuddled against him, smell the baby shampoo in her hair. The sentiment surprised and alarmed him. *God, when had he started wondering what babies' hair smelled like? Since Sarah, and the idea of family, his own family, came into his life, that's when.*

"You're taking this a lot better than your brother," he said roughly.

Liza wasn't in the least perturbed by his gruffness. "Jeff worshiped Dad," she said, the smile fading away as shadows of old sadness darkened her incredible blue eyes. "And Dad thought the sun rose and set on Jeff." She bit her lower lip. "I'm sorry. It must hurt you to hear that. Did he ever try to contact you? Ever send you a birthday card or a Christmas present?"

Margaret Alyssa had produced another handful of corn from her pocket. She held it out to Michael, uninterested in their conversation now that she saw how the geese were starting to swim toward her offering. "Throw it," she said, interrupting her mother's question, once more giving Michael a chance to gather himself before he answered.

"I don't know if he even knew I was alive." He threw the corn.

"Are you just saying that? Or do you believe it?"

He turned back to her. Liza was almost as tall as he was and lean as a greyhound. She might look like the portrait of the elegant society woman in her living room, but she had a lot of Judson Ingalls's steel in her. "I believe it. My mother wasn't a strong person. She let my grandmother pretty much rule her life. And my grandmother never once mentioned my…our father to me. I don't think he knew."

"I'm glad," she said. Her daughter had wiggled out of her arms and back onto her own two feet, and Liza spread her hands. "I'm sorry. I didn't mean—"

"I know what you meant. It helps me a little, too." He stopped himself from saying more. Liza Forrester was too much like Sarah, too easy to confide in.

"It will be easier for Jeff and Amanda to accept you when they know that."

"Maybe."

"I rebelled against my mother," Liza said, smoothing her hand across the pom-pom of Margaret Alyssa's hat, "because my father died when I was still very young. I always got along with my dad. He was good to me, but I remember things differently than Jeff and Amanda. I remember my mother was sad a lot of the time. And Dad was almost never home, always traveling on business or attending trade shows, something like that."

Yeah, something like that, Michael thought to himself, but he didn't say it aloud.

"Look at the geese, Mommy," Margaret Alyssa insisted, grabbing Liza's hand and giving it a shake. "Look at them come to eat my corn." She turned her face up to Michael, all smiles now that she had accomplished what she had set out to do. "Will you come back tomorrow, Mister, and help me feed them again?"

"I…don't know."

"Mommy, can he come back?"

"If he wants to." Liza gave him her dazzling smile again. "After all, he's part of the family now."

"Liza! Maggie girl, are you down here? What are you doing out here this late? It's way below freezing."

A tall man with a serious expression and dark graying hair appeared on the pathway.

"We're here, Cliff," Liza called, her smile turning private, even more dazzling, as she greeted her husband. "Michael is with us."

"Michael?" Cliff Forrester rose from scooping his daughter into his arms.

"Yes, Michael." She took a deep breath and held out her hand. "Cliff, I'd like you meet my half brother, Michael Kenton."

IT WAS AFTER MIDNIGHT, dark and quiet, but still Michael couldn't sleep. He padded to the window of the dingy motel room he'd rented just outside of town and looked out onto the deserted highway. *God, what a day.* He'd started out with the intention of retrieving his tools and his money and then going to ground in this room, and instead he'd come face-to-face with not only Alyssa Wocheck but her formidable father, as well, and had ended the day as a guest at Liza and Cliff Forrester's dinner table.

Amazingly, after the initial awkwardness had worn off he'd enjoyed himself. Not that he and his half sister were anything alike, they weren't, but there was something about Liza, something fresh and uninhibited, that made it easy to be around her.

"Oh, hell," he said aloud. "You sound like some pop psychology guru on 'Oprah.'"

Still, it was the truth. He had felt at home with Liza and her husband, quiet and reserved though Cliff Forrester was. And then there was Margaret Alyssa. The child was amazing, at least to him. It took real guts to be the parent of a four-year-old. It hadn't taken him more than fifteen minutes in the little girl's company to come to that conclusion. Did he have that kind of guts? That kind of stamina? Having a child meant being in for the long haul.

Making a commitment. A lifetime promise.

The traits that Sarah had accused him of lacking.

Was he taking the easy way out? If he didn't want the things Sarah wanted—a home, a family, stability and a sense of community—what was he still doing here?

He wasn't under arrest. Supposedly, he wasn't even under suspicion. He could leave right this minute if he wanted to, Brick Bauer's warning to the contrary. But he was still here. Why? Was it really to learn all he could about the man who had fathered him?

Or was it because of Sarah?

As soon as his heart whispered her name her image sprang to life in his mind's eye. He could feel the silky texture of her hair beneath his fingers, smell the sweetness of her perfume, feel the warmth of her body pressed close to his.

Michael slammed his fist against the wall, making the window rattle in its badly caulked frame. He was only fooling himself if he denied that the real reason he was still in Tyler, Wisconsin, was Sarah Fleming. Because deep down in that scared and hidden part of him, he wanted to take the risk he'd never taken before. He wanted to give himself unconditionally, and for the rest of his life, to ensuring the happiness of another human being.

But he couldn't make that commitment. Not yet. Not until he was sure of himself. Sarah was wrong about one thing. It wasn't her he couldn't trust. It was himself. Until he was convinced he wasn't flawed beyond redemption, wasn't as weak and self-pitying as his pliable young mother or as self-serving and unprincipled as his dead father, Sarah was better off alone.

CHAPTER TWELVE

"YOU'RE GOING all out decorating for Christmas this year," Sarah observed as she unwound her scarf from her neck and stuck her gloves in the pockets of her parka. She paused for a moment, letting her eyes sweep across the brightly painted play area of TylerTots. Already chains of red and green construction paper looped around the walls. Cutouts of snowflakes made a paper blizzard on the partitions that separated the toddler area from the preschoolers' space. "Where are you planning to put the tree?"

"I'm thinking of hanging it from the ceiling," Angela Murphy confessed as she took Sarah's coat. "It's the only safe place."

Sarah laughed as she was meant to. The low ceiling in the church basement would afford safety to only a very short tree. "Actually, we're going to make ornaments tomorrow and decorate the tree on Wednesday. Jonas Phillips is coming later this evening to set it up." She hung Sarah's coat on a line of child-height hooks along the far wall.

"What about Michael Kenton? Didn't you ask him to do the job?" Michael was still in the church's employ, although he'd moved out of the apartment days before.

Angela's mouth firmed into a thin line. "I'm sorry,

Sarah. I still do not feel that Michael Kenton is the right person to have working at TylerTots. Especially now.''

"Why? Have you heard something more about the fire?" When Angela gave her a sharp look, Sarah realized she'd let her own turbulent feelings escape into her words.

"You do know there's an arson investigator in town?"

"Yes," Sarah said. The weight of the knowledge had been like a stone in her middle all day. "I've heard."

"We already know the fire was set."

"There's been no official announcement."

"Be realistic, Sarah. A fire of that magnitude doesn't just happen. Someone had to have started it."

"We don't know that for certain."

"Sarah…I know you're supposed to give everyone the benefit of the doubt—it's part of your job. But Michael Kenton just looks too suspicious to me. I'm sorry, but that's the way I feel, and until someone can prove otherwise, I'd just as soon he didn't set foot in TylerTots." She changed the subject. "Come on back. Glenna and her mother and two or three others are already here. Liza Forrester might drop in later. I really appreciate your offer to help price donations for the bazaar. It's always good to have more than one opinion on what to charge."

"I'm happy to help." That she was also grateful for an excuse not to spend another lonely evening in her quiet house was a thought she kept to herself. Michael had been gone from her life for less than a week, but she felt as if it had been a year.

Angela preceded her through the big, unusually quiet and tidy room into the activities area, which had once been a Sunday-school classroom and was now filled with low tables of crafts and needlework that had been donated to TylerTots for their annual Christmas bazaar. Anna Kelsey and her daughter Glenna, as well as two young mothers, were already hard at work cataloging and pricing the items.

"Hello, Reverend Fleming," Anna said, greeting her with a smile and a wave. "It's good to see you again."

"Hello, Mrs. Kelsey. Please, won't you call me Sarah?"

"Thank you. And you must call me Anna."

"I'd like that." Sarah smiled at the other young women. "Hello."

"Hello, Reverend Sarah," Diana Thurston called from across the room. "I was just telling the others I met the arson investigator the insurance company sent to town when he came into the post office today. I'll bet you saw him too, didn't you, Glenna? He was at Marge's this morning, someone said."

"I met him," Glenna admitted.

"Really? What did you think? He's a good-looking man. A little old for my taste—"

"I—I really didn't notice."

"I wonder if he's married?"

"I wouldn't know." Glenna's tone was sharp. She turned back to her work without another word.

Anna raised her shoulders in a shrug. "I'm going to have to ask her what that was all about when we get home." She held up a beautifully crocheted afghan, already priced by the woman who'd made it. She raised her eyebrows when Sarah looked up from the ridiculously low sum on the tag. "Do you agree with the price?"

Sarah was shocked. "Goodness," she whispered. "It's worth twice that much."

"I agree." Anna smiled and picked up a blank ticket to adjust the price.

Diana had gone right on talking through the exchange. "Annabelle Scanlon thinks this Lee Neilsen person—that's his name—is going to rule the fire was definitely arson and then the insurance company won't pay out a cent to help rebuild the factory."

"Oh, no. That's what my dad's afraid of," the second young mother, whose name Sarah couldn't recall, chimed in. "He's six years from getting his pension. And way too young to retire. He doesn't know where he's going to find work if the F and M doesn't open up again."

"Of course, if they find who set the fire, then the insurance company will have to pay the Ingallses," Diana continued. "That's what's important. Finding the man Will Benson says he saw running away from the building."

"We don't know if the man Will saw set the fire," Anna reminded them, as she and Sarah tied tags to a half-dozen pairs of knitted bedroom slippers, worked in a remarkably ugly shade of green.

Sarah's stomach began to churn. She knew what Diana was going to say next—exactly what Angela had said earlier, that she believed Michael was responsible for the fire at the F and M.

"I think it was that handyman that's been working around town all month. That Michael Kenton," Diana stated flatly.

"Why do you think it was him?" Glenna asked the question that froze on Sarah's lips as she carefully arranged papier-mâché figures of the Holy Family in a carved crèche.

Diana looked flustered, a little guilty. "There's been talk."

"I think he did it, too," the other mother said. "And I'm not the only one who thinks that way." Sarah's heart started beating faster as she placed the young woman—Cassie Wiggins, a single mother with a new baby girl, who'd moved back to town from Sugar Creek and had just been hired part-time as a dispatcher at the police station.

"You mean Brick Bauer thinks he did it, too?"

Cassie's eyes grew big as saucers as she realized she'd been indiscreet. "No. No, of course not. I—I'm just repeating rumors that I've heard around town."

Was she telling the truth, or was Brick Bauer now seriously considering Michael as a suspect?

"I've only met this Michael Kenton once or twice, but he didn't strike me as a stupid man," Anna interjected in her usual frank manner. "If he started a million-dollar fire, he wouldn't hang around to see if he got arrested for it."

"Well, I heard he did it once before," Diana returned. "And now everyone knows he's Ronald Baron's illegitimate son."

Oh God, Michael's secret was out. Sarah's head jerked up, and she stared at Diana for one stricken moment before dropping her gaze to the baby bootees she was pricing.

"What?" Angela demanded, her eyes as big as saucers. "What did you say?"

The room grew silent. From the corner of her eye Sarah saw Glenna McRoberts exchange glances with her mother, but neither of the Kelsey women said a word.

Diana nodded, waving a ceramic reindeer donated by

a local craftswoman. "He's Ronald Baron's love child. Liza and Jeff and Amanda's half brother. Can you beat that?"

"Who told you that?" Sarah asked, using every ounce of willpower she possessed to keep her expression from giving away her true feelings.

"Tisha told Moira Schweinhagen. In strictest confidence, of course, but then Moira told her husband, and you know what a terrible gossip Pat is. It's all over town. I'm surprised you haven't heard it. Surely you have, Anna, with Johnny being the foreman at the F and M and all."

"Yes, I heard it. But I didn't think it warranted any discussion," Anna said in a tone that conveyed her distaste at the subject matter.

"I think it's incredible. Like some kind of soap opera. And if you ask me, it makes him look guilty as sin."

"Diana, what a way to talk. And in a church, too."

"Christian forbearance aside, I think you're also forgetting that in this country a man is presumed innocent until proved guilty," Sarah said quietly.

"I just wish they'd find out who did it. Everyone in town is scared the Ingallses won't start the factory up again," Cassie said with tears in her eyes. "I'm worried about my dad's health. He's just sick about the situation."

"We're all worried in that respect," Anna conceded. "No one more so than Alyssa Wocheck and her family. But that's no reason to start talking like a pack of vigilantes. Have faith, right, Sarah?"

"Yes," Sarah said, swallowing a knot of fear that had lodged in her throat. She was not going to be able to let this go on much longer. She better than anyone else knew Michael was not responsible for setting the fire at the F and M. She'd kept silent this long only because he had asked her to.

She had to talk to him, persuade him to let her speak before these rumors got out of hand. Even though it would break her heart to see him again.

IT WAS AFTER eleven when Sarah locked the door to the church basement and stepped out into the frosty December night. Her back ached and her shoulders were sore from bending over the low tables for so many hours, but they had priced all the donations for the bazaar and stored them on high shelves along the wall so that they would be out of the reach of curious little fingers until the big day arrived.

She walked quietly in the shadow of the old building, beneath the skeletal branches of the dying maple, her soft-soled boots almost soundless in the frosted grass. The colored lights draped over the branches of the big pine by her front door glowed softly in the darkness. Tomorrow Jonas and Randy were going to bring out the big crèche and place it in front of the church. And she mustn't forget to stop by the florist and pick up the wreath for the door. Maybe if she kept busy enough, found enough things to do, she could be this tired every night and fall asleep before she could start thinking of Michael, missing him, aching for him.

She saw him before he saw her.

Michael. She said his name silently, the word no more than a breath of smoke on the air.

He was sitting on the back steps, his back to the metal railing, his face in profile. Sarah looked up and down the street, but his pickup was nowhere to be seen.

Had he walked all the way from the motel where she'd learned he was staying?

"Michael?" This time she spoke his name aloud.

He turned his head to look at her, but even though the moon was high and bright, she couldn't make out his features.

"Hello, Sarah."

She stopped a few feet away, steeling herself against the sudden shiver of pleasure that hearing him say her name produced deep within her. She had known this moment would come, sooner or later, and foolishly she had thought she was prepared, could deal with his nearness and the longing that ran through her veins like liquid fire. She had been wrong, terribly wrong.

"It's very late, Michael," she said, resisting the urge to run to him, beg him to take her in his arms and never, ever let her go.

"I've been waiting for you." He stood up slowly, as though he had been sitting for a long time and was stiff from the cold.

"You knew where I was?"

"Yes."

"Why didn't you come to the church?"

"I think you already know the answer to that."

Three hours ago she would have said she didn't know what he was talking about. Now, sadly, she did. "Michael, we have to stop these rumors."

"Which rumors?" he asked, his voice flat. He sounded tired, discouraged. "That I'm an arsonist or that I'm Ronald Baron's bastard?"

"I'm sorry the word got around town so quickly."

He shrugged. "I hadn't expected Alyssa Wocheck to be in such a hurry to tell everyone."

"Alyssa?" Sarah shook her head. "You're wrong, Michael. Alyssa has said nothing at all."

His head came up. "Then who?"

"Judson Ingall's fiancée, Tisha Olsen, for one. And Moira Schweinhagen's husband, for another. He's a terrible gossip."

"I see."

"They aren't bad people, Michael. They just like to talk...."

"They need a life," he said sharply.

"Perhaps." She took another step closer, her feet moving with a will of their own. "Are you very upset by it?"

He looked down at her without answering, his broad shoulders blocking out the moon. She could see his face now, read his expression, guarded though it was. It had hurt him to think that Alyssa Baron was the one who might have spread the news about who he was. He was relieved to learn it was someone else. Sarah took heart at the knowledge. He had come to care, at least a little, about the family he had found.

"Michael, how do you feel about your family knowing who you are?" She shoved her hands into her pockets. It was cold, far below freezing, but she didn't have the courage to invite Michael into the house. To have him there, where she'd dreamed of a future with him, was too hard to bear.

"They aren't my family. If Jeff Baron and Edward Wocheck have their way, they never will be."

She laid her hand on his arm, unable to resist touching him, offering comfort. "They are your family, however hard that might be for all of you to accept right now. They need time. You need time. How are you, Michael? Are you comfortable at the motel?"

"How did you know I'm staying out there?" He moved a little closer. She had to tilt her head back slightly to see his face.

"I—I drove by the other day. And your truck was parked out front. Are you comfortable there?" she asked again.

Moonlight flared briefly in his dark eyes. "It's a roof over my head and there's hot water. Most of the time."

"Are—are you getting enough to eat?"

"Mother hen," he said softly, cajolingly.

Blood surged into her cold cheeks, warming them momentarily. "I didn't mean to sound like a mother hen."

"Believe me, I don't think of you that way." He reached out and tucked a stray wisp of hair back under her hat. His hand was trembling. "How are you getting along, Sarah?"

She closed her eyes against the allure of his voice. "I'm okay. I'm doing okay."

"Getting ready for Christmas?" His fingers lingered a moment at her temple, traced the curve of her cheek before he pulled his hand away.

"Yes. The bazaar is coming up soon. We were pricing items tonight." She wasn't about to be sidetracked. "Michael, they say there's an arson investigator in town. They say he thinks the fire was deliberately set. If he does, and the insurance company refuses to settle the Ingallses' claim…" She found she couldn't finish the sentence.

"This town is going to want to find who set the fire. And damn soon. Is that what you were going to say, Sarah?"

"Yes."

"And I'm the best candidate for the job."

Sarah reached out and wrapped her hands around his arm. She couldn't stop herself. The need to touch him, to convince him to heed her advice was overwhelming. "You've got to let me tell them you were with me when the fire started."

"No." She could feel the resistance in him even through the heavy fabric of his coat.

"But, Michael, why? I'm not afraid to tell the truth. I'm not ashamed of what we were doing. Nothing will happen to me if I tell the truth."

He bracketed her face with his hands. He wasn't wearing gloves, but his touch was warm against her skin. There was no anger in his face, only resignation. And deep in his blue-black eyes, so deep she knew he thought it was hidden, was a flash of pain.

"You just got through telling me I was the main topic of conversation tonight. No one had a good word to say about me, did they?"

"No, Michael. It wasn't that way."

His mouth twisted in a rueful grin. "Okay. I'll give them the benefit of the doubt. No one actually came right out and said I started the fire. But they wonder. And they'll be thinking about it. And pretty soon it won't seem far-fetched at all. And maybe Will Benson will remember a few more details about that figure he saw running away from the F and M. And damned if it won't sound more and more like me.

"It won't be the first time, they'll say. And, after all, I had a reason, didn't I? A good reason. Getting back at Ronald Baron's family, the man who knocked up my mother and then abandoned both of us."

"No, Michael." She felt like crying. He made it all sound so plausible, so inevitable. "I won't let it happen that way."

"You forget, Sarah. I've been down this road before."

"But you have an alibi. *I'm* your alibi." She placed her hands on his shoulders. "They'll believe me."

He pulled her close, gently lifting her stubborn chin with his warm fingers. Her hat fell off and her hair came free. "No, Sarah. I'll deny everything if you tell them we were together that night."

"Why?" The question was a broken whisper. Her breath came in quick little gasps that eddied like smoke between them.

"This town needs a scapegoat and right now I'm it. What do you think they'll do to me if they find out I'm sleeping with the preacher lady?"

Sarah's heart ached at his words, at the anger that was so deep inside him. Was it possible he could never learn to trust another human being? Had he been damaged that severely by his past? Maybe she was wrong. Maybe he wasn't capable of letting it go. Maybe he wasn't capable of love.

"We didn't do anything wrong. I love you...." She couldn't stop herself from saying it.

"Sarah, don't." There was anguish in his voice. "Don't say it. It won't work between us. I was a blind fool to ever believe it could. Once a con, always a con. Once a bastard, always a bastard. We have to accept that. We're from two different worlds. Worlds that can only collide."

"They'll believe me." She made the words a prayer.

The anger left his face, drained out of him like sand from an hourglass. He pulled her close and laid his cheek against her hair. "Oh, Sarah, you have the courage of a dozen angels. But it doesn't make any difference. I'll still deny it if you say we were together."

"Michael, why?" Her voice broke on the word.

"It's the only way I have of protecting your reputation."

"I don't care—"

He stopped her words with a quick hard kiss. "I care. Let me do this my way. If things get too hot to handle, I'll just disappear. I've done it before."

"You can't do that—"

"Sarah, please."

"All right." She'd say anything to keep him from leaving, from ruining whatever chance he had of proving his innocence. She stepped out of his arms, brushed her fingers across his cheek. "If you want me to stay quiet, I will. For now." If she told her story and he denied it, it would only make him seem more guilty. And worst of all, he might carry out his threat to disappear. She would stay silent, for now, but she had no intention of letting Michael be blamed for a crime he hadn't committed. She would come forward when the time was right, even if it meant losing her pulpit as well as the man she loved.

"Michael, promise me one thing."

"What, Sarah?" He moved a few feet away from her, bent to pick up her hat from the frozen ground. He handed it back to her and she took it, careful not to let their fingers touch.

"Don't leave Tyler without telling me."

Moonlight flared briefly in his dark eyes. He shoved his hands in the pockets of his coat. "No, Sarah. I care too much for you to do that. When I go, you'll be the first to know."

CHAPTER THIRTEEN

MICHAEL LEFT his pickup parked at the motel and walked the half mile to the Tyler cemetery. The burial ground was located on a small rise above town. Here, former residents of Tyler slept behind a wrought-iron fence, shaded by a canopy of oak and maple and big, old pine trees that sighed mournfully in the cold wind whistling down from Canada.

A Tyler patrol car passed by on the street as he turned into the open gates. He barely noticed it or the late-model blue sedan parked along the curb. It was late in the afternoon. Most people were hurrying home from work to warm houses and hot meals. No one was visiting the dead. He had the place to himself.

The urge to leave Tyler, to run from the trouble and the heartache, as he'd done so often in his life, was growing stronger by the day. But this time some part of him resisted the impulse to pull up stakes and head for parts unknown, to start over in a new place, among new faces. This time the gossamer strings of love and caring that Sarah had woven around his heart held him fast.

If he wrenched them free he knew they would bleed, long and hard.

Once inside the cemetery gates the noises of the outside world fell away. He could hear the soft rustling of pine boughs and the scratchy rattle of stubborn oak leaves, still clinging to the branches, refusing to fall. His footsteps loud in the silence, he walked along the gravel path, not quite certain where to go to find what he was looking for.

He headed up the hill. The red and gray granite stones nearest the street carried dates from the forties and fifties. Here and there a bronze insignia of a branch of the armed forces adorned a grave—of a Tyler boy who hadn't made it back from France or Italy or some tiny coral dot in the Pacific. Farther up the hill, the gravestones were older, more weathered. Some had angels and sleeping lambs standing guard—children's graves from a time when sickness and disease claimed too many young lives.

Then, below the crest of the rise, he found what he was looking for—the newest section of the cemetery. The trees here were small, newly planted, the paths laid out in geometric grids, the graves raw-looking, less settled, less at peace with their surroundings. The stones were new, also, the names sharply etched and easy to read. But he was no longer alone. A tall, slightly stooped man stood before a large, red-granite stone.

Judson Ingalls raised his head and looked in Michael's direction. For a moment Michael considered turning on his heel and walking back the way he had come. But something held him there, a curiosity stronger than his reluctance to meet up with this formidable old man.

"Come on down, son," Judson Ingalls called, settling his hat, a beat-up old fedora, on his head. He was wearing a red-and-black-checked wool coat that was at least as old as the hat and a wool scarf with tattered ends wrapped around his throat. "I've been meaning to talk to you."

Michael did as he was bidden. He glanced at the name on the stone. Margaret Ingalls. Judson's dead wife. Alyssa's mother.

The old man caught him staring.

"I come to see her, now and then," he said. "She was alone and lonely for a lot of years out at Timberlake. Margaret hated to be alone. I like to think she enjoys the attention."

"Yes, sir."

Judson cocked his head, eyeing Michael closely. "I don't suppose you're up here just walking for your health. You came to find your father's grave, didn't you, boy?"

"Yes, sir."

"Ronald's buried right over here. My father bought this whole section back in forty-five. Getting too crowded for all of us up there on the hill plot." He pointed a bony, gloved finger off to the left. "There. Ronald's is the gray one, third stone over. Just past my aunt Esther and my uncle Lars."

Michael's feet felt like lead weights as he followed the old man's directions. He stared quietly for a moment at his father's grave. There was nothing there, beyond the dates of his birth and death, to tell him about his father. No clue as to what kind of man he'd been, why he had done the things he had.

A cold, empty hole opened up somewhere deep in Michael's middle. There were no answers here. Maybe there were no answers in Tyler at all. Maybe he would never know who Ronald Baron had been. Who he himself was and where he came from.

His hands balled into fists. He turned away. It was time to go.

Judson Ingalls was still there, watching.

"Thanks for pointing out his grave," Michael said automatically.

"My Alyssa says you didn't know anything about your father except his name and where he came from."

"That's all." Michael wanted out of there. It was cold and getting dark. The shadows were long and blue tinged, the wind stronger, the moaning of the trees louder, as though they suffered from the cold.

"Why did you come here? To try to get money from my daughter's family?"

"Hell, no. I don't want anything from any of you."

"They say you're an arsonist." Judson leaned his weight on the cane he'd been carrying, but so far hadn't used. He looked as if he intended to stay just where he was for quite a spell.

"That's what I went to prison for." Michael wasn't about to let his guard down. Judson Ingalls might be nearly three times his age, but he wasn't a man to fool with.

"That's not what I asked you."

"I didn't burn down your factory, if that's what you're getting at."

"I didn't think you did. I wouldn't be standing here having this conversation with you if I did. I'd be down at the police station, giving Brick Bauer hell for not hauling you in."

Michael almost smiled; he couldn't help himself. "Fair enough," he said.

"Well, if you are after money, I'm here to tell you there isn't any. Ronald died penniless. That's why he killed himself. He couldn't take the shame after his business went bankrupt."

"What kind of business was he in?"

"He owned the grain elevators here in town. It was

bad times for farmers in the early eighties. Ronald got caught in the squeeze. He couldn't cope with the strain.''

"So he took the easy way out?''

"Putting a bullet through your skull ain't exactly the easy way out.''

"Maybe not. But leaving everyone else to deal with your problems is.''

Judson nodded. "That's true. Ronald was a weak man but he wasn't a bad man.''

"I wouldn't know. I never met him.''

Judson straightened, his gaze narrowed. "Ronald Baron was married to my daughter for almost twenty years. Like I said, he had his faults, bad ones.'' His face darkened. "My daughter wasn't happy in her marriage. But Ronald was a good father to his children. I'm willing to give him the benefit of the doubt. If he had known you were alive, he would have done the right thing by you.''

"You really believe that, sir?'' Michael wasn't convinced. He had hated his unknown father for so long. Hated him for what he had done to his mother. Hated him for all the times he had not been there when Michael needed him. Hated him the most for dying before he could find him and confront him with all the wrongs of the past.

Now this wily old man was painting a different picture of him—of Ronald Baron as just a man. A man who got up every morning and went to work. A man who loved his kids. A man who had made mistakes and, in the end, paid for them with his life. He wasn't a monster, he was just a ghost, pale and insubstantial, and not worth the effort to hate.

"I'd like to hear more about him someday,'' Michael

said, realizing as he spoke that he had made some commitment to himself, a promise to stay and ride this out, to make some effort to establish a relationship with his half brother and sisters.

"I'd be happy to talk with you. Walk me to my car. I always leave it on the street. Figure the noise might upset the 'old-timers.'" He chuckled at his own small joke.

Judson held out his hand. Michael took it. Judson's grip was strong and firm. "Now," he said, waving his cane in the direction of the top of the hill, "let's get out of here. It's damned cold and I want my supper."

They walked in companionable silence toward the gate. Now and then Judson would point out a tombstone, old and moss covered, ghostly white in the fading daylight, that sheltered the remains of one of Tyler's founding fathers. Schwiebert. Hansen. Wilhelm. Ingalls. Solid German and Swedish names, of hardworking people who had tamed the land and wrested a town and homes from the vast forests of the wilderness.

For Michael it was all so different from the life he'd known growing up in Miami. He and his grandmother and his mother had moved from apartment to rented house to apartment, always one step ahead of eviction, one welfare check away from being homeless. Some of the people here in Tyler had lived in the same house all their lives, farmed the same ground for four generations back. They belonged. They had roots.

That was what Sarah wanted from life. That was what she deserved. It was something he couldn't give her.

"What the devil?" Judson had stopped at the top of the rise to catch his breath, resting his hand on an obelisk-shaped tombstone with lettering so eroded it couldn't be read in the failing light. "What's Brick Bauer doing down there by my car?"

"I imagine he wants to talk to me." Michael didn't wait for the old man to keep up with him as he marched down the hill.

"Kenton," Brick Bauer said, giving him a slight nod of greeting. "I was told I might find you here. Evening, Judson." This time the greeting was accompanied by a respectful finger to the brim of his hat.

"Evening, Brick." The older man took a moment to catch his breath. "What's going on? Something I should know about?"

"Nothing much, Judson. Just want to ask Kenton here a couple of questions."

Michael remembered the patrol car he'd caught a glimpse of as he walked into the cemetery. The deputy inside had obviously been the source of Bauer's knowledge of his whereabouts.

Judson grunted a monosyllabic reply, then added, "As long as that's all you're doing, Brick. Don't harass the boy."

"I'm doing my job, sir. That's all."

"Then I'll be on my way home." He got in his car and drove away. Michael felt a fleeting, unfamiliar pang of regret. Judson Ingalls owed nothing to him. There was no reason in the world for him to stay, to stand by, to support.

"What do you want me for?" Michael asked as the sound of Judson's car engine died away.

"Like I said, I just need to ask some questions."

"Are you taking me in?"

Brick shook his head. "Nothing that official. Get in the cruiser. We can talk at your motel, if you don't want to come down to the station, but it's too damn cold to stand out here."

"HELLO, SARAH. Doing some last-minute Christmas shopping?"

Sarah turned at the sound of Alyssa Wocheck's voice behind her. "Hello, Alyssa. Yes," she said. "I've finished shopping for my parents. I mailed their box last week. I'm just picking up a few things for my brother and his wife."

It was a little after five, an hour before closing, and Gates Department Store was crowded this December afternoon. Sarah had to raise her voice slightly to carry over the background noise of other peoples' conversations, telephones ringing and the swoosh and pop of the antique pneumatic tube system overhead that carried change throughout the store. It was a relic of bygone days that, for Sarah at least, was one of the chief delights of shopping at Gates.

"You aren't spending Christmas with your family?"

Sarah smiled. "No. My parents are working at a mission in Tucson over the holidays. My oldest brother and his family are going to the in-laws and my other brother can't get away from the radio station because all of his employees want the holiday off."

"Are you going to be alone?" Alyssa's eyes were sympathetic. She laid her gloved hand lightly on Sarah's hand. "You are more than welcome to spend Christmas with us," she said.

Sarah gave the older woman's fingers a squeeze. "Thank you, Alyssa, but I don't think that would be a good idea." She thought of Jeff and Cece, and her heart contracted. They were her friends, but there was no way

Jeff would accept her involvement with the half brother he wanted no part of.

Alyssa turned her head slightly, gauging their privacy. "You mean, because of Michael Kenton?"

"Yes. Jeff has been…distant. And I won't be the cause of friction between him and Cece."

"You've spoken to her?"

"Yesterday. She says she's never seen Jeff so upset. She's worried about him."

"So am I," Alyssa confessed.

"Everyone would be too uncomfortable if I spent Christmas with you. Your family has enough problems now, Alyssa. I won't add to them." She longed to have another woman to talk to, to confide in, but Alyssa had enough on her plate without adding Sarah's heartache to the mix.

"I hate what's happened. Jeff is taking this all so hard and there is nothing I can say or do that gets through to him. I know this might sound odd, but somehow I feel responsible for Michael, too. He is Ronald's son, after all. He has no other family. I'm his only conduit to the Barons, although he's expressed no interest in wanting anything to do with Ronald's sister or her family."

"He's a very private man," Sarah said carefully.

Alyssa tilted her head, alert to the sadness underlying Sarah's words. "Will you be spending Christmas with Michael?" she asked.

The contraction around Sarah's heart tightened to pain. She shook her head, not trusting her voice for a few moments. "I don't think so."

"Both of you will be alone," Alyssa said, almost under her breath. A clerk approached with a gift-wrapped package. "Thank you." Alyssa's smile was gracious. "It's lovely."

Sarah picked up her own small package and turned away from the counter. "Goodbye, Alyssa."

"Wait, Sarah. Do you have an appointment or a meeting to go to?" As though they were discussing nothing more important than the weather, Alyssa smiled and waved to Martha Bauer, who was heading for the dry-goods department at a brisk pace that belied her eighty-odd years.

"No," Sarah said. "I stopped in on my way back from Worthington House. I always try to make extra visits this time of year. So many of the residents are alone, their families scattered here and there."

"Come with me, then. Have a cup of tea or maybe hot chocolate at Marge's." She looked out the glass doors at the lowering sky. "Yes. It's definitely a hot-chocolate day."

"I'm not sure—"

"Come with me, Sarah, please. I think we both need someone to talk to—about Michael Kenton."

But Alyssa talked only of inconsequential things as they walked along Main Street to Marge's Diner. She commented on the quality of donations they'd received for the bazaar, hoped the weather would not turn bad for the big event on Saturday, complimented the chamber of commerce on the bright new decorations that adorned the light posts along the street. Paying no attention to Sarah's monosyllabic answers, she kept up the flow of light chatter until they were settled in a booth by the front window and the waitress had set two cups of whipped-cream-topped cocoa in front of them. Then she grew silent, a little pensive.

"I love Christmas," Alyssa said finally, looking out

the window at the comings and goings on Main Street. "It's my favorite time of year." Her smile faded. Worry darkened her eyes. For the first time since Sarah had known her, she looked her age. "But this year it's been very hard to find the spirit. We're having the Christmas party at Timberlake, as usual, but it just doesn't seem right, somehow, with things still so up in the air at the plant."

"Have you learned anything more about the cause of the fire?" Sarah asked.

Alyssa shook her head. "The arson investigator has requested an interview tomorrow." She stirred her cocoa, watching the whipped cream melt. "I'm not looking forward to it."

The front door opened and closed as Pam and Patrick Kelsey, both of them coaches at Tyler High, swept in on a blast of cold air, accompanied by a group of their students. The teens were laughing and talking a mile a minute, obviously in a holiday mood. They swarmed toward a table in the middle of the room, and Sarah and Alyssa watched indulgently for a minute or two as the noisy group settled behind their menus, the boys boasting that they could bankrupt their teachers if allowed to order everything they wanted to eat.

"Pam's looking well," Alyssa remarked. "I hope she doesn't overdo, being out in this cold weather so much." Pam Kelsey had been an Olympic runner in her youth, but several years before coming to Tyler she had been stricken with multiple sclerosis, and while she allowed the disease to interfere with her life as little as possible, her well-being was always uppermost in the minds of her family and friends.

"Neither Patrick nor the kids will allow that," Sarah said, returning the wave of one of her Scripture students. The gesture caught Patrick's eye and he swiveled in his seat to face them.

"Season's greetings!" he called across the room, as his wife waved. "Pam and I have promised this bunch an early supper and then we're going caroling at Worthington House and Tyler General." Sarah had heard Patrick sing. He had a marvelous baritone voice.

"How nice," she replied. "All the residents will enjoy it."

"How about a carol or two for my customers before you leave?" Marge Phelps herself came from the kitchen to wait on the party.

"Anything for you, Marge," Patrick said expansively. "Anything, as long as you tell me there's a piece of your pumpkin pie back there with my name on it."

"There is."

"Hallelujah," the coach said with a grin. "Okay, kids, order up. We're due at Worthington House at six-fifteen."

"There," Alyssa said with a smiling shake of her head. "Marge will keep them in line. Now we can hear ourselves think again."

"I don't want to think," Sarah confessed. "I've been doing entirely too much of it lately."

"I gather from that remark you're not referring to wrestling over the wording of your Christmas Eve sermon."

Sarah looked across the booth. She saw only compassion and encouragement in Alyssa's blue eyes. "You're right. It has nothing to do with my Christmas Eve sermon."

"And everything to do with Michael Kenton?"

Sarah wrapped her hands around her mug, lifting it to her lips. "Yes."

"I said before that I feel somehow responsible for him, although he probably wouldn't thank me for saying it. I just keep thinking that what happened to Michael could have happened to Jeff if the situation had been reversed. All the love that Ronald showered on my son was denied to Michael." She traced the rim of the mug with her fingertip. She lifted her eyes to Sarah's. "I like him. I think beneath all the barbs and prickles he's a good man. You're in love with him, aren't you?"

The question took Sarah by surprise. She answered without thinking. "Yes." She set the mug down very carefully. "Is it so obvious?"

"No," Alyssa said. "Only to someone who fell in love again herself not so long ago."

"We aren't seeing each other anymore."

"Why not?"

Sarah looked out the window for a moment. Darkness had fallen while they talked. The lights on the trees in the square had come on, green and red and gold and blue. They shimmered like fairy stars in the tears she didn't dare let fall. She couldn't speak a word.

"Michael Kenton isn't an easy man to love, is he?" Alyssa offered.

Sarah shook her head. "Sometimes." There was a funny little catch in her voice, and she took a sip of cocoa to bring it under control. "Sometimes I'm afraid he isn't capable of loving anyone."

Alyssa reached out. "Don't ever say that, Sarah. Don't think that. I know there are people out there who truly aren't capable of love, but I don't believe Michael Kenton is one of them."

"He keeps pushing me away. He won't let me help. I was with him when the fire at the F and M started, Alyssa. But he won't let me tell anyone."

Alyssa closed her eyes for a moment. "I'm glad to hear you say that. I didn't want to think—"

"See, Alyssa, even you had doubts. I can't let this go on. But Michael doesn't trust anyone, and he won't let me risk my reputation by giving him an alibi. Nothing I can say or do will convince him that Tyler people won't tar me with the same brush."

"Most won't," Alyssa agreed, though her tone was rueful. "But some will. One or two I can think of in your own congregation, if you want the unvarnished truth. You're being naive if you believe otherwise, Sarah. Michael is trying to protect you the only way he knows how."

"He doesn't trust me, Alyssa." The tears were very close now. "I can't accept that. When a man and woman love each other they must trust, as well. I trusted Eric with my life."

"You loved Eric very much, didn't you?"

"Yes. I loved him from the first moment I saw him."

"Have you ever thought that it was easy to love Eric because Eric was an easy man to love?"

"What do you mean?"

"I mean he was a good man. A simple man, with no rough edges, no excess emotional baggage. Michael Kenton isn't that kind. He's intense, stubborn, scarred in heart and soul. It will take a very strong woman to love him and to heal him enough for him to love her fully and completely in return. Do you have that strength, Sarah? Because if you don't, it will only mean heartbreak for both of you."

Was what Alyssa said true? Was she strong enough

to break through the walls that Michael had built around his heart? Was she brave enough to try?

The door opened again, letting in another blast of frigid air that swirled around their feet and ankles and sent a shiver skating down Sarah's spine. She looked up, distracted from her thoughts. Three men had entered the diner. One of them was Cassie Wiggins's father, Hoyt, the other Joey Schmidt and his brother, Walt. All three were employees of the F and M. They crossed the room, looking around as if in search of a friend. Alyssa's back was to the men, her slender form hidden by the high booth. She didn't even glance their way as she waited for Sarah's reply.

"What you boys doing here?" Marge called from behind the counter.

"We're looking for Howie Carson and Bill Smith. You seen them around?"

"Not tonight. You look pretty agitated, Joey. What's up?"

"We just heard a call come in over the emergency scanner at the Hideaway. Will Benson signed a statement down at the police department. Says the man he saw running away from the fire could fit the description of that guy that's been hanging around town here of late."

"Brick Bauer's out at the Green Woods Motel. He's questioning that drifter—that Kenton fellow—about the fire," Walt Schmidt added excitedly.

The diner was suddenly very quiet. Patrick Kelsey exchanged glances with his wife, then shifted his gaze to where Sarah and Alyssa were seated, still hidden from the newcomers' view.

"We're going to drive on out there. Maybe make

sure Brick's okay," Joey Schmidt interjected. "With any luck, he's getting ready to arrest the SOB."

"Yeah, by tomorrow the whole town will know that Ronald Baron's bastard kid is the one who set the fire. Then the insurance company will call off that damned investigator they sent down and Alyssa and Judson can get started on rebuilding the plant. Get us back on the job."

"C'mon, Patrick. Come with us. See what's going on. Your dad's job is on the line, just like ours."

"Don't be fools," Patrick said. "Let Brick do his job. If Kenton's the man who set the fire, we'll find out soon enough."

"Don't waste your time talking to him," Hoyt said, tugging on Joey's coat sleeve. "Howie and Bill are probably at the Pine Tree Bar. We'll try there. It's right on the way to the Green Woods. Let's go."

The door whooshed shut behind them, leaving silence in its wake. Alyssa's expressive blue eyes were filled with apprehension. Sarah's heart slammed against her rib cage. "Oh God," she said. "They sounded like...like the beginning of a mob."

Alyssa reached out, covered Sarah's shaking hand with her own. "Don't worry, Sarah. Brick can handle this."

"But there were three of them. And they're looking for two more men. I can't let this go on. I'm going out there right now to tell Brick Bauer what really happened."

"From what you just told me, Michael won't thank you for it."

Sarah choked back a sob. "I don't have any other choice."

CHAPTER FOURTEEN

WHEN THE THIRD PICKUP pulled into the parking lot of the motel, Michael began to wonder if the whole situation was going to get out of hand. Now there were six or seven men milling around, shuffling their feet, refusing to meet his eyes. At least they weren't armed, although he'd glimpsed a shotgun or two hanging on gun racks in the back windows of the trucks. And he was outside, not trapped in his room. He could make a run for it if he had to. He doubted if half of the beer-belly-toting agitators could keep up with him for more than a few blocks.

One thing he knew for certain: he wasn't going to jail. Not even for his own protection. Not for one minute. Not for one second. Never again.

Brick Bauer leaned against the door of the cruiser, his pose nonchalant, his eyes watchful and alert. "Evening, boys," he said pleasantly enough. "What can I do for you?"

"We want to know when you're going to put this son of a bitch behind bars where he belongs," Hoyt Wiggins said belligerently, his breath coming in spurts that wreathed his bald head like steam from a locomotive. Michael wondered how many beers the man had had before he got there? Not enough to get him drunk, probably—just enough to make him reckless and a little bit mean.

"I've got no reason to arrest Mr. Kenton," Brick said, his tone still pleasant but his stance no longer quite as relaxed. "I'm just here for a friendly chat." He moved away from the cruiser, putting himself between Michael and the angry men confronting them.

"What about Will Benson? We know he was in earlier to sign a statement about the man he saw running away from the fire."

"Where'd you hear about Will Benson coming down to the station?"

"They got a scanner down at the Hideaway," Joey Schmidt informed Brick, naming a local bar.

"Damn things," Brick muttered under his breath.

"Will Benson give you a statement and then you hightail it out here to talk to this bastard," Hoyt insisted. "Two and two add up to four, in my book."

"Well, you're wrong this time," Brick said, his tone no longer quite so pleasant. Several of the men shifted restlessly, tugging on hat brims, looking at Brick, at Hoyt, but not at Michael.

Michael recognized one or two of them from working around town. The one doing all the talking, Hoyt Wiggins, he'd seen at the fire. And Joey Schmidt. The others were strangers, but he'd bet his last dollar they were employees of the F and M. All of them were worried and afraid for their livelihood and their futures, and that made them dangerous if they were provoked.

"Then what are you doing out here?" one of the other men demanded.

"Just talking."

"You're talking about the fire."

"Among other things."

"About how Kenton here is a firebug?"

"That's got nothing to do with it," Brick said flatly.

"The hell it don't. Once a firebug, always a firebug. Let us alone with him for five minutes and he'll tell you where he was that night."

Michael shifted his weight. He didn't want a fight. He'd be a damned fool to think he could take on this bunch. And he didn't think Brick Bauer would pull his gun on men he'd known all his life. He might be an honest cop—maybe there was such a thing—but Michael wasn't about to stake his life on it.

"Don't push me too far, Hoyt, or I'll take you in for obstructing an officer in the line of duty."

For a moment Hoyt looked as if he would challenge Brick's pronouncement, but one or two of the other men urged him to slow down, take things easy. Hoyt waved them off with a slashing motion of his hand, but did as he was told. "Then tell us what the hell you were doing that night, Kenton, and we'll go home. Leave you alone."

Michael ground his teeth. He'd be damned if he told this bunch anything. He flicked a glance at his truck, but three of them were standing between him and freedom. He was going to have to tough it out. Or run.

"Where were you, Kenton?" Wiggins demanded. "Where were you when all our jobs went up in smoke?" Two or three of the men glanced off to their left. If it weren't for the trees edging the fields behind the motel, in the daylight you could have seen the ruins of the F and M from where they were standing.

"That's enough, Hoyt. I'm taking Kenton down to the station where we can talk without being interrupted."

"No." Michael ground out the word between clenched teeth. His gut tightened, his hands clenched.

He started to sweat, even though the temperature had dropped below freezing an hour before.

"Don't be a fool, Kenton," Brick said under his breath. "We're outnumbered and I'm not going to pull a gun on these unarmed men."

Michael knew he was being unreasonable, but it didn't make any difference. His loathing of returning to jail was stronger than his fear of the mob. "I'm staying here."

"Damned, stubborn fool. I said get in the squad car or you'll get us both hurt."

A car pulled into the parking lot in a spurt of gravel, a dark-colored, late-model sedan that Michael recognized from the cemetery. A woman in a business suit and trench coat got out of one side. Judson Ingalls unfolded himself slowly from behind the driver's seat.

"Any trouble here, Brick?" Amanda Trask asked. She moved into the glare of the security light mounted above the office door, her chestnut hair swirling around her shoulders, her expression serious. Her grandfather followed close on her heels. "Does this man need an attorney?"

"Hell, no, Amanda." Brick crossed his arms over his chest.

"It looks that way to me," Amanda said, unruffled.

"I just want to ask him a couple of questions, that's all. Now what?" Brick's gaze flicked past the assemblage to the street.

A second car—an older, noisier one—pulled into the parking lot. Sarah's car, followed by Tyler's other two police cruisers.

"What are you doing here?" Brick asked his deputies, one big and heavyset, jovial looking, the other a woman, lean and lantern-jawed.

"Just out patrolling, Chief."

"Both of you?"

"Nice night for a drive," the woman drawled. "Saw the crowd. Wondered what was going on."

"Nothing's going on. I'm just trying to have a conversation with Kenton, and this bunch of yahoos think they have the right to listen in."

Michael barely heard what was being said, had eyes for no one but Sarah. She was still standing beside the open door of her car. Her face was pinched with fear, her hazel eyes huge in her white face. Alyssa Baron was with her, but her being there made no more impression on him than the others did.

"Do you wish to retain my services as your attorney, Mr. Kenton?"

Michael tore his eyes from Sarah's face and focused his attention on his sister. They had spoken only once, at Timberlake Lodge the day he'd delivered the Bentley to Devon Addison. The day of the fire at the F and M. A few words only, meaningless stuff. Now she was here offering to defend him. He looked at the ramrod-straight old man behind her and knew it was his doing.

"Yes." Michael's face was stiff with cold and tension. The word came out a bark, an animal sound. She didn't seem to notice.

"Good. That's settled." Amanda smiled, that same high-voltage smile she shared with her siblings. The Baron smile. "What is it you're so hell-bent to ask my client, Brick? If it's in his best interests, I'll let him answer. If it isn't…" She shrugged slender shoulders. "Well, you know the drill."

"Yeah, ask him," Hoyt Wiggins demanded. "Ask him where he was when the F and M burned to the ground." The others were silent. The appearance of

Judson Ingalls and his daughter seemed to have dampened their enthusiasm for baiting Michael.

One of the men who hadn't spoken before raised his voice. "If you have an alibi, why don't you say so?"

"If you have an alibi, I suggest you answer the question, Michael," Amanda said in a softer, less-businesslike tone. "It would save everyone a lot of trouble."

"I told Bauer—"

"I was with him when the fire started," Sarah said, shaking off Alyssa Wocheck's restraining fingers. She moved forward. The crowd parted as though choreographed by a master hand. Sarah stood among the angry men, looking small and fragile in her fur-trimmed, hooded parka. Alyssa moved to stand beside her father, her hand on his arm, her face expressionless, her eyes guarded.

"Sarah."

She ignored the command in Michael's voice. "We were together all that day." She took a deep breath. "And all that night."

"She's lying," Michael said. He couldn't let her do this. He could almost see the wheels turning in Wiggins's head. Joey Schmidt had the beginning of a sneer on his face.

"I'm not lying." Sarah avoided Michael's gaze, looked directly at Brick. "Michael Kenton was with me at 2:15 a.m. on the morning of the fire at the F and M."

There was a buzz of voices among the would-be mob. A snicker of laughter was cut off abruptly by a warning growl from Michael. His hands balled into fists. By morning the news would be all over town— hell, long before then, the way rumors traveled in this burg. By midnight everyone would know that the Reverend Sarah Fleming was carrying on with the drifter, the arsonist, the man who claimed to be Ronald Baron's bastard son.

"Are you willing to sign a statement to that effect?" Brick asked kindly.

"Yes."

"The insurance investigator will probably want to talk to you, as well."

"You know where I live, Brick," Sarah said with a brave, faint smile. "My door is always open."

Brick watched her for a long moment, then nodded. "Come down to the station whenever it's convenient."

"I take it we have your word that no formal complaint will be filed against my client," Amanda prompted.

"As far as I'm concerned he's free as a bird."

There were mutters of discontent here and there in the crowd, but even Hoyt Wiggins kept his mouth shut. Michael wasn't fooled for a moment. It wasn't Sarah's protestation of his innocence that had spiked his guns. It was the arrival of Alyssa and Judson that had brought on his sudden return to sanity.

Brick raised his hand and his voice. "Okay, everyone, let's go home." It was a command, not a suggestion. "It's colder than a witch's thorax out here and by now, so's my dinner."

Three of the men headed for their pickup. A second truck pulled out of the parking lot right behind them. That left only Hoyt and Joey and another man, who looked enough like Joey Schmidt to be his brother and probably was.

"Go home, boys," Judson said, the first words he'd spoken. "There's nothing you can do here that won't make things worse than they already are." He looked old suddenly, every day of his eighty-plus years, as he leaned slightly on Alyssa's arm for support. "We can't take the law into our own hands. So help me, if anything happens to this man or anyone else, I'll pull the rest of that building down myself, with my own hands. Go home!"

They went.

"I'll leave one of the patrol cars here, just in case," Brick said, opening the door of his cruiser.

"Don't bother," Michael said. "They won't be back." He wanted to believe it, for Sarah's sake.

"I don't think that's a good idea," she interjected.

Michael didn't take his eyes off her pinched, cold face. "I don't want any more attention drawn to me than I've already got. Just go away. All of you."

"Michael." Sarah's tone held the faintest hint of censure, of disappointment.

He lifted his eyes to his half sister. "Thank you, Amanda. I—I appreciate what you did for me tonight."

"It's my job." She smiled again, making her not just pretty, but really beautiful. "I'm glad I could help." Michael searched her face for some sign of himself, some link to their shared heredity. He found it in her eyes, as blue-black as a midnight sky. Like Jeff's. *Like his own.*

He smiled, too. "Just like the cavalry, arriving in the nick of time."

"That's me. Come on, Granddad. Brick's right. It's cold and I'm hungry. What do you say I buy you a burger at Marge's before you drop me at home? Ethan's working late tonight at the courthouse. He won't be home for hours."

Judson was watching Michael. "You sure you're all right, son?"

"I'm fine, sir." Michael held out his hand. "Thank you for getting Amanda. I—I never expected your help."

"Least I could do." His grip was strong and sure. "Tisha and I... Well, we're sorry that word got out about your father like it did. It was awkward."

"It's all right."

"We'll work this out...." Judson looked for a moment as if he might say more, then thought better of it. "I think I'll take you up on that burger at Marge's, Amanda girl. Will you join us, Alyssa?"

Alyssa, too, was watching Michael—and Sarah. Her blue eyes were dark with concern. "Sarah? Do you need me?"

"I'm fine, Alyssa. I...Michael and I have to talk."

"I understand. In that case, I'll join you and Amanda, Dad. I think it's a good idea if the town sees us together. We are going to have to talk about the F and M soon, you know. People will only get more and more anxious and suspicious, if we don't."

Judson patted her hand where it rested on his arm. He looked down at his only child. "I know, Lyssa. I know. If only that damned investigator would get it over with. Then we'd know where we stand."

"We have to rebuild, Dad. Regardless."

"I know. I just don't know where the money will come from if the insurance company won't pay up. Maybe Edward's company..." Judson shook his head and looked around, recalling that they were not alone. "We'll find it somewhere."

Amanda helped her grandfather into the passenger seat, then slid behind the wheel. Alyssa hesitated a moment before following them into the car. "Michael, I'm sorry. This isn't… Those men tonight. That's not Tyler. Not really.''

''It's okay, Alyssa. Thanks for coming with Sarah. I wouldn't have wanted her to be alone.''

Alyssa smiled. ''She has faith, Michael. She's never alone.''

A minute later Brick Bauer and the other two Tyler cruisers pulled out of the parking lot. The sound of idling car engines and angry voices was replaced by the silence of a cold, country evening, with the promise of snow before morning, but for Michael, the faint tinge of menace still hung in the air.

''I'll follow you home,'' he said.

Sarah shook her head. ''I'm not going home.''

''What do you mean, you're not going home?''

She glanced over her shoulder at the door of his motel room. ''I'm not leaving you alone in this place. They might come back. You should never have sent Brick and his deputies away.''

''Sarah, I can take care of myself.''

''I'm not leaving.'' She set her chin at a stubborn angle.

''This is no place for you.''

She sighed. ''Michael, I'm an adult woman. I make my own choices.''

''This place is a dump.'' He couldn't take her inside. He wanted her so much, had missed her so much, he couldn't be certain he could control his need. Nothing had changed between them. The last thing he wanted to do was compound the heartache by making love to Sarah, only to see regret and remorse later in her eyes.

''Then come home with me, Michael.''

He thought of the drafty old house by the drafty old

church and his heart contracted with a new, sharp pain. A house like that could be home. But not for him.

He wrenched his thoughts away from fantasies of what might have been. "I can't." He'd sent Brick Bauer's deputy away, but he had no intention of relaxing his guard. Desperate men did desperate things, and Hoyt Wiggins, at least, was a desperate man.

"Then I'm staying here, too."

"No." He spoke too quickly, too intently.

A tiny smile curved the corners of her mouth. "Alyssa was right. I'm strong because I have faith. In God. In you. In myself. I'm not leaving you."

He was too tired to fight. Too tired to argue and he wanted her too much, needed her too much to have the strength to send her away again. "God, Sarah, don't do this to me."

"Shh, Michael. There's no reason for us not to be together now." Her eyes were bright with reflected tears. She touched her finger to his lips, and he could feel the warmth of her skin, imagine the softness, even through the fabric of her glove. "I'm not asking for anything. I'm not talking about forever. Just tonight. Just let me be with you tonight to keep you safe."

He did smile then at the thought of this small, determined woman proclaiming herself his bodyguard. He pulled her tightly against him. "You can stay."

"Just tonight," she whispered, her breath warm against his cheek. "Just to keep you safe." The words were sweet and low, a prayer, a benediction.

You don't know how much I want it to be forever, he said inside his head, but the cold, hard hurting place in the middle of his chest closed his throat and the words stayed bottled up in his heart.

SARAH AWOKE cold and confused. She lay quietly a moment on the unfamiliar bed, bringing her thoughts and her surroundings into focus. The room was dark and musty smelling, the bed beneath her hard and lumpy at the same time. The only light came from the reflection of a street lamp outside the window.

"Michael?" She reached for him, realizing that it had been the loss of his warmth, of the comfort of his arms around her that had wakened her from her restless dreams.

"I'm over here." He was standing near the room's only window, his hand on the frame, his profile etched sharply against the gray-yellow background, looking out into the darkness.

Sarah's heart began to pound. "Is something wrong? Is someone out there?"

She could see him shake his head. "No. It's snowing, that's all."

"Is it? Perhaps this time it will last. It would be nice to have a white Christmas." If she didn't speak of such ordinary, everyday things, the silence would be overwhelming.

Michael said nothing.

"I—I fell asleep."

This time he answered her, although he didn't turn away from the window. "So did I, for a little while."

Sarah glanced around her. There was no clock. She couldn't see her watch in the murky light. "What time is it?"

"After midnight."

Sarah sat up on the bed and wrapped her arms around her knees. Something in his voice, in his stance, told her he had made up his mind. Her heart slowed down and began to shrivel up inside her chest. He was going to leave. Maybe not tonight. Maybe not even tomorrow, but he was going, as surely as the sun would rise in the morning, and there was nothing she could do to stop him.

She had suspected it from the moment he'd closed the door to the shabby motel room behind them and taken her in his arms. They hadn't talked. They hadn't made love. He had only held her and kissed her and warmed her with the heat of his body, lying beside her on the narrow bed until she had fallen asleep from sheer exhaustion. He had made her feel safe and secure enough to sleep, when it was he she wanted to protect.

"What are you thinking, Michael?" she asked very quietly. She loved him, would always love him, but sometimes love was not enough. She held her breath. If he didn't answer her again, ignored her plea for understanding, she would leave, never look back. She would have to for her soul's sake. For her heart's sake.

"I was thinking that I should wake you," he said after a moment. "Take you home."

It was the way he said the word, *home,* the way he let her hear the longing in his voice, that made her heart flutter in her breast, gave her hope.

"It could be home, Michael. For both of us."

"You still believe that after what happened tonight?" He turned away from the window. Now his face was hidden in shadow. "The way they came after me tonight? Your friends, your neighbors?"

"They're worried and frustrated. Scared to death that their jobs are gone, their futures, their families' security. They lashed out at you because you're a stranger and they need someone to blame."

He was beside her now. He sat down on the bed, his thigh against hers. "Are you defending them?"

Sarah reached out and touched his face. She couldn't stop herself from wanting to be near him, to hold him and be held by him. "No," she said. "I'm not defending them. I'm only telling you I understand them." She closed her eyes as a fundamental truth took root and blossomed inside her. "I'm one of them."

"And I'm not, Sarah," he said in a rough whisper. He bracketed her face with his hands. "I have no roots here. I have no place."

"You could." She was desperate now. She could think logically, know she'd made the right decision not to marry him when she was alone, when he wasn't beside her, when she didn't have to look into the emptiness behind his eyes. But when they were together she could only feel, and ache for what couldn't be, and try to change it, to make it right somehow for both of them.

Michael took her by the shoulders, searched her face. "God, Sarah. You're so damn sure of yourself." He smiled, a faint upward curve of his lips, a darker, more-somber version of Jeff Baron's killer smile. But Michael was devastating to her heart.

"I try to look for the best in people, if that's what you mean."

"Faith. That's what Alyssa called it." His words were thoughtful, rough with suppressed emotion. He looked down into her face, his eyes searching for proof of something she sometimes found hard to put into words.

"I have faith in God."

"And in yourself. And in your fellow man."

"Yes," she said. "All of those things."

"Do you think some of that faith can rub off on me?"

Sarah's heart jumped into her throat. Was he going to stay? Was that what he was trying to tell her?

"Michael?"

He tightened his grip. "I want—"

There was a squeal of brakes in the parking lot, the sound of a car door slamming, then the sound of breaking glass.

"Michael? What's going on?"

"Damn it. My truck."

He stood up so quickly that Sarah lost her balance and fell sideways just as a brick slammed through the window, shattering the glass and slamming into the wall two feet above her head. It fell to the pillow with an ominous thud. Before she could pick herself up, Michael was back, hauling her into his arms.

"My God, Sarah! Are you all right? Are you hurt?" He held her so tightly she couldn't answer, could barely breathe. She wiggled to be free of his iron grip. The sound of squealing tires was almost drowned out by the rush of blood pounding in her ears.

"Michael, stop. I can't breathe. I'm fine," she managed to croak. "I'm fine. What happened?"

"Someone must have pitched a brick through the window of my truck. I don't know if the second one was meant to go through this window, but it sure as hell did." He turned his head toward the gaping hole through which cold air and snow now swirled into the room.

"You're bleeding." Sarah stared in horror at the blood on his cheek.

Michael lifted his hand to his face, which had been cut by flying glass. "It's nothing. Just a scratch. Call the cops. I'm going to see if it's too late to get a look at that truck."

IT WAS TOO LATE. The truck was long gone by the time Michael ran outside to the street. So two hours later, as Sarah stood at her living-room window, watching the dark bulk of the police cruiser Brick Bauer had set to guard her home, she still had no idea which of her friends or neighbors, or even parishioners, had wished to do Michael harm.

Had it been one of the men who had confronted them at the motel? Or was it someone else at a bar or the supermarket who had heard about Will Benson's statement? Someone angry and frustrated enough by the fire at the F and M to take it out on the only man among them who was a stranger, an outsider?

She had told Michael she was one of them, part of the community. Now she wasn't so sure. But it was too late to speak of her doubts. Michael was gone and nothing she could say or do had changed his mind. He had waited patiently for the police to arrive—first a deputy then Brick Bauer himself, looking sleepy but alert. He had given them his statement and then requested that a deputy be assigned to watch over Sarah until Brick was certain she wouldn't be the target of any further attacks. That was when she felt the first crack in her heart.

The second came when he refused any medical treatment for the cut on his cheek because Jeff Baron was on duty at Tyler General. The third and, she suspected, ultimately fatal blow came as he swept the glass from the seat of his truck, repaired the broken window with cardboard and duct tape and loaded every earthly possession he owned under the tarp in the back.

"Michael, Brick will find who did this. They'll be punished for it," she had pleaded. "You don't have to go."

"That brick could have killed you."

"It was an accident. I'm sure they only meant to damage your truck." It was the only defense she could muster and it wasn't a very good one.

"It doesn't matter. By daylight I'll be long gone from here."

"Michael!" She didn't dare cry. She had promised herself she wouldn't, but she had come so close, so close to making him believe in Tyler, in her, in himself, and now all her hopes and dreams were gone, shattered like the window glass. "Where will you go?"

"I don't know. It doesn't matter. I'm going, Sarah. That's all there is to it." He yanked so hard on the rope holding down the tarp that it broke in his hand. He turned toward her, but made no attempt to touch her. The look on his face kept her from going to him. "I told you I wouldn't leave without telling you."

"You're going now? Tonight?" It was too soon. She needed time to get used to the idea, time to get used to the pain.

He nodded. "I can't fool myself any longer. There's no place for me here. There's no place for us." This time he did touch her, a finger to her cheek, a fleeting caress over in a heartbeat. "Goodbye, Sarah. Let Brick Bauer keep you safe. God knows, I did a damn poor job of it."

"I can take care of myself." She wouldn't cry. If she started crying now she would never, ever stop.

"Sure you can." He opened the door of the truck. "Sarah?"

"Yes?"

"When you get a chance, say a prayer for me."

But she couldn't pray. All she could think of was that once more she was alone, and this time she was afraid she could never be whole again.

CHAPTER FIFTEEN

SOMEHOW, SARAH GOT through the next few days. On the third night the squad car parked on the street outside her house she called Brick Bauer at home and asked that it be sent away. Michael was gone. She was safe. She didn't need a bodyguard, and when she refused to hear any more discussion on the matter, he agreed to do as she asked. The insurance investigator, Lee Neilsen, went about his business. Bulldozers and backhoes came to knock down the damaged walls of the F and M and bury the debris in a huge hole behind the plant. No clue as to who had vandalized Michael's truck and the motel window was found. No one came forward to claim responsibility. Perhaps it was better that way.

Saturday dawned cold and clear, the day of the TylerTots bazaar. Christmas was ten days away. Angela was hoping for a big turnout of browsers with long lists of last-minute gifts to buy. Glenna McRoberts brought several children to the festivities with her and videotaped them wandering among the displays, the little girls oohing and aahing over the dolls and stuffed animals. The boys were less interested until they found the baked-goods table and got to sample the cookies and candies. Annie and Belle Baron were among the group, and Sarah felt a quick, familiar jab of pain that she hadn't seen either Jeff or Cece in church or socially since Michael Kenton's identity had become known.

Michael. Thinking of him brought a new, sharp wave of pain washing over her heart and into her soul. She couldn't think about him. Wouldn't think about him. Not today. Not when everyone would be watching her, gauging her actions and her behavior with a critical eye. For Sarah the bazaar was a trial by fire. Since Michael had gone she'd rarely ventured out of the house except to make her usual visits to Worthington House and Tyler General. She couldn't eat, she couldn't sleep and it took all her strength and energy to keep up a pretense of any kind of holiday cheer.

Thankfully, she was so busy that she was able to forget her troubles for most of the day. By three o'clock in the afternoon the crowd had begun to thin out, and Sarah was counting receipts from the morning's sales in the kitchen when the president of the church board, Leon Hansen, a distant cousin of Britt Marshack's first husband, walked into the room. Sarah looked up from her seat at a small table at the back of the kitchen and smiled, hiding her dismay.

"Hello, Leon."

"Good afternoon, Reverend Sarah." Leon was a small, fat man, nearly bald, with an impressive belly hanging over the waistband of his slacks. He was a hog farmer from out near Willow Lake, conservative and rigid in his thinking, but a good man, honest as the day was long. He had never approved of the ordination of women and never missed an opportunity to say so. He'd been a thorn in Sarah's side for as long as she had been at Tyler Fellowship, but although they didn't see eye-to-eye on many things, in all fairness, he had never stood in the way of her ministering to her flock.

"Have you come to buy something for Mary for Christmas?" Sarah asked, although she doubted that was why he was here. Mary was Leon's wife, a kind woman, whose influence on her husband went a long way to soften his sharp edges.

"No, Sarah. I've come to talk to you. I tried to call you on the telephone several times but your machine always picked up. I don't like leaving messages on machines. I like to talk to people face-to-face."

Sarah secured the stack of five-dollar bills she'd been counting with a paper clip. She wished she were standing. She was at a distinct disadvantage, seated at a table with nothing more impressive than a kitchen sink at her back and the smells of noodle soup and German potato salad still heavy in the air. She laid the money in a metal box and shut the lid. She folded her hands in front of her. "I'm here now, Leon. What is it you want to talk to me about?"

Leon looked around. They were the only ones in the kitchen for the moment. "I think we should discuss this in your office."

Sarah felt a flutter of anxiety start deep in her stomach and begin to work its way up into her throat. Her hunch had been right. She took a moment to make sure her voice was steady and wouldn't betray her anxiety. "Whatever you have to say, Leon, you can say here."

He looked around once more. Through the open doorway Sarah saw Myra Allen sorting through an assortment of wooden Christmas ornaments, her eyes frequently darting in their direction, her head tilted, as though she might be able to overhear what they were saying if she only concentrated hard enough.

Leon saw her, too. His lips thinned and he shifted position so that his back was to the door. "There's been talk, Sarah. Talk about you and that Kenton fellow. The one who left town the other night."

"What kind of talk?" Her heart sank.

"That you were spending way too much time with him."

"He's gone, Leon," she said wearily. "And may I remind you, my private life is my own."

Leon wasn't moved. "It's not seemly," he said. "Getting him off the hook for the Ingallses' fire by saying you spent the night with him."

"We were together when the fire started," Sarah said carefully. "I told the truth. That was all."

"I accept that. We haven't always gotten along, but I've never known you to tell a lie."

"Thank you."

He nodded but stuck to his guns. "But it was two-thirty in the morning. People get ideas of their own about what goes on at that time of night. Do you deny you were in his room at the Green Woods Motel the night he left town?"

"No," Sarah said. "I was with him."

"It's not a good example for a Christian woman to set for the youngsters."

"I have done nothing to be ashamed of." All she had done was fall in love—a wonderful thing, a desirable thing unless the man you loved was so badly scarred by life that he ran from commitment.

"That may be. But there have been complaints. You'll have to explain yourself to the entire board. There's a meeting planned for tomorrow. After services. The bishop is sending a man down from the district office to sit in on it."

"What's going on in here?" Nellie Phillips came limping into the kitchen, supported by a strong cane in one hand and a sturdy grandchild on the other side. "Leon Hansen, what are you doing here? I've never seen you at a bazaar before unless we were serving food. And lunch was cleaned up and over with an hour ago. Are you bullying Reverend Sarah, here?''

Sarah stood up, bringing her almost eye-to-eye with Leon. He puffed out his cheeks. Nellie Phillips was not a woman to be trifled with. ''I'm conducting church business with the Reverend, Nellie,'' he said, attempting to mollify the old lady.

Nellie would have none of it. ''Church business, my eye. You're out to get Reverend Sarah sent down from her pulpit. Well, I won't stand for it. Those rumors about her and that Kenton fellow are not true.''

Sarah smiled, despite the dread in her heart. ''Thank you, Nellie. I appreciate your support.''

Nellie limped closer to Sarah, and Leon took the opportunity to make his getaway, saying, ''We'll discuss this matter tomorrow. After services.''

''I'll be there,'' Nellie informed him. ''Don't you think I won't.'' She glared at him until he retrieved his coat from the entryway and disappeared up the stairs. She turned back to Sarah with a militant gleam in her eyes. ''We're behind you, Sarah. Me and mine. Don't you worry.''

''I'm not worried. I've done nothing wrong.''

''Of course you haven't.''

''Am I interrupting?'' Alyssa Wocheck asked from the doorway. She was dressed in wool slacks and a simple silk blouse. She looked calm and collected, unless you looked deep into her eyes. Alyssa was a troubled woman. The signs showed through the veneer, if you knew what to look for.

''No, of course not.''

''C'mon, Grandma,'' the Phillips youngster urged.

"I want to buy some of the fudge I saw at the baked-goods table."

Nellie snorted. "Humph. In my day you wouldn't call that fudge. Made out of a box, that stuff, with a little water and not single drop of real cream."

"Grandma." It was almost a whine.

"All right, all right. I'll be sitting in the first pew tomorrow morning, Reverend Sarah, come fire or flood." She reached over and patted Sarah's hand. "Merry Christmas, Alyssa," she said, making her slow, painful way out into the crowded playroom.

"Merry Christmas, Nellie." Alyssa waited for a moment until she and Sarah were alone. "Are you okay?"

"I'm fine."

"You don't look fine."

"I'm tired, that's all." Sarah tilted her head to look past Alyssa's shoulder. "Did Cece come with you?"

"No, I'm afraid not. Jeff is still upset. It's… awkward for her."

"It shouldn't be, now that Michael is gone."

"He'll be back, Sarah."

She looked down at her hands. "No. He won't be back."

"I'm sorry, Sarah. I know how hard this is for you."

"You saw Myron Hansen, I take it."

"Yes, I saw him. He's the president of your church council, isn't he?"

"Yes. Evidently, there have been complaints about my behavior. There's to be a meeting after services tomorrow. The bishop is sending a representative from the district office."

"You've done nothing wrong."

"No. I only fell in love." She lifted her eyes to Alyssa's. "But perhaps Michael was right. I'm not sure

I belong here anymore, either. Maybe it's time I leave Tyler, too.''

IT WAS QUIET among the deserted campsites of the small Kentucky state park. Cold, but not the same kind of bone-numbing, teeth-rattling cold he'd experienced in Tyler. There was no snow this far south, but a thick layer of frost covered the ground and trees each morning, when he left his primitive cabin to eat breakfast at a diner out by the main road, and there was ice along the shoreline of the lake.

Michael was beginning to know the park well. For three days he'd walked through a thick carpet of fallen leaves, uphill and down, following first one trail and then another, never stopping to admire the stark beauty of the winter woodlands, the high thin arc of clouds across the sky or the haunting chorus of geese calls as they settled onto the placid waters of the lake at sundown. He walked to bring on exhaustion so that he could sleep at night and keep his thoughts at bay, at least through the long, cold hours before dawn. He stayed away from the lamplit cabin until late at night to avoid that homecoming. It only made him think of Tyler and Sarah and all he had left behind.

But this time of sanctuary was coming to an end. This morning a uniformed park attendant had knocked on the cabin door and reminded him that he must be out of the park by noon on Saturday. The cabins were not winterized and therefore not habitable during the coldest winter months. He was going to have to move on, and soon.

He wasn't certain exactly where he would go. There was nothing and no one for him back in Miami, or anywhere else, for that matter, but the shipping season on the lakes was months away and he might as well head south as any other direction. He was a man alone, without family or friends, and he had never been more aware of that fact than he had been these past three days. He looked into the future and the utter bleakness of it weighted his heart and his body. Maybe that was why, today, sundown had caught him unaware, too far from the cabin to make it back before dark unless he took the path that skirted the small lake.

The sun was a low, red ball of fire hovering just above the tree line, its light breaking into shards of orange and gold that soared upward into the sky and lit the water of the lake with sparkles of copper and bronze. The geese were already patrolling the surface, aware, perhaps, of some weather change coming that his human senses could not discern.

They might have been the same geese that Margaret Alyssa had fed along the shores at Timberlake Lodge. He had no idea how far south they moved in their wanderings. For a moment in his mind's eye he saw his half sister's child, her face a study in determination as she marched up to the water's edge, intent on feeding her geese, as stubborn and loyal as her great-grandfather. For a moment he couldn't help but imagine picking up her sturdy little body, savoring her warmth and the baby-shampoo smell of her hair.

His niece. A beautiful, wonderful child, who shared his blood.

And then unbidden, unwanted, his thoughts skipped past Margaret Alyssa to Sarah. Her babies. Their babies would have been just as beautiful and quick and bright as Margaret Alyssa. If he had had the courage to stay and make his life with her.

"Dammit!" Now that his thoughts had breached the

barriers he'd erected, he would never be free of memories of her. Her taste, her scent, the sweet sound of her voice, the feel of her in his arms. He would go to his grave with the echoes of her laughter in his ears and the pain of leaving her in his heart.

"God, Sarah. I don't want to be alone." He picked up a rock and hurled it out into the lake. It landed a hundred feet away from the geese, but the explosion of sound and fury frightened them and they sailed off, honking in agitation.

Michael watched them go. He didn't want to be like those geese, always on the move, always just beyond the reach of the ice. He wanted to be a partner, a lover, a husband and father. And if he didn't have the courage to reach out for those things, he would be no better than the man who'd fathered him. An unhappy shell of a human being, too weak to fight for what was good and true, too afraid to make right what was wrong.

Michael turned away from the lake and the geese and the cold beauty of the December sunset, walking into the shadows that surrounded his cabin. He had already proved himself Ronald Baron's son. He had driven away from his dreams and the woman he loved without a backward glance, taking the easy way out. He had learned nothing from loving Sarah, a woman of faith and character, who loved him in return.

Running away was easier than staying to defend his name and build a place for himself in Tyler.

Running away was easier than loving and sharing not only good times but bad.

He had run away from Sarah and everything he'd come to hold dear because that was what he had always done.

It was a pattern he'd never had the courage to break.

But this time when he got into his truck and headed south, he would know for certain and for always that it had cost him his future and the woman he loved.

THE CHOIR WAS FINISHED singing. The last strains of "O Come, O Come, Emmanuel" echoed among the rafters and faded away. Sarah sat quietly in her high-backed chair to the left of the lectern, nearly hidden from the assembly by a bank of festive red poinsettias. She remained seated for another moment or two, while the singers settled back into their pews.

Then she stood up, smiled and mouthed a thank-you. Finally she turned to the congregation, unconsciously squaring her shoulders beneath the warmth of the beautifully pieced and quilted Advent stole that had been her gift from her young-adult Sunday-school class the year before.

"Wasn't the choir wonderful?" she asked. "I think we should give them a round of applause." The applause was warm, but perfunctory. It was obvious the members of Tyler Fellowship had something else on their minds. Sarah took a deep breath. "There are several announcements to be made after I pronounce the benediction," she said carefully. She didn't have to look down at her notes, but she did anyway, fighting to get control of the sudden, cold wave of fear and anxiety that threatened to swamp her. "Please bow your heads. May the peace of Our Lord, Jesus, be with you today and always. Go in peace." She opened her eyes and gazed out at the sea of faces staring back at her.

She should have called her parents or one of her brothers to be with her today. She shouldn't have tried to face this alone. But none of them, so rock-solid in their faith, their relationships, would have understood the uncertainty in hers. *Thy will be done,* she said silently to herself, and raised her head. "The dress rehearsal for the Christmas pageant is Thursday night at six o'clock sharp. Don't forget. The performance will be directly after services next Sunday. Then Christmas Eve service will be at seven p.m. and Christmas Day will be at the regular time for morning service."

Usually by this point in the announcements there was some fidgeting, searches for purses and misplaced gloves, hymnals being slipped into the racks attached to the backs of the pews. Today there was silence. Sarah took a deep breath and went on. "For those of you who haven't heard, there will now be a meeting to air the concerns of some of our members who feel that I have been conducting my personal life in such a manner as to reflect badly on this pulpit." She folded her hands together on top of the lectern to still their sudden trembling. "Reverend Aronson has been sent by the district office of the denomination to hear those concerns."

"I have no concerns," Nellie Phillips called loudly from the first pew, exactly where she had told Sarah she would be. "She's doing a fine job of ministering to me and mine." The old lady was surrounded by Jonas, Randy and Darryl, their wives and children and grandchildren—all the vast Phillips clan, three pews deep on each side of the aisle. Sarah blinked back tears of gratitude at their strong showing of support.

"Some of the rest of us do," said a voice from farther back in the church. *Myra Allen,* Sarah thought, and sighed. Several heads nodded in agreement, but no one else spoke.

Leon Hansen stood. "Reverend Aronson will conduct this meeting in accordance with the rules of the denomination. You'll all get your chance to speak. Reverend.'' He motioned toward the dais where Sarah was standing.

Sarah had met Reverend Aronson before the service. He was a jovial-looking man with thinning gray hair and the practiced smile of a politician, but his eyes were kind and intelligent, and Sarah had felt confident that he would not be rushed to judgement. That was why, when he had asked her earlier if she wished to confront her accusers in private, she had said no.

"Ladies and gentlemen," he said, mounting the three shallow steps to where Sarah stood. "Let us have a moment of silent prayer that all our hearts may be guided by Our Lord's fairness."

Once more, Sarah sought the words to ask God to help her make the right decision. All last night she had lain awake, wrestling with her decision. Should she stay, fight to regain her pride and her pulpit? Or should she leave, as Michael had done, to start over again where no one knew who she was or why she had left Tyler? Did she have the strength to stay and fight to redeem her good name? Without Michael, did she want to?

Sarah lifted her eyes and looked out over the congregation. There were the Phillipses, strong and united. There were the members of her teen study group and her Sunday-school class, Angela Murphy and her parents.... Suddenly her doubts began to slip away, one by one. Calm settled over her spirit. No ringing voice spoke inside her head, but her prayer had been answered.

She would stay. She would fight for her good name. She had done nothing wrong but fall in love with a man who couldn't love her back. Tyler was her home and she intended to remain for as long as she could.

"Amen," Reverend Aronson said, raising his head. "Ladies and gentlemen of the congregation, it has been brought to the attention of the bishop that Reverend Fleming may have been conducting herself in a manner unbecoming to her calling as a minister of Christ's gospel. If any of you here can verify those remarks, do so now, in my hearing."

There was a rustle of movement as people craned their necks to see who would come forward. Others looked down at their hands or up at the ceiling. Those members of her congregation were undecided, Sarah realized. They wouldn't speak against her, but neither were they ready to rise to her defense. Finally Myra Allen stood, then one or two others—employees of the F and M, people with great pain and great uncertainty and no one to blame for those travails. Her heart fluttered in panic again but she pushed the new doubt aside.

"Reverend Sarah has been seen visiting the motel room of a man in the dead of the night," Myra announced into the stillness. She cleared her throat. "And she has admitted herself that she was with this same man at two o'clock in the morning the night Ingalls F and M was burned to the ground. It's not fitting. They aren't married. They weren't even engaged."

"We will be engaged by the time she leaves this church if I have anything to say about it."

Sarah's eyes sought the figure at the back of the sanctuary. "Michael." Distracted by her thoughts, she hadn't even heard the church doors open and close.

He came striding forward, his footsteps loud on the bare, hardwood floors. Heads turned to watch his progress, but Michael ignored them all, his eyes fixed on hers.

She had feared she would never see him again, had steeled herself against that possibility, had congratulated herself on every minute of every day that she managed to survive without him. But now he was back, and she knew she'd been fooling herself. She would have gone on living, eating and breathing and going through the motions, but without him she would never truly have been alive again.

"Who are you?" Reverend Aronson inquired, blinking in surprise.

"My name is Michael Kenton." He halted at the bottom of the steps. His clothes were rumpled, his face beard-roughened and drawn from lack of sleep. "I'm the man Sarah was with."

"Then sit down, young man. You will be given a chance to speak at the appropriate time."

Michael barely glanced his way. "Now is the time," he said. His tone brooked no argument. He turned his head, glanced out over the congregation. "You're fools, all of you, if you think badly of this woman. She has honor and integrity. She's good and kind and better than most of you deserve." His eyes sought and held Sarah's. Now he was speaking directly to her. "She taught me that hatred and revenge were not an option. She showed me that I could belong somewhere. She showed me how to love."

His voice was rough around the edges, the words halting, but strong and clear. "I love you, Sarah Fleming. I want to marry you. I want to stay here in Tyler, make a life, raise a family with you. But if the lot of you are fools enough to let her go, then I'll take her away from here, to a place where she's appreciated and honored, and you will all be poorer for her loss. But not me. I'll thank God every day of my life because I'm the luckiest man on earth.''

He stepped forward, his eyes still locked with hers. He held out his hand. For a moment Sarah couldn't speak, couldn't move. Panic flared briefly in Michael's midnight eyes. His voice dropped to a whisper. ''I love you, Sarah. I came back for you.''

For a heartbeat, then two, then three, she searched his gaze, looking for something—what, she wasn't quite sure. And then she saw it. She saw that the barriers were down, the shadows gone from his eyes. His thoughts were laid bare for her to see—the love and the promise. She could see into his heart, almost into his soul. He meant it. He loved her and he would honor that commitment for the rest of his life.

She held out her hand, no longer concerned with Reverend Aronson or the judgment of her congregation. Everything would be all right. Michael's hard, warm fingers closed around her hand. ''I love you,'' she said, smiling up at him. ''Welcome home.''

CHAPTER SIXTEEN

"LYSSA, GIRL? Are you still awake?"

"Yes, Dad." Alyssa rose from the window seat in the big bay window in the living room. The only light came from the Christmas tree in the corner. All around her in the quiet town of Tyler, her friends and neighbors slept, dreaming their Christmas dreams, reliving the memories of the holiday now past. But she couldn't sleep and she didn't want to waken Edward, who had to leave for England early in the morning, so she had slipped out of bed and come downstairs.

"I couldn't sleep, either. Too much turkey and mince pie," Judson grumbled. "I hate mince pie, but for the life of me I can't make Tisha understand that. She just keeps baking them. I saw the lights from the tree when I came downstairs looking for the antacid. There's none in my bathroom."

"I'll get you some."

He waved her off. "No need. I can find it myself. What's troubling you, Lyssa girl?"

"Just post-Christmas blues, I think." It was much more than that, but she didn't want to trouble her father.

"Don't try and bamboozle me. You couldn't when you were five and you can't now. Out with it. What's wrong? Is it Jeff and that Kenton boy? You can't make them feel like brothers, Lyssa, no matter how hard you try."

She shook her head, although she didn't think he could see the gesture in the near darkness. "You're right. They'll have to work it out on their own."

"Then what is it? The F and M? We'll be fine, girl. We've always worked through the hard times before."

"Dad, what if it was arson?" She thought of the horror of watching the building go up in flames, of realizing that someone she knew might be the cause of that destruction. She remembered the anger and frustration on the faces of the men she had known for years, men who had been on the verge of doing violence to Michael Kenton because they feared for their lives and their futures. "What if the insurance company refuses to make good on our claim?"

Judson's shoulders slumped for a moment, but he straightened again, moving across the floor slowly, a little stiffly, because the room was cold and his arthritis had been bothering him of late. "There's no use borrowing trouble. We've got enough of the real McCoy without making it worse. We've just got to have faith in the Good Lord and in ourselves."

He came to stand beside her, put his arm around her. She laid her head against his shoulder. For fifty years he had been there for her, and though, sometimes lately, their roles were reversed, he was still here for her when she needed him most. "No matter what that insurance investigator comes up with we'll find a way to get the F and M up and running again. We'll find the money someplace," he repeated under his breath. "Some way."

IT WAS CHRISTMAS NIGHT, almost midnight, but Michael couldn't sleep. He stood at the window of Sarah's bedroom—their bedroom—looking out into the moon-bright darkness. Snow covered the ground. Here and there, red and green and blue Christmas lights still twinkled on porches and shrubbery, but most of Tyler was asleep.

They had been married three days earlier, and now they had spent their first Christmas together. He twisted the wide gold band on his finger. Its weight was strange, but also strangely comforting. It was a symbol of love, of commitment, of bonding. All the emotions he had spent so many years denying and now embraced.

"Michael?" Sarah sounded sleepy and a little confused. "Are you all right?"

He turned away from the window, seeking the source of her warm voice. "I'm fine. Just not sleepy, that's all."

Sarah still worried about the brick-throwing incident at the Green Woods Motel, but he had decided to put it out of his mind. He'd refused to press charges and had even paid for the window at the motel, so the owner did the same. Some of the townspeople might not be ready yet to welcome him with open arms, but he didn't think too many of them considered him an arsonist anymore.

"I told you not to have the second piece of pumpkin pie for dessert," she said, holding out her arms. She was wearing the buttercup-yellow nightgown Liza had given her as a wedding present. The color suited her hair and eyes, and the gown was soft and silky and very, very sexy. Sarah had blushed like a teenager when she'd opened it, and Liza had laughed, delighted by her confusion.

Of the Baron/Ingalls family, only she and Cliff, Amanda and Ethan Trask had attended the simple dignified ceremony. Jeff still refused to acknowledge their relationship, and although they'd sent best wishes, Alyssa and Judson stayed away, as well.

"Michael? Come here, tell me what you were thinking about."

Ten days ago he would have made an excuse or side-stepped her request with a curt answer. But those days were gone, as was the cold ache of loneliness he'd carried around inside himself for so many years.

"I was thinking about how much things can change in a very short time," he said, stepping out of his jeans and sliding under the covers, into her arms. "And I was thinking how glad I am Liza gave you that nightgown as a wedding present."

"You're cold." She giggled, wrapping him in her arms, the dull gold of her wedding ring catching a stray beam of moonlight when she moved.

"Warm me," he said, his voice hoarse with longing he no longer tried to hide.

"Again?" she asked, but she moved against him with slow, deliberate movements, her lips brushing over his, her scent and her touch making his head swim with longing and desire.

"Again and again and again."

She slid her leg between his. "It's very late and you have to be up early tomorrow. Jonas Phillips is bringing that man by. What's his name?" Her tone was growing distracted as he slid his hand beneath the silk skirt of her gown and over her thigh.

"Dayton Hartman."

"What a name," she said.

"He's very rich." He brushed his mouth across the satiny skin of her throat. "He has three vintage Cadillacs he wants restored." It was a beginning. If he could regain his reputation in the rarified world of restoring classic cars, he could make a good living for them both, make a place for himself in this town that Sarah had chosen to call her home.

"However did Jonas meet him?"

"Who cares?" he said, moving to cover her body with his. "If he gives me the commission, I'll have work for the rest of the winter."

"Is that what you want?"

"Yes," he said. "It's what I want. How many times do I have to tell you my wandering days are over. I'm here to stay. You'll never get rid of me now."

"Promise?"

"Promise," he said fiercely.

"Then I will consider Mr. Hartman and his Cadillacs our own private little Christmas miracle." He could feel her smile against his mouth. "I'll remember to say a prayer."

Michael rested his weight on his elbows, held her face with his hands so that she could see his eyes, see his thoughts and his love in the reflected light of the moon. "You are my miracle," he said, lowering his head to taste her lips again. "You are the answer to my prayers."

HOMETOWN REUNION

continues with

The Reluctant Daddy

by Helen Conrad

Here's a preview!

THE RELUCTANT DADDY

"Do you want to dance?" Lee asked.

Dance? Glenna looked at him, bewildered, then looked out at the dance floor. The music playing was a popular jazz standard and a few adult couples were out there, taking advantage of a melody they knew. But why would she want to dance?

She looked at him again and he held out his hand, his eyes soft as velvet, and suddenly she realized what he was doing. He didn't know how to comfort her, but on the dance floor, he could take her in his arms and hold her in a way he couldn't anywhere else. She smiled at him, her eyes still shimmering with moisture, and she took his hand and rose with him.

She sank into his arms as though they welcomed her into a haven from all the cares of her life. The music was low and seductive, and he held her like a precious jewel. As they moved together, Glenna felt every doubt and every worry shrink and fall away like magic.

And just like magic, it seemed to go on and on. Her eyes were closed and she felt herself melt against him as though they were alone. The scent of his after-shave mixed with the smell of the coffee, and his hand spreading across her back made something fall away inside her with a shiver.

She knew she was flirting with danger, but right now she didn't care. She could feel the length of his thighs against her, feel how hard and muscular they were, and she thought she felt the beat of his heart. She pressed closer, feeling the heat rising from beneath his shirt, and suddenly she remembered the kiss and how everything had turned to silver, and she knew how it would be if they made love. Everything would turn to gold.

And still she didn't pull away. It was too good, too smooth, too warm right where she was. She wanted to stay there forever, to let the dance go on and never stop, to hold him closer and closer...

He dropped a soft kiss on the top of her head, so light, so quick, she almost thought she'd dreamed it, but she could tell he was breathing in the scent of her hair, and that was when she knew she had to stop it.

Drawing back, she stared up into his eyes and slowly shook her head. "I have to go," she said quickly, turning and heading back to the booth for her parka and her purse.

"Okay," he said. "Drive carefully."

"I'm only going a few blocks," she muttered as she closed the window and drove off. But his admonition warmed her.

"He is such a nice guy!" she wailed, and then she laughed loud and long.

It was only later that she remembered she had never gotten around to finding out why he didn't like children. And that he still hadn't come up with a definite suspect in the arson case, and until he did, she had serious worries along those lines.

And then she didn't laugh anymore.

THE MACGREGORS

4 BOOK COLLECTION ON THIS
WELL-LOVED FAMILY

BY

NORA ROBERTS

Book 1 - Serena and Caine

Book 2 - Alan and Grant

Book 3 - Daniel and Ian

Book 4 - Rebellion

READER SERVICE SPECIAL OFFER

AUGUST 2000

Receive the first book FREE
when you preview this collection.

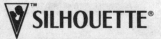